BESTSELLER

BESTSELLER

ALESSANDRO GALLENZI

ALMA BOOKS

ALMA BOOKS LTD
London House
243–253 Lower Mortlake Road
Richmond
Surrey TW9 2LL
United Kingdom
www.almabooks.com

Bestseller first published in UK by Alma Books Limited in 2010
This mass-market edition first published by Alma Books Limited in 2011
Copyright © Alessandro Gallenzi 2010

Cover design: Jessie Ford

Alessandro Gallenzi asserts his moral right to be identified as the author of this work
in accordance with the Copyright, Designs and Patents Act 1988

Printed in Great Britain by CPI Cox and Wyman, Reading, Berkshire

ISBN: 978 1 84688 128 2

BESTSELLER

for Elisabetta

Having books printed at your own cost and selling what was born from your own imagination is to me like eating pieces of your own flesh... I would sooner endure poverty than offend virtue by turning the liberal arts into a trade... Those who seek profit should become merchants – and those who act as booksellers should renounce the name of poets... Please print these letters carefully, on good quality paper – that is the only recompense I want...

Pietro Aretino to his publisher, 22nd June 1537

Publication is the auction
of the mind of man
Emily Dickinson

1

Jim's destiny was to be a great writer, to write a bestseller. His first novel – little more than a long short story – was written about fifteen years ago, under the encouragement of his creative-writing tutor, a retired university lecturer who had ended up committing suicide a few months later by tying a plastic bag around his head.

Just before the sad event, the man had recommended his student to a notoriously sharkish London literary agent, who had immediately decided to take him on and represent his next work, which they agreed would be a thriller called *Appointment with Death*. Unfortunately, writing under commission to a deadline wasn't the same as dabbling with words for an hour or two in the afternoon, and the thought of the high stakes on the table – and the agent's huge expectations – grounded Jim's flights of inspiration. As a result, *Appointment with Death* was somewhat lame, so that the agent asked one of his henchmen to chop it back, cut it up, sort it out and then put it back together – in other words, to rewrite it from scratch. "You see, Jim," his agent had said, wrapping him in a huge cloud from his cigarillo, "style is all very well – but we need to get to the nitty-gritty, y'know: less description, more death and a bit of bonking. How many copies do you want to sell? A hundred or a hundred thousand?"

Strangely, for all his wisdom and influence, the agent failed to place the eviscerated script – and so it was on with the second novel, this time a murder mystery set in Paris, *The Woman with Three Faces*. And after five months of painful silence, the agent had called to give him the good news: an American publisher – not one of the biggies, admittedly – had shown interest. Well, the advance wasn't great, in fact it barely crested four figures, but – everybody needs a springboard, right?

Jim could distinctly remember the day when he had received the black-and-white catalogue of the Pink Hippopotamus Press, with his happy, smiling young face on page twenty-four, where the book was announced for release in the following autumn. He took that catalogue everywhere – to the café, to the library, to the toilet – and looked at page twenty-four for ten or fifteen minutes at a time. Sadly, two weeks later the Pink Hippopotamus Press was declared bankrupt. That was the end of *The Woman with Three Faces*, and his agent stopped returning his calls.

But Jim wasn't overly disheartened: he immediately set himself to write two more works, a science-fiction book with a telepathic robot as the main protagonist, and a historical novel set during the Time of Troubles, *The Warrior of Kiev*. With great hope and enthusiasm, he sent out manuscript after manuscript to agents, publishers and renowned authors, confident that an opportunity would soon arise. But the agents answered in unison that they were not interested in taking on any new authors; the publishers lamented that their programmes were already overstretched and that the work in question did not "fit in" with their lists, and suggested that he should contact an agent; the renowned authors didn't bother to reply.

At this point there was something of a hiatus in Jim's literary career, a pause that coincided with a series of weekly meetings with a Belgian doctor at a private psychiatric hospital. At the end of this difficult period, Jim's primal impulse was still to write – perhaps out of spite, revenge, anger, or maybe just as a sort of cathartic tool. The works written during this time – two free-verse poetry collections, a very short semi-autobiographical romance, a humorous novelty book and an experimental play – bore "all the marks of the author's deep emotional and mental turmoil". At least, that was the judgement of the Belgian doctor, who was still keeping an eye on Jim at three-month intervals. These books – coming as they did from Jim's tormented period – were never loosed upon the teetering slush piles of agents and editors, but remained stuffed in a drawer, underneath Jim's socks and underpants.

It was the run of subsequent novels that rekindled a glimmer of hope in Jim's faltering career. He felt he was entering upon his mature, creative prime, and that his latest works carried a new authority. And every now and then, in reply to all the manuscripts he sent out, a slightly more authentic letter of rejection would crop up. Jim would extract the titbits of encouragement from these letters and attach all of them, in detail, to every new proposal and submission that he sent out. One day he would get published, he was sure about this.

With his tenth novel, a naturalistic work à la Zola, he adopted a more proactive submission technique, following up the initial proposal with a phone call to editors and editorial directors. In a short time, he became a well-known figure in every publishing house. Although the editors and editorial directors were always busy in some meeting or other, or on a lunch break even at four in the afternoon, sometimes there was a secretary or assistant he could talk to about his publishing history and current situation. Little by little, he began to exist in the collective mind of the book industry as a well-defined, three-dimensional, slightly unpleasant entity: a kind of blowfly that no one can be bothered to shoo out or swat.

Jim's next novel remained unfinished, and his visits to the Belgian doctor, who issued a total ban on "any kind of artistic-creative-compositional activity", took on their former frequency. It was suggested to him that he should go on a long trip abroad, which he immediately did – though not forgetting to take a notepad and pen with him. The result was a travel book entitled *Grand Tour*, nearly three hundred pages long, which agents and publishers turned down with much more vehemence than any of his previous works.

He really couldn't understand these rejections, so he decided to delve even deeper into the mysterious workings of the creative process. For three months he moved into the British Library on a near-permanent basis, and devoted himself to reading and researching, making his nest at desk 372 of the Rare Books and Music reading room, where there were only a few bookworms and an air of hypnotic stillness. One late afternoon he fell asleep on a quantum-mechanics textbook, and the security guard had to shake him hard to wake him up. Another time he was caught underlining a passage with his pencil. It was his own book he was defacing, but he very nearly got ejected and banned from the library for life.

After this period of profound study, he began to spend long days in bookshops, browsing hundreds of books in a bid to answer this fundamental question: "What is the difference between a published and an unpublished book?" Is it the quality and originality of its content? Is it the title? The author's fame? The fact that it is printed and bound? That it is sold and read by other people? Jim came to the conclusion that there's no difference between the books that get printed and the infinite number of works that remain unpublished. "The only variable is chance," Jim would argue with himself. "A manuscript landing in front of the right editor at the right time. Sure, it can help to have good contacts among the editorial mafiosi, but a bit of good luck is all it takes." And yet, despite this fatalistic vision of the publishing world, he would still devour the newspapers' book-review pages, drop by the library to read books like *The Writer's Bible* or *How to Grow a Novel*, and scan through the bestsellers' charts trying to draw some conclusions from them.

On the day the *Evening Standard* reported that the Belgian doctor had been extradited after being accused of giving teddy bears and cotton socks to five-year-old boys, something happened to Jim. It was as though all the years of experience, the months of studying and the deep-rooted questioning of what makes a successful book came together in a brilliant fusion of creativity. He locked himself in his room and started dashing off words, inspired by a new, unknown feeling of joy. He carried on for weeks on end, hardly pausing, rarely leaving his room.

And so it was that at 3.45 that morning – in a nondescript West-London flat swallowed up by rows and rows of terraced houses sheltering their sleeping occupants, in the tomb-like silence of his writer's dungeon – the last words of his masterpiece had finally blinked on the screen.

* * *

Jim sprang up in his bed as the front door was slammed shut. He looked around for a few seconds, perplexed, then decided to sink his head back into the pillow. It was probably Janet, his landlady, dashing off to a Tibetan yoga class. Or perhaps Tom, her boyfriend, coming back from his night shift at the post office. What time was it, though? He scratched the tip of his nose, eyes still closed, as a tentacular arm stretched towards the candlewick curtains blacking out the room. Light: there was light outside. He opened one eye and strained to look at his watch, but one of the hands seemed to have fallen off. Then he understood – it was twelve o'clock – and he stretched his jaws in a soundless yawn.

There was an unpleasant smell in the air, something like scrambled eggs. The tentacle gave another little tug at the curtains, letting a white strip of dust into the room. The dim light tentatively explored his figure lying crumpled on a folding bed, the cheap pine furniture huddled in the corners, and the piles of books scattered everywhere – on the floor, on shelves, even under the bed.

Then it all came back to him: his features twisted into a smile that cheese-wired his face in half, and his fists clenched so hard under the duvet that the bed gave off a sinister creaking noise.

"Yes!... *Yes!...*"

Writing "The End" always gave him an intense joy, but the night before, when he had tapped those words on his computer keyboard, he had the definite feeling that this was the novel that was going to yank him out of obscurity and into a successful writing career.

He got out of bed, yawning, and put his ear to the bedroom door. It sounded like no one was in, so he ventured out in his usual tracksuit-trousers and pyjama-jacket nightwear. His kitchen cupboard was as empty as his stomach, and when he opened its door that same rotten smell of scrambled eggs assailed his nostrils. He wondered whether he should check out the other cupboards, but he knew that Janet kept a detailed inventory of the food situation down to the last frozen pea, and that Tom did not take kindly to that kind of liberty. There was nothing for it: he had to get down to the corner shop. Since he was going out, he could also drop by at the post office and order the stamps, and maybe pay a little visit to the library and the bookshop.

In front of the bathroom mirror, shaving himself with a razor blade past its best, he grinned at himself and muttered.

"A bestseller, yeah... a chart-topper..."

Afterwards he sauntered about the flat in his underpants for a while, improvising a little jig and whistling *Aida*'s 'Triumphal March' as he cavorted into his room. He had not felt this happy, this perky, for months. He tugged at the curtains, allowing light to trickle in, and emerged from his room wearing worn-out jeans, a green mock-alpaca jacket and bright-red trainers.

It was a decent day outside, at least by London standards: mild but overcast. Jim hated the English weather, and was sick of the city's eternal pall of cloud. He'd much prefer to live in the south of France or on the Costa del Sol, tapping away on a laptop under the shade of a beach umbrella, sipping at some exotic cocktail on the seafront – but London was the place to be for an aspiring writer like him, the place where one could make useful contacts and, above all, the centre of the publishing universe. So he didn't plan to move abroad until he had established his name as a writer, which he hoped would be very soon.

Until then, he had to endure the situation a little longer, renting the dismal little room in Janet and Tom's flat. Shepherds Bush was an up-and-coming area, they'd said – well, maybe so, but Jim knew he didn't belong in a place like *Shepherds Bush...* His natural habitat was only a few hundred yards away – beyond the huge roundabout which divided the rich and the poor – in the elegant villas of Holland Park and Notting Hill. So many famous writers lived there – and with a bit of luck he'd soon be catapulted into one of those sumptuous, high-ceilinged houses, among the braying grand people, the glossy posse, the chamber-music quartets, the crystal glasses warbling with Cordon Rouge. Janet and Tom had said that they intended to get married soon, in July or August, and wanted him out. They'd been repeating the same old thing for three years now, but this time it looked as if they were serious, because he had seen them writing invitation cards. God willing, he would be turning his back on the two Irish love birds and Shepherds Bush by the end of the summer.

He put the manuscript in his rucksack, unchained his bicycle from the wrought-iron fence and set off for the Fulham Post Office. On the way, he mulled over which strategy he should use this time for the proposal to publishers and agents.

* * *

Charles Randall, the editorial director of Tetragon Press, had had a dreadful weekend. The head of a small but prestigious independent publishing house that had somehow managed to survive – even if in a state of continuous near-bankruptcy – for thirty years in a fragile shell of literary quality despite the crushing advance of the corporate giants, he had decided to take some work home over the weekend: a handful of submissions to read, a script to be edited and a couple of galleys to be proofed. But once he'd got home, the mere sight of piles and piles of books, papers, catalogues, letters, bills and other rubbish had drained his will to live.

His lank figure had collapsed into a dusty old sofa, also covered with unspecified paper trash, and his gaze had wandered into the void as he looked through thick lenses encrusted with little white dots. He had retraced the entire arc of his existence, and had lingered on a distant, slightly blurred point, from which emerged the image of a young university student with long hair and an unkempt beard, a poet full of dreams and ideals who used to print political flyers and poetry pamphlets with an old hand-cranked cyclostyle. Then the beard disappeared, the hair became shorter and withdrew around the temples, and a pair of black-framed glasses sprang up onto his nose. Now he was sitting behind a desk in a tiny room in the basement of a run-down property in South-East London, surrounded by heaps of paper and books, with an ancient telephone that rattled the furniture when it rang. Newspaper clippings began to float around him: the first reviews, the first interviews. Then a femme fatale with long auburn hair, a volcano of sensuality and passion, entered the scene. And all of a sudden his desk flew into an elegant Mayfair reception room, papers and books disappeared, to be replaced by dozens of hunching, tottering figures who were gossiping whilst sipping wine and champagne in the dim smoky light. Some of those figures lit up momentarily with a halo of sanctity, showing the faces of famous poets and novelists, Nobel Prize winners, journalists and critics of a generation now forgotten. The auburn-haired woman was then spirited away by a Paris train, and a grey-haired forty-something reappeared in a dark office on the Southbank, submerged by cardboard boxes, books and other clutter, which sedimented around him. After that, a lanky figure began to run from the door of his flat to the station, catching the train at the last minute, arriving at the office, gulping down a cup of instant coffee, and then proofs, manuscripts, coffee, deadlines, phone calls, coffee, meetings, invoices, book covers, coffee – and the same lanky figure put on his coat and ran to the station again, for ten years in a row, until his hairline receded to reveal a shiny bald pate, his remaining hair went hoary, the lenses in his glasses thickened, his clothes got shabbier and mangy.

When he came to on that Friday evening, he found himself holed up in his lower-ground-floor London flat, surrounded and oppressed by the printed word. So he had grabbed a bottle of Cabernet and... had descended into a calamitous bender, waking up on the Monday morning with three-day stubble, his shirt tails flapping over his open flies and his tie lapping his back. One hour behind schedule, he had just enough time to shave and force himself under a cold shower, then he dashed off to the station with long, desperate strides, his briefcase bulging with books and paperwork.

The minute he stepped into the office, he had to face the ghost-like appearance of Pippa, his new editorial assistant. This "great addition to the team" had been ratified from above… at the time when the *above* was created above him, a few months ago.

"Nick Tinsley has been waiting for half an hour."

"Brrnnff," grunted Charles.

"What?"

"Cof-fee!"

Pippa wrinkled her nose, turned round and waddled to the kitchenette, leaving a strange trail of garlic behind her.

"What the heck do these girls eat in the morning?" thought Charles, shaking his head and striding along the corridor towards his little room.

Nick Tinsley, aka the Shark, was waiting for him there, sprawling on a fold-back chair, absorbed in the sports pages of his *FT*. In front of him, on Charles's desk, lay a fuming mug of black tea.

"A-ha!" The publishing consultant sprang up and stretched out his hand. "Good *moorning*. How are we today?"

"Trrnff," replied Charles, turning over his hand and stretching out three fingers in a kind of Masonic greeting gesture.

Nick squeezed the three fingers for a second, then let them slip away and, performing a half-pirouette, sucked in his paunch to let Charles pass between him and the wall.

"Everything all right?" added Nick, folding his newspaper and putting it back into his briefcase, whilst Charles trudged past another fold-back chair and struggled to sit down on the black-leather chair wedged between his desk and the wall.

"Everything in the garden is lovely," Charles mumbled, letting his case drop heavily on the floor. "Lov-eh-ly," he repeated, pretending to sort out some heaps of paper scattered on his desk, without deigning to grant the Shark a single glance.

Nick mustered a strained smile. He'd grown inured to this kind of childish strop. Sometimes the directors of a company would be as meek as lambs, sometimes they would stamp their feet on the ground and shout and scream. It was natural. Sure, it wasn't nice having to announce to fifty people, or even to five people, that they would be losing their jobs within a week. And it wasn't nice having to sack the founder or the managing director of a company for being surplus to requirements. But that was part of his job. And there was no task which was too awkward for him. As he loved to repeat: "Shit always goes to the top". And this, perhaps the highest philosophical concept that he would ever express in his long career as a company butcher, had almost become his motto.

"Well, Charles, have you done your homework?" Nick's smile had turned into a grimace.

Their eyes finally met, and they stared at each other for a few moments. Charles and Nick were almost the same age, although the former looked at least fifteen years older than the latter. Yet the publishing consultant had a bad habit of talking to Charles with an openly patronizing tone, to emphasize the new hierarchies that had been put in place at Tetragon Press.

"No."

"What do you mean '*no*'?"

"No. I didn't have time, I had other things to do," Charles shifted his gaze onto an old submission, which after a quick glance ended up in the bin under his desk. "Someone has to see the books through to publication... mmm."

"Look, perhaps I haven't been clear enough." Nick straightened up in his chair. "If you don't start engaging with the new situation, there will be no more publications, all right? From now on, everything must be approved by myself: from expenses to print runs and discounts."

"What about the titles?" Charles threw in casually, still looking away, and busying himself with pencil and sharpener.

"No, not the titles, for the time being – but the days of Hungarian and Chilean poets are over."

"Bolivian."

"You know what I mean. The idea is that we give you a little leeway with the editorial choices, and in return..."

"You give *me*? Oh, so who is giving *me* 'a little leeway'?... I thought I was still the MD of this company... I won't let an accountant and... and—"

"Then it's true," Nick interrupted him, "it's true what Roger says – you still haven't got to grips with how things work here..." and he snorted in irritation, turning his face to the wall for a moment. "It's very simple: if you want to keep the business afloat, if you want to carry on printing your nice little books, you have to let us do our job. We need cooperation. Is that asking too much? You should consider yourself lucky that with all the debts you've accrued you've found someone who's taking on the risk—"

"I am not going to pull Naruszewicz's book, that's for sure," said Charles. "And we are not going to print our books on toilet paper."

"We'll discuss this later."

"No, we'll discuss nothing."

"Listen to this: next week we'll sit around this desk – Roger, you and me – and we'll go through all the titles for next—"

"Next week I won't even bother to come to the office, and you'll have to do everything yourself... You'll sit here, on this chair, and you'll start reading the books, editing the texts and proofreading them..." And he slammed four fingers on the only empty space in front of him.

Pippa came in with a cup of coffee, a mock-polite grimace clotting her washed-out face. She left the cup on a book blotched by circular tea stains, and before leaving the room she made a sudden turn and hissed:

"Holly called this morning, she can't come in... She's got a migraine..." and making another sharp turn she waddled out of the room.

"Prnnfff," Charles grumbled, shaking his head.

"What's that?" said Nick.

Charles gave a shrug.

"What's wrong with the girls these days? What kind of names are these? Pippa... Holly... Where do you find them?"

The Shark seemed to smile for a moment.

"Right... can we start talking business here? We haven't made a penny since I walked in."

Charles stifled a curse.

Nick opened a slim folder labelled TP and pulled out a couple of sheets of paper. "So, for example..." he murmured, with a patient tone of voice. "I understand these are the expenses for last quarter's titles... mmm... what's this?" and he pointed to a minute box in a huge spreadsheet he had in front of him.

"What?" said Charles.

20

"What is *this*?"

"What, that?... I don't know... What's that?... What is it?..." Charles showed a sudden interest in the first sheet of paper he could get hold of. "That one is..." – he cast a sidelong glance – "that one is the expense for... second proofs of—"

"*Second* proofs?!" snarled Nick. "Second proofs? Are you joking? This isn't bloody Random House – we didn't publish Ruth Rendell or Dan Brown last month, did we?"

"Actually at Random House..."

"This is bad... this is really bad..." and this time it was the Shark who slammed his fist on the desk, making Charles jolt back in apprehension. "You must get it into your head that this is a company, not a charity... At the end of the day what matters is the bottom line, the sales, the costings, the forecasts, the budget, the cash flow, the margins..."

"The page margins?"

"Listen," Nick continued, after a good long shaking of his head. "Listen... I'm here to help you, all right? Is that clear? Someone else in my place would have kicked you out a long time ago, OK? I am your best friend here, do you understand?"

"Well, Nick..." – he pulled out his glasses and scratched the bridge of his nose – "...it doesn't work like that, you know? Not here..."

"What do you mean?"

"Well, for good or for bad I've kept this business afloat for thirty years, you know? I've seen all sorts of things, I've seen a lot of people come and go... and you can't just turn up here with a business card saying 'Publishing Consultant' and expect me to spring to attention... I've published more than five hundred books, including a couple of Nobel Prize winners, so I've got a little bit of experience myself. It's easy to come from God knows where and terrorize people with numbers and the spectre of bankruptcy..."

"Look, if I'm here today, it's not to advance your interests or mine. I'm here because I represent the interests of the majority shareholders, OK? I don't give a damn if you publish a book by Tom or Dick – or Harry. I don't give a toss if you win the Nobel Prize or an Olympic medal: all I care about is that at the end of the year I can go to Mr Goosen and tell him: 'The company has made such and such profits...' 'Who is the editorial director? What books have been published? Which paper was used?' 'I don't know, I don't give a damn – but here are the profits...' Do you understand?"

The telephone rang.

A few seconds later Pippa peered through the doorway and announced, raising her eyebrows:

"Craig Mortimer for you."

"Craig Mortimer?" Charles turned this over in his mind for a moment. The name didn't ring a bell.

"Oh *yes*, Craig Mortimer... yes, yes, put him through..." With an apologetic gesture, Charles picked up the phone and selected line one, under Nick's withering gaze.

"Hello?"

From the other end of the line emerged a confused stammering, and the story of a manuscript sent the previous week...

"Mm-uh, mm-uh..."

"I mean, I know you must be very busy... but, er... I just wanted to check... that you got it... that's all..."

"Mm-uh…" Charles's glance landed on a babel-like heap of submissions hidden in the corner of the room, then intercepted the bloodshot eyes of the Shark, who snorted ostentatiously, fished out his *FT* again and opened it.

"The novel… the novel I sent you… no hurry of course, but… when do you think you'll be able to… I mean… there may be interest from other publishers and…"

"Mm-uh, mm-uh…" Charles looked around again in despair: everywhere paper, paper, paper… Words, words, words… Money, money, money… Numbers, numbers, numbers… The struggle for survival… everyone for himself…

The Shark raised his eyes abruptly and produced a cracking noise as he snapped the newspaper wide open at a new page.

Charles signalled to him with his index finger that he'd be only another minute, just another minute… And as Nick, clenching his teeth, went back to his newspaper, Charles let his index finger fold back down whilst raising the middle finger at the same time, in a gesture of protest which had been used many years ago by the long-haired young man, that young idealist still lodged in some unfathomable recess of his soul.

"Turd," thought Charles.

"The fun is over, pal… time's up…" thought the Shark, pretending to read.

* * *

Jim's bicycle screeched to a halt in front of a shabby café on the North End Road. He used to go there a lot, looking for a quiet place to work. The café owners, two sisters from Glasgow, regarded him as something of an odd fish, a philosopher, with his ponytailed head in the clouds and his bright-red shoes. They were used to seeing him hunched in a corner, reading or writing in absolute silence. Every so often they would bung him a cappuccino and a croissant, as if he were a harmless tramp.

"Ah, Jim... long time no see..." said the youngest of the two, Helen, as she saw him come in.

Jim grunted a greeting and went to sit at his usual table, near the shop window.

"What would you like, cappuccino?" asked the other sister, craning her neck from behind the coffee machine.

There was no answer from the philosopher, who was pulling out his manuscript from the rucksack. The two sisters exchanged glances and a few whispered comments, then burst out laughing.

"Chocolate on top?" shouted Helen. No answer. Jim was already rereading the beginning of his novel, and was deaf to the external world, a placid expression of beatitude stamped on his face. Helen shrugged and walked with her tray towards him. He lifted his eyes from the manuscript only when she was standing right in front of him.

Two years ago – in the spring, it had been a Sunday – Helen and Jim had gone for a walk together. Helen didn't remember whose idea it was, only that it had been one of the most cringingly uncomfortable experiences of her life. They had walked in silence side by side in the park. Jim was wearing a headset, which was connected to an elderly walkman hanging from his belt, and looked off into the distance, smiling to himself. From time to time Helen cast a sidelong glance at him, pouting in dismay.

"What are you listening to?" she finally burst out.

"Er... Radio Four."

Then rain had come, and they ran at once into a bus shelter. He kept listening to the radio, she started reading *Anna Karenina*. At around two thirty they had parted in front of Victoria Station, and that was the last time they had met outside the North End Road café.

For Jim, the female gender was a mystery. He had, in some ways, a medieval idea of woman. He regarded her as a frivolous, whimsical being, constantly bent on the most trivial aspects of life, such as clothes, perfume, jewellery, the home, children, electrical appliances, laundry... Just think what a downright curse it would be to spend an entire life with such a mean-spirited enemy of promise, whose only purpose in life is to drag down man's ideals with the deadweight of her pragmatism and reproductive imperative. It would be impossible to write with a woman around. It would be difficult even to read or to have one minute for thinking freely in.

Helen, on the other hand – who described herself on her Guardian Soulmates ad as "attractive, early thirties, hazel eyes, light-brown hair, 5' 6", into reading, movies, creative writing, restaurants, cooking, going out and staying in with a good DVD and a bottle of Pinot Grigio" – was in full nesting mode. She had recently finished rereading the *Huntress' Handbook* after spending her third Valentine's Day in a row on her own. One thing was for sure: she didn't want to turn into a bitter, overweight forty-something one-night-stander like her sister Sarah, with whom she shared the studio flat above the café.

"So where have you been all this time?" Helen said, smiling, placing the cappuccino on the table.

"What? Well, I've… I was finishing my novel…"

"Which novel, the one you were writing last year?"

"No, another one, a new one… it's called *A Thorn in My Side*."

"What's it about?"

"Well, you know, it's impossible to sum it up… it's a story… a story… how can I put it… it's the kind of story that is very popular these days, yeah… very commercial. There are already three publishers who are interested," lied Jim, raising his nose and his voice, "so… let's keep our fingers crossed…" And he accompanied the words with the appropriate gesture and a half-smile.

"Yeah, fingers crossed," Helen repeated, as she turned to go back to the counter.

"Helen?" Jim stopped her.

"Yes?"

"Nice of you to ask. And thanks for the cappuccino."

"Not at all."

"We should catch up one of these days. Maybe go out for a beer?"

"Sure," Helen said, with little conviction.

A few seconds later, the philosopher had buried himself again in the first few pages of his novel.

* * *

Later in the day, as he sat on a low wall outside the Fulham Post Office, Jim's eyes were fixed on his watch. He knew that his landlord Tom, who was a postman, had already finished work at that time, so they were in no danger of bumping into each other. It would have been slightly embarrassing for Jim to explain his presence there. A few minutes after one o'clock, as he had anticipated, out ambled Gautam, his Indian friend with a secret passion for off-piste photocopying and stamp larceny. Gautam was a bit surprised to see Jim again after many months, but he immediately understood the reason of his visit.

"How many do you need this time round?" he murmured with a wink.

"Seventy," Jim answered.

"Seventy?" repeated Gautam. From his pocket he pulled out a calculator. "How many pages?"

"Four hundred."

"Four hundred?"

"Four hundred," Jim said, nodding. In fact, the page length was closer to five hundred, but he thought he could play a bit with margins and line spacing, and save a few quid. "Printed on one side or on both sides?"

"One side."

"With or without envelopes?"

"With."

"SAE enclosed?"

"Yep, second class."

Gautam tapped on the tiny keypad with nimble fingers, whispering to himself from time to time: "One penny per sheet... four hundred... times seventy, equals... right... plus envelopes, stamps, franking... mmm..." The Indian shook his head.

"Payment terms?"

"Cash."

"Mmm..." And Gautam's head began to swing one way and the other. "Well, that'll be... two hundred and eighty...

plus the stamps… I'll need a little bit of time, at least a few days…"

"No problem, I'll be tinkering with my novel. I'll need a few days too."

"I'll see what I can do."

* * *

The Shark was sitting to attention: shoulders pushed back, stomach held in and buttocks tense as violin strings. In front of higher-ranking sharks, Nick Tinsley could turn into whitebait.

He was sitting in the lounge of one of the most exclusive hotels in central London with the majority shareholders of Tetragon Press, who had flown in for the meeting. After the customary handshakes and polite grins, Gustaaf Goosen – fifty-seven years of age, two metres of pure Dutch bacon fat, bald pate, greying goatee, Pantagruelian paunch – had sunk into a jet-lag-induced nap. Perched at the top of an international paper manufacturer's – a company of around two thousand souls which he had clawed into shape through an unstoppable series of acquisitions, buy-outs and double-digit-growth years – he ruled over his empire from the cocoon of a Jumbo Jet, constantly travelling in the opposite direction to the earth's rotation in order to nibble at the time zones of various countries, and taking a bit of shut-eye at four-hour intervals like a newborn baby. This gave him the illusion that his days were thirty or forty hours long, and that he could be more productive and live longer.

The other majority shareholder, Samson Mulu, a middle-aged Ethiopian with an infinite sense of his own worth and a barely visible moustache above his damp lips, was one of Goosen's most trusted business partners and his emissary in the Afro-Asiatic regions. Towards the end of the '90s, taking advantage of a distant cousin's connection to the clan of the former Emperor Haile Selassie, Mulu had assisted his Dutch partner in the purchase of a valuable land plot in the country's Free Zone. On this land he had built, under Goosen's instructions, a kind of Taj Mahal of paper manufacturing and printing, an architectural colossus with no precedent on the African savannahs, used predominantly for the printing of tourist guides and postcards. Business rivals hissed that it was nothing but a cover-up for money-laundering activities; others swore that deep among the interminable rows of containers brimming over with books and stationery were stacked AK47s and surface-to-air missiles; still more claimed that some corrupt African UN grandee was keeping that marble monster up and running as part of a complex kickback operation. No one knew for sure, but the aura of mystery surrounding the true scale and nature of Goosen and Mulu's dealings on African soil only increased Nick's admiration for the two men – the more so as his fully loaded invoices were always settled punctually and without a quibble, via a transfer from a Maltese bank into his offshore Jersey account.

As Goosen wheezed in the dim light of the muzak-filled lounge, the Ethiopian was engaged in a couple of calls on his mobile. Nick followed him with interest, munching some nuts as he sipped from a trumpet-shaped glass of beer, waiting for his moment.

"OK... OK... mm-mh... OK... mm-mh... mm-mh... One moment pleeze." Samson pressed a key and began a heated conversation in Amharic, shouting instructions at some unfortunate minion somewhere. Then he pressed the key again and resumed his sing-song negotiations: "OK... OK... Yes, yes pleeze... mm-mh... mm-mh... thirty million... mm-mh... mm-mh... letter of guarantee... pleeze..." while scrawling indecipherable notes on one of the sheets of paper scattered in front of him.

At the end of his call he looked up slowly and rested his watery, indifferent, sickened gaze on Nick.

"How are you, Nick?" he said in a grieved voice.

Nick thought this was his go-ahead, and wriggled on his chair as he geared up to say his bit, but Samson went back to his mobile phone again, pressing a dozen keys and shouting new orders convulsively.

"Tell me, tell me," he urged Nick during the first pause. "How did it go with Dr Randall?"

"It was all right... I mean, we'll have to take it step by step... Today he was in a bad mood and he just wouldn't listen."

"I see, he was in a bad mood... Mr Harris, pleeze... Nick, just a second... yes pleeze... OK, OK. And... how did he react to the news?... Yes, I'm holding."

"The news? Well, like I said it was impossible to talk to him properly today... he arrived late and did nothing but complain about this and that... as usual..."

"I see... yes, I'm still holding... And when do you think..."

"In a couple of weeks, maybe? It's better not to give any warning, otherwise he might do something stupid – come up with a revenge plan, destroy some important papers or something... And of course we need a publishing programme for next year..."

"I see, the programme..." He hung up and dialled another number. "The programme... and... and where is his..."

"His replacement? He's sitting at that table over there. Shall I wave him over?"

Samson nodded, then turned away to whisper something into his phone.

The Shark signalled to a young man sitting at the opposite corner of the lounge, who jumped to his feet and trotted towards their table. He had long, flaxen hair, an earring in his left ear and glasses of a vaguely intellectual description. His face might have borne a striking resemblance to Kurt Cobain's had its symmetry not been spoilt long ago by a head-butt to the nose during a college rugby match. He had tried to dress up smartly for the occasion, but his orange tie and brown belt hinted at fundamental aesthetic deficiencies.

He exchanged a meaningful look with Nick, who invited him to sit down on the only available chair and eat a few nuts while Samson finished his call.

"One moment, one moment pleeze... Good evening, Mr..." The Ethiopian stretched a drooping hand towards the newcomer.

"Payne-Turner," chipped in Nick, in support of his protégé.

"Bane-Turner..."

"Payne... Payne..." pointed out Nick.

"Bean..."

"Payne."

"Bain... One moment pleeze..." Samson continued talking for a few minutes in his mother tongue, chortling noisily from time to time. At the end of the call he raised his blood-shot eyes slowly from his papers and rested them on the well-built individual who sat across the table.

"Mr Bain…"

"Mr Mulu?"

"Mr Bain, what is the most important thing in this job? Did Mr Tinsley explain it to you?"

There was a long pause.

"Confidentiality…" Samson rasped. "Not even the left hand should know that there is a right hand doing something completely different. Is that understood?"

James threw a startled glance at Nick, who replied with a reassuring and discreet wink.

"Another essential thing is always to follow orders, especially…" – and here Samson's voice turned into a whisper – "…especially if they are coming from Mr Goosen. Is that understood?"

"Sure…"

"Good, Mr Bain, good… Hello? Hello hello hello?… Yes?… Yes, just one moment, I'll put you on hold… Now, Mr Bain, if someone asked you to—"

Goosen roared himself awake, and silence fell around the table. He propped himself up with some difficulty and grabbed at the documents in front of him. At first he didn't seem to understand what they were, but then his piercing eyes narrowed in comprehension. For some moments he scanned the figures with ferocious processing power as the other three men watched deferentially.

"Ha!" he snarled at last. "This is completely unacceptable!… The situation is out of control… We must cut the dead wood… start sacking people… Who did this bit of creative accounting? Who did it? If we carry on like this, the company will go into liquidation by the end of the year…"

Nobody dared speak or move.

"This is a limited company," Goosen muttered, "not a charity... No loss is no good: I want profits, OK? Pro-fits. Otherwise you all go home. And you've kicked out that good-for-nothing at last – what's his name, Randall?"

"We'll do it on Friday," said Samson with assurance, stretching a finger to silence his vibrating mobile, which was ready to erupt with a shrill ring. "We need to get the publishing list from him for next year, Nick says."

"I don't care about his list. List or no list, just sack him, OK? Fuck him. He's wasted enough of my money on Hungarian epics and shit like that."

"No problem. Friday will be his last day," confirmed Samson, making a series of hieroglyphic notes on his doodle-bespattered diary.

"Good... And who's this?"

Nick jutted forwards eagerly, his chin almost brushing the rim of his beer glass.

"This, Mr Goosen, is Randall's replacement... the new editorial director of Tetragon Press... James Payne-Turner..."

"Editorial *director*? Why 'director' and not 'manager'?"

Silence.

"Who authorized this?"

There was another long pause, during which Goosen cast a beady eye on his latest blinking employee, scrutinizing in particular Payne-Turner's hair, earring and orange tie. Finally, he adjusted his gigantic mass and stood up with a condescending grin branded on his face.

"Good. We'll meet next month. Nick, Samson... can we talk for a few minutes in private?"

Nick sprang up and, fully satisfied with the result of the interview, nodded reassuringly at James. Samson gathered up his papers chaotically, shouting something into his mobile in an incomprehensible mixture of languages, while James remained sitting at the table on his own, his heartbeat regaining a normal rhythm, his eyes lost on the swaying bottom of a well-furnished waitress.

* * *

After meeting Gautam, Jim went browsing in a bookshop on the ground floor of a big shopping centre. He wandered around the tables covered with piles and piles of novels, plastered with "3 for 2" and "Half Price" stickers on their covers. He fantasized over posters, tried to imagine what cover his book might have, what kind of publicity campaign...

By now it was two o'clock – but he wasn't peckish. When he was among books or writing, he lost awareness of time and space. He could forget to eat, forget to sleep... it was almost as if he could become an incorporeal being, a pure spirit.

Later in the afternoon, he went to the local library. He was relieved to see that there were very few people. But the *Bookpage* magazine was in use, even if Jim couldn't see anybody reading it. He leafed through the TLS for a long time, and was reduced to reading a short review of a nineteenth-century Romanian poet by the time he at last observed an eccentric-looking man in a striped suit placing *Bookpage* back on the shelf. Jim followed the man with his eyes as he queued up at the borrowing desk. Flaunting a long white beard and Leonardo-style hair, a broad-brimmed hat, thick glasses and a purple-veined nose, he was holding a tall pile of books in his hands, all by the same author. He gave the books and his reader's card to the librarian, then took the books back, turned round and went across to the opposite counter, where he appeared to return the books he had just taken out on loan.

"Some nutter…" Jim said to himself, with a shrug. But any preoccupation with the outside world dissipated the moment he got his hands on the magazine. He turned to the bestsellers' charts at once and surveyed the whole section, making comments to himself from time to time.

"Jamie Oliver… 25,435 copies sold in a week… Maeve Binchy… 21,273 copies… mmm… Arrow, Hodder, Corgi, Arrow, HarperCollins, Hodder, Hodder, Picador, Orion, Orion, Black Swan… Bantam, Abacus, Hodder, Penguin… mmm… Penguin… Canongate… feisty young independent… mmm…"

He freewheeled around in his daydreams for a long time, even after leaving the library, so that his bicycle seemed to fly him back to the flat.

At home there was the usual muffled silence. He took shelter in his room and turned on his computer. He immediately got on with finalizing the pagination and the typeface of his novel, fiddling with the word-processor's commands for hours. At seven o'clock, his eyes now strained by the effort, he felt he had reached Bodonian levels of typography. Satisfied with his work, he decided to print the final copy that would go out to publishers and agents.

From under the bed emerged a 20 cl mini-bottle of Moët & Chandon, which he had zealously kept from time immemorial for some great event. Without much difficulty, he silenced the pop of the cork: no one could have heard that faint gassy gulp, nor taken that moment of rarefied happiness from him.

2

The telephone was ringing with raucous desperation: dring-drriinnng... dring-drriinnng... The other phones echoed it with different ringing tones: tarara-tarara... tarara-tarara... tuuuuuuuu... tuuuu... He picked up receivers one after another, answering as best he could, but his tongue remained anchored to the depths of his mouth: "Hul... hulllll... hulllllllll..." He started throwing his arms about, scattering sheets of paper to the right and to the left as he frantically gestured to Helen's sister to pick up the other ringing phones. But she was shaking her head: she giggled and let the phones ring on and on for an age, wasting God knows how many good offers from publishers and agents, until she answered at last:

"HarperCollins on line two... Random House on three..."

But he still couldn't speak, and kept on mumbling, with a paralysed tongue: "Hullll... hulllll..."

"Hello?... Hello?..." Gautam was saying down the line, getting no answer.

Jim inched his head up from the pillow and realized that he had a talking mobile phone in his hand.

"What? Who's that?" he could only say, floundering in the waters of his awakening.

"Gautam... it's Gautam, hello?... Are you there, Jim?"

Jim jolted up on his bed and looked at his watch. It was twenty-past twelve.

"Yeah..." he mumbled, still half-unconscious.

"Everything's ready."

"Ready?"

"Yes, everything's ready... Bring me the envelopes and labels, it's D-Day."

"D-Day?"

"Dispatch Day... but are you there, Jim?"

"I'm coming..."

In the last few days, he had done little but wait for that telephone call. The text of the letter for publishers and agents had been prepared a week ago, in a sudden gush of epistolary inspiration. Then he had spent two whole days double-checking names and address details, calling up whenever possible to make sure the recipients were all still there, because it was six months since he had last thrown himself over the barbed wire of the publishing trenches – and a lot can change in publishing in six months. Then he had carefully chosen the writing paper and written down each address by hand, to give his submissions a personal touch, as if they were wedding invitations. Finally, he had spent half an hour experimenting with an appropriate signature and even the best pen to be used.

Gautam came out for his lunch break bubbling over with winks and smiles, holding the calculator in his hand and a bunch of sheets under his arm.

"There you go, this is yours... it's all ready to roll, seventy copies... bam... the Normandy Landings..."

"Here's the stuff you need," said Jim, ignoring him. He had pulled out a bunch of signed letters, the self-addressed envelopes and the labels from his rucksack. "What's the total cost?"

"Four pounds times seventy is two hundred and eighty pounds... let's say two hundred and fifty – plus two pounds' postage for each parcel – is three hundred and ninety – plus the second-class SAEs for the rejection letters, heh heh heh, let's say ten pounds to keep things simple, and the grand total is..." – Gautam's forefinger hit hard on the equals key – "four hundred pounds exactly... inclusive of labour..."

"Crook," Jim thought, with a slight twitching of his eyebrows, but he started taking his wallet out.

"No, no... not here," said Gautam. They withdrew to a more secluded place, at the back of the nearby church, where Gautam watched in surprise as eight fifty-pound notes rained one after the other onto his open palm.

"Whooa... have you won the lottery?"

"No, not yet..." replied Jim, as banknotes and calculator vanished into his friend's trouser pocket. "Not yet..." he repeated to himself.

* * *

There was an oppressive atmosphere at the Tetragon Press offices that morning. The gloomy London pall, together with the usual climate of depression that envelops the world of books, had combined to create a kind of greenhouse effect of dissatisfaction within the cramped walls of the small publishing house. Holly was still suffering from migraine, and was dawdling over a useless letter to some individual who kept on posting his CV, looking for non-existent editorial openings. Pippa was very busy playing furtive solitaire – and what's more, without much joy. And a world-weary Charles was sitting in his small room, sucking on his smouldering pipe in blatant contravention of the smoking ban, watching the nearby urban horizon through the window while a loquacious translator – a skeletal man with tartar-ridden teeth and welder's goggles for glasses – tried to persuade him to publish a collection of poems by an obscure Hungarian writer of the early twentieth century, who had committed suicide at the age of twenty-three.

"I've devoted fifteen years of my life to this poetry."

"Grrnff."

"I beg your pardon?"

"The name…" said Charles, laying his pipe on the desk and sighing.

"Excuse me?"

"The translation is good, but the name… the name's a problem – it will be difficult to market. Compared to that, pronouncing Laszlo Krasznahorkai or Deszo Kosztolany is as easy as pie. Why is it that all the authors I'm asked to publish are unpronounceable? Zoshchenko, Gombrowicz, Krzhizhanovsky, Pszcisziszewszki… Look at the French instead," Charles added, becoming briefly animated. "Proust, Gide, Sartre, Balzac, Dumas…"

The translator gave a smile full of uncertain bonhomie and tartar.

"I've spoken with the Director of the Hungarian Foundation – she said that she could help us get a subsidy or a grant for the publication of the book. And if the grant falls through…"

"Grnf."

"…and if the grant falls through, I would be willing – how can I put it – I would be happy to help, with my own savings…

You don't get rich with this sort of thing, it's a well-known fact... I'm not doing this for money, it's a labour of love... fifteen years..."

"Stop it, stop it, stop it!" cried a shrill voice inside Charles's head. "Why?... why are people so desperate to get into print? Everybody wants to publish a book, everybody wants to change the world with a sheaf of printed papers..."

The entryphone croaked, and Charles heard Pippa shuffle along the corridor and answer it in her usual snappy tone.

"...and we could submit the book to all the major translation prizes. I believe that a book like this, even though it's not by a very famous author..."

Charles pulled out a stapled document from a tower of papers, and passed it to the translator, who gave it a bewildered look.

"Brnf."

"Pardon?"

"The contract."

The translator looked at it, trying to hide a mounting excitement.

"No advance and no royalties. We'll publish it at our expense. This poet ought to be better known in this country. If there's a grant from the Hungarian Foundation, we get all the money. Here's a pen."

"Can I have a look at this at home?" asked the translator, trying to speed-read the pages crammed with clauses and sub-clauses.

The door opened without any notice, revealing the figure of the Shark, followed by a tall, short-haired young man who had the look of a door-to-door salesman.

"Hey, Charles."

"What's this? We didn't have an appointment today, did we?"

"Surprise surprise."

"I'm busy now. Can you come back later?"

"Sorry, we've got to talk now, can't be put off."

"But can't you see I'm busy? Don't they teach good manners any more? Without even calling or knocking at the door? And who's this?" asked Charles, pointing at the young man peering at him from behind Nick's shoulders.

"Your replacement, James Payne-Turner."

"My what?"

"Your replacement. You're fired."

There was a very long pause. The translator, who had followed the ping-pong exchange attentively, drew the contract closer to his bag with a barely perceptible movement.

Charles burst into wild laughter. Behind James's shoulders appeared Pippa and Holly.

"Ha ha ha... how funny! Now get out."

"This isn't a joke, Charles... game's up."

"Go away!... Out!... Out of my office, immediately!"

"Charles..."

"I said *out*! This is *my* office, this is *my* publishing house!"

The Shark gave him a letter signed by Gustaaf Goosen himself.

Charles cast a quick glance at the letter and threw it on his desk.

"This doesn't mean anything. I am not leaving."

"Yes you are."

"No I am not."

"Oh yes, you are."

"Oh no, I am not."

"Excuse me," chipped in the translator. "If it's OK, I'd better be on my way, as we've already discussed our contract and there's no…"

"What contract?" asked Nick, firing a petrifying glance first at the translator and then at Charles. "What contract?"

"Well, this… I mean…" And the translator passed the stapled sheets to Nick, who leafed through them briskly.

"What's this!?" he finally exclaimed, pointing at a long sequence of unpronounceable syllables.

"The author's name…" the translator answered timidly.

"Is he from Poland? Serbia? Montenegro?"

"He's Hungarian," said the translator, venturing a yellowish half-smile.

"Hungarian? Hungarian?" And he turned his stare on Charles. "Didn't we say that the days of Hungarian and Chilean poets were over?"

"Bo-li-vian!"

Nick crumpled the contract into a ball and threw it in the bin. "Enough with this crap."

"I'll… go…" the translator said with a reedy voice, and he zigzagged out of the room.

"If you don't mind…" the Shark said to Pippa and Holly, who were watching wide-eyed in the doorway, and he slammed the door behind him.

"I am not leaving."

"Charles…"

"I-am-not-leav-ing!"

"Charles…"

"I'll chain myself to the desk. I am the founder of this company. You cannot take it away from me like this."

"Let's try to make this as painless as possible…" Nick said in a soft, persuasive tone, as James kept nodding in silence. "It's in everybody's interest to sort this out without making too much fuss."

"Who gave you permission to throw that contract in the bin and kick out the translator?"

"Charles…"

"How can you humiliate people like that? I'm going to sue you, you can be sure about that."

"Charles, Charles… try to calm down and see things from an objective point of view. The red warning light has been on for years. This company guzzles like a Ferrari and performs like a 2CV… We need a new… a new… thrust…"

"Prrnf… Spare me your plebeian metaphors."

"We need new blood, new ideas… Times have changed and we need more…"

"More ignorance, that's what you want. Ignorance and brazen cheek."

"We need a less old-fashioned approach, a more modern…"

"You can save your breath, I am NOT leaving. This is my life. You can't kill a person like this, in cold blood. People are sent to jail for this kind of thing."

"Look, this is the final offer from the two majority shareholders. Take it or leave it. If you want to make a fuss, then I should warn you that Mr Goosen and Mr Mulu have a very good legal team and you'll end up with nothing."

Charles threw a desperate glance at the letter Nick had handed him.

"I'm not interested in making money. It's the emotional value that—"

"Yeah, we all know you don't care about making money. Or losing other people's. This is why it's time for you to retire."

Charles collapsed into the chair. "If it's a matter of money, I can invest my own savings in the company."

"It's not *simply* a matter of money."

"Keep me as an editor at large."

"No."

"As a consultant with a reduced salary."

"No."

"As a consultant with no salary."

"No."

"I see."

Charles scrutinized the letter more closely, lifting his glasses to bring the numbers and the terms into focus.

"That's chicken feed."

"What?"

"I mean, I've worked here for thirty years to get such a pittance? If I really am to leave, I expect at least three times as much."

The Shark snorted, losing his patience.

"Charles, you really are pushing it. This is an extremely generous offer, considering that the company has been unprofitable from just about day one."

"Yes, OK, but the reputation, the name, must have a value!"

"Well, you can stuff the name and the rep—"

The founder of Tetragon Press snapped around and swept his arm across his desk, from one end to the other, sending to the floor most of the books and papers that had been lying there from time immemorial.

"Rrrrrgh…"

"Whooaaahh…" Nick warned, while James Payne-Turner took a step forwards, as though he might intervene physically.

"This won't be the last you'll hear from me…" Charles said finally, his voice trembling, his hands shaking, as he picked up his pipe from the floor.

* * *

Jim was pedalling homewards with hardly any feeling left in his legs. It seemed as though the pedals were pedalling his legs, not the other way round. Even the rest of his body, including his long ponytail, was pervaded by the same sense of limpness. He had written the book: now he had sent it out and could only sit in a corner and wait. He felt like a pitted olive.

Once he got home, he laid down on his bed. He spent a few hours examining the ceiling, letting himself be meekly swallowed up by the slavering mouth of night. From time to time some fragments or unconnected words emerged from his lips – the erratic spasms of a galvanized dead frog:

"That's good… that's also good… maybe the ending…"

And that was his last half-conscious glimmer of thought until he awoke with a growl in the middle of the night, at the end of some scary dream. He was still wearing his clothes, and an icy shudder ran first down his spine and then through his arms. The darkness was total, the silence was tomb-like, and his body was motionless – it dawned on him that he might be a thinking corpse. Was this what death was like? A gloomy solitary place, a limbo which is not illuminated by the glow of earthly – or posthumous – fame? He tried asking the darkness around him, holding his breath and swallowing bitter spittle, but there was no answer. In the end, the shouts of a gang of boozers going past outside, throwing empty bottles around, dragged him back into the land of the living and the losers. But a certain anxiety had crept into him, and he struggled to go back to sleep.

The following day the sun didn't seem to rise at all. The room was still dark when, around one in the afternoon, he woke up with a splitting headache. He peeped out of his room, with a vague hope that Janet and Tom might be away. And in the kitchen he found a brief message explaining that the two love birds had gone off on a sponging mission to see their friend Daphne in Dorset. They would be back on Sunday night. Jim closed his eyes for a moment in relief, nursing his temples with his fingertips. At the bottom of the message there was a detailed PS in which Janet reminded him about opening the windows of both the kitchen and his room, taking out the rubbish bag, watering the basil pot and, above all, being careful not to flood the bathroom floor if he decided to shower.

In front of him were hours of liberty, during which he could finally breathe freely, read, relax and devote a little time to himself. But the problem was that the limpness which had pervaded him the day before was still running through each particle of his body – a kind of murderous nausea which turned everything he looked at into a repulsive sight. So, without washing his face, combing his hair or shaving, without eating his usual buttered slice of bread with marmite, he decided it was best to get out of the flat.

The sky was like a smooth concrete slab, even though an icy drop, from time to time, rained down from some hidden chink. Perhaps, if there was any meteorological justice in the world, it was pouring down in Dorset now. The people who walked past him on the Uxbridge Road seemed to have emerged from the set of a horror movie: grim faces eroded by hunger, toothless mouths, bald heads, double-decker necks, washed-out tattoos, gangly zombies in shorts tottering around with cans of Fosters in their hands, human carcasses wrapped in shrouds of rags, lying in street corners waiting for the great sweeper.

Leaving the BBC and White City on his left and the filthy Green on his right, past the Tube station and across the huge roundabout, Jim walked under the trees lining Holland Park Avenue. Then up to the top of Notting Hill, where he met hordes of tourists flocking to Portobello market. And then on and up again, first coasting Kensington Gardens and then Hyde Park, until he reached Speaker's Corner, where knots of people loitered around the usual oddballs. He momentarily saw his own ghost standing on one of those stools and reciting his novel in a loud clear voice – a misunderstood genius crying out to deaf ears, pelted down with rotten eggs and tomatoes hurled by the pitiless hands of the ignorant masses. But the ghost jumped off the stool of its own accord and Jim, passing by Marble Arch with his head lowered, crossed the street and joined the nameless crowds walking up and down Oxford Street.

There thronged a different human brood from the one he had left behind at Shepherds Bush. It was an overflowing of health and energy, an uncontrollable explosion of vitality, youth, sex and credit cards; a triumph of designer clothes and accessories, branded shoes and watches, fashionable hairdos. It was the land of consumerism, of the mass-market stores, the big chains, the multinationals, the land of endless possibility and excess. It was in this seething frenzy, Jim knew, that all successful products were seeded, including best-selling books. From there, they would then spread out and colonize the rest of the capitalist universe. People seemed happy, their well-being bubbling over merrily in public: they queued up in front of the cashiers to buy the latest gadgets, paying promptly and without haggling. The more expensive the purchase, the happier they seemed.

It was this monstrous mass that fed on pulp fiction and all the latest bestsellers, allowing a happy few writers to live lives of unfettered luxury. But how could *he* speak to that mass, how could *he* appeal to it? Jim had the presentiment that, after all, all those nameless people walking past him really couldn't give a hoot about what he had to say to them. His murderous nausea grabbed him by the throat again, whilst his feet were beginning to ache.

As he walked past the long window of a shopfront, he caught his own bobbing reflection out of the corner of his eye and stopped dead. He saw a famished figure in front of him, with a dead man's shadows under the eyes and chiaroscuroed cheekbones. He felt old, he felt uncool. He looked at the way he was dressed: he had been wearing the same jeans, jacket and trainers for the last ten years. He didn't even have an iPod. In pursuing the hollow dream of success, he had lost touch with reality. While his contemporaries had been busy enjoying themselves and making the most of their youthful years, he had wasted the best period of his life. He walked on in self-disgust.

He ended up spending the whole afternoon on a bench in Trafalgar Square, watching the pigeons pecking away at any sort of food or excrement, under an intermittent drizzle which made no ripples in the fountains' water.

When he got home, all he did was take his shoes off and slip into bed, hoping that the night would soon be over and that a better day would follow.

But the following morning, as he woke up in the clothes he had been wearing for two days, a terrible sense of apathy swept over him, and he barely managed to drag his carcass in front of the television, where he spent eight hours watching cricket. When night approached, he retired in good order to his den and sank into a dreamless sleep, which not even Janet's giggles and Tom's guffaws on their return from Dorset could interrupt.

3

Monday came, and the waiting was over. It was only eight o'clock when Jim turned on his PC to check his email, even though he knew that the sun had not risen yet in the world of publishing, and that his typescript could not have been delivered by that time. But this was only the first in a long series of well-oiled propitiatory rituals, such as wearing his lucky T-shirt, using only his left hand and opening Shakespeare's *Complete Works* at random in order to take the auspices for the day from the line on which his forefinger fell. On that day, the Bard had decreed from the poetic depths of *Henry IV*:

> *Do nothing but eat, and make good cheer.*

So, after deleting a couple of spam messages, he opened the door of his room with his left hand and sneaked into the kitchen looking for something to eat. His cupboard was still empty, so he resigned himself to pilfering a can of tuna of doubtful provenance, which he had been eyeing for months in the corner of a cupboard. In the rubbish bin he spotted an entire pack of Hovis bread, which Janet must have thrown away the previous night for being past its use-by date, and fished out a couple of borderline-mouldy slices. Always using his left hand, he poured water into his personal mini-kettle and filched a spoonful of instant coffee. Then he sneaked back into his room and, sitting on the edge of the bed and being careful not to drop crumbs on the floor, he munched his crude sandwich with satisfaction, relishing the thought that many little secretarial hands would soon be opening his submission and passing it on to whomever it concerned...

Somehow or other ten o'clock arrived. Then eleven o'clock arrived, then twelve. Still no email, no telephone call. "Be patient," he said to himself. "It's way too early... the internal mail-sorting system... and it's a Monday, they're busy... and it'll take them days to read anyway..." Around one o'clock he started checking his email every five minutes. At two he adopted the crossing position, which involved keeping his arms, legs and fingers crossed, chin leaning on chest. After a few minutes, as he dozed off at the height of his concentration, a gentle tapping at the door made him jump off the bed. He hastened to open the window and hide the empty tuna can under the bed, behind a pile of books.

"Ah, you're back..." Jim said, opening the door a little and trying to block the fissure with his body. Janet gave a start and flared her nostrils. She had a worn-out look, as if she had only found rain and hail in Dorset. All her yoga lessons, her weekend trips, her herbal teas and her anti-stress creams didn't appear to have any effect on her gecko-skin complexion.

"Yeah, back last night, as the message said... Listen, Jim, I'm off to Tesco's to get a few bits and pieces – and a new pot of basil..."

"Eh? Oh... Ah, sorry-sorry-sorry..." and he slapped his head. "I just... I forgot to..."

"Doesn't matter, don't worry... Do you need anything?"

This was a gentle way of reminding him about paying his share for the dishwasher powder, the refuse bags and all the other communal items.

"What? Er… no, thanks… I'm going out myself later on… How much is it for the washing powder and stuff?" And he pulled out a crumpled note from his pocket.

"That'll do. See ya later." And throwing a worried look over Jim's shoulders and into the room, she turned on her heel and strode to the front door, which resounded with its customary *bang* a few seconds later.

"Bitch," said Jim.

He shut the door and hunched himself into the crossing position again. His figure resembled that of a strange, rickety mummy.

A few hours went by. Offices would be closing by now. Even the most workaholic of editors, together with their flunkeys, would be joining their colleagues down at the pub for their daily booze-glugging. And Jim had not received a single response. "How it possible," he said to himself, "in this age of instant communications, that not even one publisher out of seventy – yes, seventy – has deigned to email a brief acknowledgement of receipt, or pick up the phone to say if they are interested or not? There's something wrong with this world…"

At eight o'clock in the evening, his belly rumbling louder than his thoughts, he decided to give up for the day and grab something to eat, and refrain from checking his email until the following day. But it took him another couple of hours before he could tear himself away from his room to breathe again the air of the living. On his way back, while his stomach struggled to cope with an ill-digested mass of spicy food, he convinced himself that he shouldn't worry too much, after all: "Of course... publishers are old-fashioned... They reply by letter..." He was sure that the following morning he would receive a few replies through the door – and with this thought he at least managed to get something close to a quiet night's sleep.

But the following day was a poor copy of the previous one, with the aggravating circumstance of the morning-post false alarm, delivering him only flyers, dodgy competitions and offers of zero-rated credit cards. No letter, no message and no phone call. Day three was wrapped in a black cloud of silence which heralded a horrible storm. On Thursday Jim felt a spurt of energy, which made him spring up from his bed and pace up and down his room all day. On Friday he was seized with a fever and spent most of his time in bed, checking his email only from time to time. And in bed he remained for the entire weekend, in a state which can only be described as unreal, popping out of the room only to collect some pizza or Chinese takeaway.

On Monday morning he decided to grab the publishing bull by its horns, once and for all. At nine o'clock sharp, taking advantage of Janet and Tom's absence, he picked up the phone and dialled the first number on his list.

"Sorry, our editors don't start until 9:30," was the first answer.

"No, I don't think I've seen it..." was the second response. "Could you resend it please? No, not by email, we don't accept email submissions, sorry..." Next to the name of this publisher he wrote: RESEND.

"Sorry, wrong number... There's no Free Will Press here." DOUBLE-CHECK ADDRESS AND TEL. NUMBER. CHK IF FREE WILL PRESS STILL EXISTS.

"What? Ah, yes, yes... I think so... but we are inundated, you know, we're so much behind... it'll take at least six months for us to get back to you." SIX MONTHS.

"Mrs Buckley is in meetings all day." TRY AGAIN TOMORROW.

"Oh yes, of course... I have read it and enjoyed it very much... I was just about to write you a letter... Sure, of course we can help you publish your book, that's no problem at all. All we need is a little contribution from you, just for direct expenses... How much?..." – *tap tap* – "Four and a half thousand, all inclusive... What?... A thousand copies, paperback... Sorry, what did you say the title was?" £4,500.

"Sorry, we only consider agented authors. Our submission policy is clearly stated on our website." ONLY THROUGH AGENTS.

"Please leave a message after the long tone... beeeeep." – "Er... eer... Hello... my name is... er... Jim Talbot and... er... and I've sent you... er... a manuscript last week... I mean, two weeks ago... called... called... er... er..." He hung up.

DELETE.

* * *

So that was it. He was dead and buried. He was history. No, not even history: a *footnote* in history. The world had moved on and had already forgotten all the books he had published, all the battles he had fought in the name of culture. He was a discarded pipe, a broken conveyor belt.

Charles had thought that the news of his sudden departure from Tetragon Press would generate, if not a hullabaloo, at least a ripple of interest in the media. He imagined that one of his journalist friends would persuade a broadsheet to run a piece, creating a little stir, or that *Bookpage* or *Publishers Today* might cover the story for the book trade. The day he was kicked out of his office, he had gone home and furiously prepared a very eloquent press release, full of venom against the bottom-line-driven contemporary publishing scene, bracing himself for the inevitable publicity storm that was to follow. But ten days had gone by and no one had bothered to call. A tiny mention had appeared in a couple of London newspapers, and the few letters he had received were from translators or the Society of Authors, who were worried that their books might be delayed or cancelled as a result of "the termination of his contract", as one of the articles had put it. He wondered whether Mr Goosen and his cronies had paid a PR company to spin the story their way, or bribed the journalists to have him engulfed in silence.

For the past few days, Charles hadn't stepped out of his flat. He was growing a beard and had been wearing the same clothes all week. He had lost his appetite and had stopped cooking for himself. Dishes and mugs piled up in the kitchen, while the rubbish bag smelt as if it contained a dead cat. Insomnia had crept in. He turned over and over in his bed, obsessing about that third-floor office in central London which, from the infernal depths of his flat, now seemed to him a lost paradise. He remembered his small room at the end of the corridor, with all his books and dictionaries, the framed photos of his authors hanging on the walls... and he saw that cocky young man sitting in his place, still wet behind the ears, that good-for-nothing who – he was sure –

could barely string a literate sentence together. He clenched his sheets at the thought that his young successor might have already rearranged the furniture, cleared his desk, used his pen, thrown away some important submissions...

Torn from his thirty-year-old habits and his ingrained nine-to-six routine, he would wake up very late in the morning and remain in bed until noon, frittering away his long days in apathy, sucking at an empty pipe. He didn't know what to do with himself, or even how to keep himself occupied. He had no interest in listening to the radio or to his classical-music records, and didn't have the strength or the courage to begin sorting out the mess around him. What could he do with his life now? He realized there was a world out there that did not know and did not care about books, but he was too old to explore it or start out on a new path. Perhaps he could look for another job – but who would employ him at his age? And he could do no other job than the one that had kept him busy and cocooned for the past thirty years. His head was full of idle facts and pedantries that were completely useless in real life. Maybe he could start the book of poetry he had never written? No: it was too late now, far too late. There was a time when he had nurtured his own poetical ambitions, when he had pledged to join the great poets of the past, those courageous minds who had devoted every fibre of their beings and every moment of their lives to writing. But he was too old now. He had wasted his life pushing mediocre scribblers and ambitious, wheeler-dealer, two-faced, whorish, money-grabbing, vampiric self-promoters – writers who as soon as they got a whiff of success would try to get a better deal from other publishers and jump ship at the earliest opportunity, without even saying "thank you" or "goodbye". His own talent had always been his lowest priority. He had always made time for other writers and their neurotic concerns, and now it was too late for him. The Muse had gone... gone for ever. Maybe he could write a few reviews, or obituaries – or an autobiography, a kiss-and-tell memoir about his thirty years in publishing? But who would read it, if no one had even noticed that he had vanished from the surface of the earth? And would he be able to find a publisher? Probably not. He was alone now. Alone with his memories, with his books and authors, most of them dead.

He spent hours and hours hovering around the sagging bookshelves that ran around his rooms, picking up at random some of the books he had published and others from his rare-book collection, turning them over in his hands, inhaling the musty smell of their jackets, fingering the paper, reading short bits aloud to himself.

That Monday evening his hand landed on one of the first books he had published in the late Seventies, the *Selected Works* of Lord Byron, a lavish hardback edition with gold foil stamped on black cloth. Byron... had he lived to a ripe old age rather than dying in his thirties as he set off to fight for the Greeks, who knows how many more masterpieces he might have penned. Whereas he, Charles, would be equally unremembered were he to live to sixty, seventy or a hundred-and-twenty years – just like John Murray, Byron's publisher, the only difference being that he had no offspring to perpetuate his name, no successor to continue his work. At this thought he grew even more melancholy and depressed, and heaved a portentous sigh. He continued leafing through the book, and his eyes fixed on a line from the second Canto of *Don Juan*:

'Tis never too late to be wholly wreck'd.

He gave a little grunt and, listening again and again to the inner reverberations of these words, a deep sense of pride swelled up in his heart, and a watery rim formed around his eyes.

No, he wasn't dead. He was still alive inside: they could not kill his enthusiasm, his joy, hard as they tried. So they could slot it between their arse cheeks, that paltry redundancy offer with its odious tiny-print non-compete, no-claim and non-disclose clauses. True, he didn't have money in the bank, but maybe with a little bit of help from the Arts Council or some other grant, or from an enthusiastic backer, he could spring back to his feet, set up another imprint? After all he didn't have a family or dependants... he had no wife, no sons, no daughter, not even a cat... he could get by on very little money.

"Trrnf... what an incurable fool... always daydreaming..."

He closed the book, wiped his eyes with the back of his hand and sank into the sofa, where he fell asleep.

* * *

Jim's mood was gloomier and more impenetrable than the cloud-crowded sky weighing down on him. As he walked along the bank of the river, near Hammersmith Bridge, he asked himself if, in all honesty, after his twenty-odd unsuccessful calls, he could still launch a tiny, flying pig of hope across the bleak expanse of his future, and secure a contract for his book. He shrugged and stopped to watch a line of ducks gliding gently across the surface of the water. It was foolish to keep that pig alive. It was absurd to carry on with this life. Why was it so difficult to get a breakthrough, or even a chance? In the old days all you had to do was to dash off a few pompous sonnets about resplendent sunsets while your valet trimmed your mutton-chop whiskers and – bam! – a kindly gentleman-publisher cove would gather them together and produce a handsome gilt-edged volume, without anyone having to swim through a stinking slime of agents and editors...

His thoughts became dark and philosophical. Why write? Who had decreed that the written word was superior to the spoken one? For millennia, man had let his ideas evaporate around him without feeling the urge to inscribe them into stones, scratch them across wax tablets or ink them onto papyri. What evil God had given man this gift – the written word? Wouldn't it be better if man had remained an illiterate brute? What was the point of deep-freezing your thoughts for the sake of future generations – people of other times and cultures who would only misinterpret them? And after all, what was the written word's contribution to the history of mankind? It had only led to laws, wars, scriptures and oppression...

The hazy outlines of a grand treatise on the history of the oral and written word started to take shape in Jim's mind: a paper that could be sent to some prestigious literary or scientific magazine for publication, and later appear in a distinguished collection of essays – and for a second he saw himself in Stockholm, an elderly, revered, cotton-haired figure receiving the Nobel Prize for Literature with natural modesty. But the swirl of images dissolved at the ring of his mobile. His hand fumbled in his pocket.

"Hello?"

"Jim?"

"Mum?" His Adam's apple descended a couple of notches.

"How are you?"

"I'm all right... how are you?"

"What happened last week? Why didn't you come, dear?"

"Well, you know... I was busy at work..."

"Work, work, always work... Don't work too hard, Jim... or you'll end up like your father..."

"All right Mum, I know."

"Listen, I went to my GP this morning... you know, there was that pain under my armpit..."

Jim started listening with a new attention.

"...And he wants me to check into a clinic for some tests."

"Who?... W-what?..."

"Dr Iqbal – he asked me to go for some clinical tests."

"What clinical tests? What Dr Iqbal? What... Are you all right?" He crouched down on the wet, shabby grass, under a tree.

"Don't get upset dear, it's just to be on the safe side, you see. And I wanted to ask you, I need the number of my health-insurance policy."

"The number? Your health policy? No problem, Mum, no problem... Don't worry... I'll call the... I'll... I'll sort it all out. You don't worry." His middle finger was burrowing deep into the damp earth without his knowing it.

"Could you post it to me, dear? The policy? Better still, why don't you come over this evening? Uncle George is coming from Bristol, and we can have dinner together."

"Uncle George is coming?" The burrowing finger became more violent and agitated. "But why do you need it so urgently, this policy, Mum? I mean, can it wait a couple of days?... It'll take time to fish it out from all the papers, from my folders..."

"Well I need to show it to Dr Iqbal tomorrow morning. He called Bupa, but they can't seem to track it down. They need the policy number."

"They're useless..." Jim's middle finger had now tunnelled a whole series of mini shafts in the earth. "OK, Mum, look, I'll bring it over tonight, the Bupa thingy... and I'll talk to the doctor tomorrow morning. You just put your feet up. Don't worry, it's going to be all right, Mum... it's going to be all right..."

But was it going to be all right? As she started talking about Uncle George again, Jim's mind circled over a morass of past deceits. It wasn't wholly deniable that for several years he'd been siphoning his mother's private health-care contributions into his personally administered aspiring-writer fund. To make matters just a tad trickier, when it came to some of her savings and ISA money – which had also been entrusted to his able financial management – he would probably find it awkward, in a strictly empirical sense, to disprove that a significant portion of those funds had somehow oozed out of her accounts and into his. And as if that weren't bad enough, it seemed that Uncle George – Jim's nemesis through many years and interminable disputes – was coming all the way from Bristol in his rotten Morris Traveller to poke his very long and pimpled nose into this cataclysm.

The moment his mother hung up, Jim exhaled a primeval death-wish grunt. He looked up, and since nobody was around he hurled himself towards the riverbank wall and kicked it as though it were a brick arse.

"Shhhhit. Shit, shit, shit, shit!"

He rested his head on the concrete top of the wall and tried to calm down. There was no time to lose. He had a quick look at his watch and dashed towards his bicycle. On the way, his foot connected with an empty Coca-Cola can on the ground, catapulting it into the river, where it scattered the innocent ducks.

* * *

Holly did not suffer from migraine these days. Her morning ailments had dissipated, worming their way into the head of her colleague Pippa, who sat opposite her with an increasingly drawn expression and sunken eyes. To be perfectly honest, Pippa had never liked Holly all that much anyway – maybe because she was so pretty and seemed to have a happy and active sex life. But from the minute James Payne-Turner had made his appearance in the office, Pippa's natural dislike had turned into gnawing resentment. Holly's skirts had been shrinking, her stilettoed shoes craning up, and her blouses were showcasing ever more cleavage by the day. But what really drove Pippa mad were Holly's long and gratuitous visits to her boss's office. She was sure the two of them were up to something in that room. She could hear Holly's piercing voice and cluck-cluck-cluck even over the noisy whine of the shredder, and it was putting her off her solitaire. What hope of advancement did Pippa have now, with Holly and JPT making eyes at each other all day long? When she had joined Tetragon Press a few months ago, after a short work placement in the marketing department of an academic publisher, she thought she'd soon be editing and proofing the most wonderful books by the greatest writers, and attending exclusive literary parties frequented by the crème de la crème of the British intelligentsia. But working for the gruff and moody Charles Randall had been a nightmare at the best of times, and her greatest achievement, in her six months at the Tetragon Press, had been the cover copy for the reprint of a 1987 book by a female Armenian poet. But at least Randall – eccentric and old-fashioned as he was – had been a gentleman, and he had hinted that in due course she might be entrusted with more stimulating work to enhance her editorial skills. But this new glam-rock idiot who didn't even know how to spell his own name and yet still called himself a publisher – he was a different beast altogether. He treated her like a mere cipher, bossed her around with a soft tone of contempt and a false smile on his twelve-year-old face, told her to file this, photocopy that, put this into a box, type that up, book this ticket, call that translator – leaving all the interesting stuff to Holly, who had started at the press only two months ago and was, technically, her junior. Pippa couldn't stomach working in that office for a day longer. She was going to write a letter and give notice that very minute.

In the adjoining room the shredder was moaning away. In little more than a week, Randall's old office seemed to have doubled in size. The walls had been painted white, the authors' photos had been brought down, and all the papers boxed up or destroyed. Most of Randall's extensive reference-book collection, and even his beloved desk, was up for sale on eBay. The new desk – with its glass top, slick wireless phone and top-of-the-range laptop – showed no trace of paper other than a brightly coloured Post-it pad, and the last few stacks of Tetragon's immense and in parts years-old slushpile were being slowly digested by James Payne-Turner's most trusted assistant.

"Trouble is," Holly was saying, her right leg resting at an angle on the wall, a coffee mug cradled in her cupped hands, "trouble is I don't know where to have it, this tattoo… My sister's got it on the ankle – nice. Or on the shoulder, or here—" and she looked down at her left breast, or seemed to.

"Yeah," said Payne-Turner appreciatively.

"They say it hurts… and I get all squeamish and squirmy when I see a needle… but it's only a small tattoo, a small butterfly, or maybe a Celtic shamrock…"

"Yeah." Payne-Turner was feeding page after page in the shredder, toying with a number of lascivious thoughts.

"My sister now, for example, she's into body-piercing… she's more studded than an Elvis jumpsuit… she's got a ring in her belly button, another in her eyebrow, a stud in her tongue, and one in her—"

There was a gentle rap on the door. Holly straightened up and fell silent.

"Come in!"

The door opened cautiously to reveal Pippa's death-pale, mask-like face.

"Can I talk to you for a minute, James?" she whispered, as Holly squirted a quick smirk of acknowledgement.

"I'm actually busy right now," said Payne-Turner, turning to feed another wodge of papers into the shredder.

"It's very important," insisted Pippa.

"All right. Give me ten-fifteen minutes," and he gestured to close the door.

But as she did so, Pippa thought she heard something:

"Nosy cow..."

She froze for a second, then cautiously reopened the door.

"Did you say something?"

"What?"

"Did you just say something to me?"

"No no, nothing." And he gestured again with his hand to close the door, while Holly's stifled giggles followed her out.

Pippa walked slowly back to her desk, heart thumping, ready to detonate.

A couple of minutes later the buzzer rang, and Holly went to the door to let Nick Tinsley in. As she returned to her desk, she put her mug on the mat next to the galleys she was proofing, studiously avoiding her workmate's stare and resuming her work as if she had only interrupted it a few seconds ago to look up a word in the dictionary.

The Shark was feeling good that day. He had just wrapped up, over a long and very alcoholic lunch with an old business pal, a multi-million deal for the supply of some electrical-testing equipment on behalf of a company he had rescued from insolvency the previous year. The notion of being a few hundred thousand pounds better off always had an extraordinary effect on his outlook on life and general well-being.

"How are we today?" he boomed in an alcoholic voice as he tottered into the room, dropping his briefcase on the floor and casting a quick glance around. "Hey, this looks *good*."

"Yeah." Payne-Turner rose to pump his hand. "Getting there."

Pippa admitted herself into the room without announcement.

"Nick, sorry to interrupt, but... can I have a word with you for a second?"

"What's up?"

Her eyes darted swiftly from Nick to James and back again to Nick.

"Could we talk for a minute in private?"

"What's going on? Let's talk here."

"It's..." she hesitated. "I've decided to leave."

"Oh. Well, Pippa... Um..."

There was a long pause, then Nick said: "Can you at least make us a cup of coffee before you go?" and the two men burst out laughing.

Pippa's jaw dropped. She tried to find something to say, but she was also striving to check her tears. She walked out, slamming the door behind her.

"We didn't even have to sack her," Nick said in a wondering tone. "And has Dr Randall been in touch? Has he signed the redundancy offer? Has he tried to jemmy into the office?"

"Nope. He's disappeared. Maybe he's gassed himself or something."

"Oh well. I am glad I had the locks changed though. You never know."

The front door banged wildly.

"We may have to change them again now..."

The Shark grinned.

"So how's tricks, James? How's the new programme coming along?" Nick fumbled in his briefcase and drew out his TP folder, a notepad and a pen.

"It's looking good, looking good. Got in a few very commercial proposals already from big agents... I'm working on them. I can show them to you if you want. But I've got a nice little surprise for you first... Our Arts Council application—"

"What Arts Council application?"

"The one submitted by Charles Randall Esq. a few weeks before he left."

"No shit?"

"They've been knocking him back the last few years, but it wasn't a bad application this time, and I know someone there – we were at college, you know."

"And?"

"Well, with a bit of a shove from my contact, I'd say it's pretty much in the bag. I've got lunch with her tomorrow. We're probably looking at 120K."

"Jesus Christ..." Nick sprang up, went round the desk and slapped his protégé on the back. James could see and smell that he was half-drunk, but didn't resist his effusions. Nick went back to his chair, wrote down "AC +£120K" in his notepad, high-fived James across the table and sat down again. The day was getting better and better...

"As long as the Arts Council believe that we are going to publish the books listed in the application—"

"So we just do a short print run..."

"E-xac-ta-mun-do... get them typeset and proofed in India."

"Genius."

"Yeah. And then, as for the programme—"

Nick closed the notepad with a brisk snap.

"Next time, mate, next time. Let's go down the boozer for a couple of jars... We've made enough money for today. Ask Holly if she wants to come along."

"You sure?"

"Go on… she deserves a treat too."

* * *

At ten to six, en route to his mother's house, Jim came out of Twickenham station with a springy step to his gait, a cappuccino in his hand and a slim yellow folder under his arm. He had had what one might have described as a challenging day, but for now everything was under control. He had called Dr Iqbal, and found out which tests his mother needed. Then he had explained that he would deal with Bupa himself and find out which hospital his mother would attend, so that Dr Iqbal could write the appropriate referral. The next step had been to find a private clinic that offered the tests on a pay-as-you-use basis, and after some confusing phone calls and a lot of googling he had discovered a London clinic providing same-day, walk-in clinical testing and screening. His mother wouldn't suspect a thing.

He found himself looking at a brightly lit shop window. Every time he went to see his mother, he combed all the estate agents on the high street for the latest house prices in the Twickenham Green area, with a particular interest in three-bedroom semis with gardens and off-street parking – it had been wonderful to see house prices soar, and worrying to see them falter. After the death of his father, he had convinced his mother to let him manage her financial affairs, relieving her of the burden of settling her utility bills, paying in her state pension and filling in her Tax Return. And a few years back, as the crowning achievement of his early-retirement scheme, he had persuaded her to register the family home under his name in order to avoid inheritance tax. How much longer could the old lady last? Three or four years maybe? Perhaps even a matter of months, if the tests picked something up. Not that he was wishing her dead...

Preoccupied with such fantasies, he only realized he'd arrived when the familiar grating sound of the doorbell made him come to. His mother opened the door.

"Jim! You're early..."

They exchanged kisses.

"Well, I took the afternoon off... you know, when you told me about your tests, the problem with the policy number... I was worried. Look, I've got all the documents here..."

"Later, dear, later... I still haven't finished preparing dinner..."

"Listen, Mum, before we go in..." Jim lowered his voice, pointing back to the light-blue Morris Traveller parked in the driveway. "What's Uncle George doing here? I mean, you've got enough on your plate, haven't you?... surely you don't want him around at a time like this?"

"Oh come on, Jim, don't be silly. I know there's no love lost between the two of you, but don't you think it was very sweet of him to jump in the car and come all the way from Bristol to see me, at his age?"

"Yes, but what for? I'm here to look after you, right?"

"He's my brother, dear..." she whispered. "Now let's go inside. And try to be polite to him. Not like last time."

"He always provokes me," grunted Jim, closing the door behind him.

The living room was engulfed in a crepuscular half-light. At the far end, leaning back in Father's easy chair with a copy of the *Daily Mail*, sat the bespectacled, rubicund-nosed figure of Uncle George. There was a long, long history of settling old scores, one-upmanship and vengeance between Jim and his mother's brother. Like that time – Jim must have been fourteen or fifteen – when Uncle George, then living in Kingston, had caught him as he was peeing on his car; or the occasion when his uncle had slyly tripped him up as he was racing down the lawn, making him fall awkwardly onto the gravel; or the infamous incident when Jim had phoned the police and tipped them off about a dirty old kiddy-fiddler living in Bristol. With the years, their disputes had gone beyond mere personal animosity to become ideological and philosophical too. George, a staunch conservative and later on a rabid immigrant-bashing member of UKIP, could hardly bear the sight of his long-haired, bohemian, shambolic, lefty nephew. Not to be outdone, Jim loathed George well beyond the old boy's political convictions, as if his uncle were an active part of the great conspiracy that was operating against his success as a writer. And Jim's hatred had matured with time: whereas once he would have slashed his uncle's car's tyres in retaliation for some minor act of aggression, now he could as easily torch the whole car without remorse.

"Hiya," Jim said.

"Hello! The big boy's here – we haven't seen each other for a while, eh?"

"Yeah."

George lifted his glasses to have a better look at how time had treated his sister's only son.

"Interesting haircut," was his comment.

Once they were sitting at the dinner table, Jim explained that everything had been sorted out for the following morning.

He had spoken to Dr Iqbal and contacted Bupa, and the tests were taking place at a clinic near Cavendish Square.

"I'll take the day off tomorrow, Mum. I'll pick you up at nine-thirty and we'll go to this clinic. It'll take only a couple of hours, they say..."

"Strange," intervened George, spreading butter on a piece of bread, "strange that they couldn't find a record of your mother's policy. We even called up the Bupa helpline this afternoon, didn't we Anna? No trace of it. Really strange."

"Well, here it is," said Jim, waving his yellow folder around cautiously.

Uncle George seemed impressed.

"Idiots... Bloody NHS... That's all thanks to Gordon Brown..." he commented, munching away.

The main course arrived. His mother's baked salmon with dill mustard sauce was one of the most dreaded and dreadful offerings from her cuisine. He still remembered how sick he had been the last time he had endured it.

"Just a little bit for me... not all that hungry."

As soon as the very first morsel went down, the salmon seemed to acquire a second life in Jim's digestive apparatus. He could feel it swimming up and down his digestive tract.

"So how is it going with your job?" said Uncle George in a casual way, later on, while Jim's mother was in the kitchen preparing coffee, as if striking up an idle post-prandial conversation.

"All right," replied Jim non-committally.

"Still the same company?"

"Yeah." Jim's nostrils flared: this was dangerous terrain.

"Peculiar... The other day my next-door neighbour had a query with her Tax Return and I gave her your number – you know, your work number – but she couldn't get through to you."

"Maybe it's an old number you have."

"Yes, maybe. But you're definitely still working with Hollis & James in Piccadilly, aren't you?"

"Yeah?" Jim felt his anger rising like hot, bitter coffee spilling over from the narrow pipe of an espresso machine.

"That's what I thought." Uncle George scratched his pimpled nose. "So yesterday I gave Hollis & James a call myself. And they've never heard of a Jim Talbot there. Funny, eh?"

"Must've got the wrong department."

"That's what I thought." He gave his nose another good scratch. "So I spoke to the receptionist—"

"She's new."

"Well, she put me through to the Human Resources department, you see? And—"

"All right, you nosy old coot," said Jim, raising his voice, "suppose I don't work there any more... suppose I've never worked there... suppose I'm a fraud... is it any of your bloody business?"

Jim's mother shuffled in from the kitchen with a shaky tray of coffee.

"Are you having another of your arguments?" she screeched.

"No, just talking... just talking, Anna," said Uncle George in a conciliatory tone.

"Yeah, just talking," repeated Jim, taking his steaming cup and sipping from it.

But that was a big mistake. He had forgotten just how strong and nerve-racking his mother's special-blend, French filtered coffee could be. The minute it went down his throat to scorch the tail of the salmon, the reincarnated beast started wriggling and jumping in his belly. He felt a seismic commotion down below, then a violent pang – more than a pang: the irrepressible cramps of a colic attack. He was running to the loo within seconds.

Half an hour later he emerged from the bathroom with the uncomprehending look of a plane-crash survivor, still shaken by the odd spasm. Uncle George had been so moved by his plight that he had dozed off in Father's easy chair. There he was, mouth wide open, tongue almost sticking out, calmly and unconsciously digesting the vicious salmon with his notorious stomach of steel...

"Why don't you stay over, dear?" said his mum as Jim made for the door.

"It's all right, Mum, I've got stuff to do tonight. But I'll see you tomorrow morning, at nine-thirty. We have to look after you, eh?" he managed weakly. He gave her a limp hug and disappeared down the driveway.

On the way back, a brand-new car parked by the roadside had the ill-advised notion of provoking him by brushing its rear-view mirror against his elbow, and ended up with a double scratch on its immaculate metallic-blue flank. And a black cat, whose only misdemeanour was to cross the street from left to right in front of him – premonition of further calamities – had to climb for dear life up the first available tree.

But as he got off the bus on the Uxbridge Road, his greatest torment wasn't his occasional stomach cramps, or his uncle's prying, or his mum being screened for cancer and on the verge of discovering he had been cleaning out her finances for years – no, what bothered him most was still the indifference of the world to his masterpiece.

"One day…" he whispered to himself grimly. "One day…"

When he opened the front door he could hear peals of laughter from the upstairs flat: Janet's unmistakable turkey shrills followed by Tom's haw-haw-hawing. Jim went up a couple of steps and pricked his ears: silence. Then he went up a few more steps and laughter exploded again. What was going on? The love birds were having a little bit of fun? He stopped in front of the flat's door and tried to understand what was happening inside. Again – convulsive giggles, wild guffawing and long pauses. The minute he slotted the key into the lock, there was a bit of a hubbub within, some frantic whispering. He tiptoed towards the kitchen and peered his head around the door. Janet was suppressing a giggle and wiping a tear from the corner of her eye, while Tom was sitting at the table in shorts and vest, a bottle of red wine in front of him, reading what looked like… what could only be… his manuscript!

"Isn't that… isn't that my…"

"Oh… Jim… Ooops…"

"Where did you get it?"

"Bought it," said Tom, recovering his brashness. "First copy sold, Mr Talbot."

"What the f… who gave it to you, Gautam?"

"Good guess, Jimmy. Lots of freelance photocopying going on in our office at night… And it sounded so interesting: listen here…" He winked at Janet, who was struggling to contain herself. "*They were standing on the lawn, amidst a forest of croquet hoops and cucumber sandwiches…*"

Janet burst out laughing.

"Give me my manuscript back," Jim shouted, wincing as his stomach cramps came back to torment him.

"Hang on, hang on... we're just having a laugh, you know... *They'd wake up together at the crack of dawn and sit outside their bungalow to contemplate the cloud-laden sky as it gradually changed from purple to violet to a rich hibiscus hue...* Uuuuuuu..." howled Tom, improvising an unusually high-pitched note. "What colour is a hibiscus, man? Heh heh heh..."

"Give it back to me, it's mine!"

"Hey, hey, slow down pal..." Tom said, blocking his arm. "Since you wrote it in my flat, and since you've not paid this month's rent as yet, I can confiscate it, right?"

"I'll call the police," shouted Jim.

"Yeah, call 'em," Tom hollered back in his face, rising to his feet a good six inches above him. "From *your* mobile. Nine-nine-nine. And start packing."

They stared hard at each other for a few seconds, the tips of their noses almost within touching distance, then Jim mumbled something and did an about-turn. Just after slamming the door of his room he heard from the kitchen:

"That's what he does all the time, the fucker. That's why there's rising damp in there."

He sat down on his bed holding his head in his hands, and stifled a horrible growl down his throat. His stomach cramped again for a few moments, making him groan. He jumped to his feet and looked around in despair, then he saw a plastic bag full of old books and emptied it on the floor. For one brief moment, with the bag in his hands, he thought about wrapping it around his head and calling it a day, just like his creative-writing tutor... But no, he mustn't give in: his destiny was to be a great writer, to write a bestseller.

4

Somehow Jim managed to wade through the dire days. His mum kept him busy on several mornings with blood tests, hospital visits and X-rays, resulting not only in bank-breaking bills from the clinic, but also in the discovery of a little lump in her left breast – which meant scans and treatments and more private-health blood-sucking. What really drove him insane, though, was Uncle George, who never let a chance go by to escalate their disputes. One day, at his mother's house, as Jim was heading for the door with the strained face of an undertaker loading a heavy coffin into the hearse, George popped up from the kitchen – a glass of gin-and-tonic in his hand, his carbuncular nose aflame – and stared at a spot on the floor, as if looking for something he had just dropped.

"What?" said Jim, grabbing the door knob and giving it a half-turn.

"Nothing," replied the old man with a mischievous smile on his face.

"*What?*"

"Nothing, nothing… You've got some spanking red flippers on your feet, eh?"

A couple of days later the Morris Traveller emerged from the long Twickenham night with a flat tyre and graffiti sprayed on both sides. When Jim and his mum returned from the clinic that day, they found Uncle George jumping up and down around the car.

"Unbelievable, un-be-liev-able... in our own driveway!"

"Bloody yobs..." commented Jim, nostrils flared up to suppress laughter.

"Probably some foreign immigrant."

"Yeah, a drunken Eastern European on benefits and stuff... or some asylum-seeker."

"Precisely. And the police do nothing, nothing! Under their very noses. Bloody idiots. I'll have to park the car somewhere safer."

But taking it out on Uncle George and his car was cold comfort, a pyrrhic victory: his real enemy – the publishing world – was still churning out all sorts of crappy books at twice the speed of light and in the most brazen fashion, showing a complete disregard for his work. After three weeks, his submission campaign had generated only a handful of laconic replies, duly posted back in his stamped self-addressed envelopes. Some editors had had the cheek to scribble their refusals along the margins of his letter: "Sadly we are not considering new work at present", or "The project you suggest is well outside our area of competence", or "As we are nautical publishers, your novel is not of interest to us". No one had wasted more than a short paragraph on him – no one except a publisher from the north, a desperately small independent who had sent him the faded photocopy of a five-page philippic. It started with the usual "I regret that we are unable to consider your work for publication because our programme is overcommitted" and it continued for a couple of pages lamenting the current degradation of the British book trade, which prevented them from "taking on any more books by authors from Britain and Ireland who are new to our list for the next seven years". It went on to explain how the main reason for the current position was the "alarming decline in book sales through bookshops, resulting from the dumbing-down of the UK book trade which has gone hand in hand with the demise of the Net Book Agreement and Waterstone's takeover of Ottakar's". This had forced publishers to cut back on the number of fiction titles they published and shrink their print runs, with big book chains reducing at the same time their stock range. This apocalyptic vision was crowned by the claim that bookshops and distributors nationwide were "clearing out huge numbers of slower-selling titles by indiscriminate computerized returns, including books which have only been on their shelves for a very short time". The handwritten post scriptum, barely legible and ungrammatical with frustration, read: "If you would like your manuscript returning, please send sufficient postage and packing, or it will be destroyed after two weeks".

Jim convinced himself, even though with some difficulty, that he shouldn't give up. After all, he had recently read an old article about an aspiring writer who had secured a major publishing contract after receiving dozens and dozens of rejections. He could have been reading his own life story: the author had dropped out of university, worked for a communications-consultancy firm, then given up his job and sold his London flat in order to write. And after four years of struggle, his gamble had finally paid off: now he had a six-figure contract with a top publisher and Hollywood studios vying with each other to obtain the film rights.

"Not all is lost," he said to himself as he walked down the Uxbridge Road, returning to the squalor of his room. He was still in his mid-to-late thirties – much younger than many other debut novelists – and at the zenith of his creative powers.

His mobile phone warbled a serendipitous ring.

"Hello?"

"Hello, is that Mr Talbot?"

"Yes?"

"Hello, Mr Talbot, this is Dr Oldfield from the clinic."

"Oh hello." Jim's legs went slack, and he stopped dead in the middle of the pavement.

"I'm ringing you about your mother's case. She said we can discuss this with you – do you have a minute? All the results are in now, and you've seen the way they've been tending..."

"Well, I er..."

"I realize it might be something of a shock, but our recommendation is to operate. A lumpectomy."

There was a long pause, as a vortex of totally absurd and disconnected images whirled in Jim's mind. He saw sheets of his manuscripts blowing in the wind, the corpse of his mother in a black coffin, Uncle George reading his paper in Father's easy chair, the police knocking on his door in the middle of the night, a "FOR SALE" sign outside the Twickenham house, his mobile phone ringing and ringing and ringing...

"Is it serious?" Jim said at length, trying to inject some filial zeal in his tone.

"Serious? Well, no cancer is good, as I'm sure you're aware, and no operation is without its attendant risks. On the other hand, we've caught your mother's cancer early and the biopsy results indicate that it's of a relatively slow-growing type. And a lumpectomy is far less invasive and traumatic than a mastectomy. So don't worry – it could be a lot worse. She'll need a six-week course of radiotherapy afterwards."

"Is it going to be very expensive?"

"My secretary will write to you about the costs, Mr Talbot. Unless you decide to do it via the NHS…"

Jim zombied his way back to the flat. This really was the last straw. As his limp hand opened the door of his room, he noticed an envelope on the floor with a silver special-delivery label on it. He immediately ripped it open and scanned the letter inside. Jesus Christ, it was from Penguin!

31st March 2008

Dear Mr Talbot,

Many thanks for submitting your novel, A Thorn in My Side, *to Penguin. It has been passed on to me for consideration. I must admit that, in my many years at Penguin, I have rarely enjoyed a book as much. I can't remember the last time I felt so disoriented and engrossed at the same time, with no idea where the author was taking me until literally the last sentence.*

We see so much potential in this book that we would like to make an offer. I look forward to discussing the terms in more detail with you at your earliest opportunity (please feel free to call me on my direct line below).

G.T. Hanley, etc.

Jim read and reread in disbelief. He had made it. He had *made* it! He was going to be famous. He was going to be rich. He knew it would happen. He had always known. An offer... an offer! The thought of his mother's operation had fizzled out of his mind. He sat down on his creaking bed and started crying from happiness, slapped his face twice to see if he was awake or not, then jumped up and started walking around the room. Ah, if only Janet and Tom were in! He wished he could scrunch this letter straight into their faces, this very moment. He tried to calm his nerves and summon the courage to ring Penguin. He did some deep-breathing exercises and waited for the perfect moment to make his call. He wanted to sound cool and relaxed. After a few minutes he dialled the number and got through at once.

"Hello?" answered a male voice.

"Hello... Can I speak to G.T. Hanley, please?"

"May I ask who's calling?"

"Jim Talbot."

"One moment please."

Jim could hear some excited murmuring in the background. A few seconds later another male voice said:

"Hullo?"

"Oh hello, is that G.T. Hanley?"

"Speaking."

"Oh hi, this is Jim Talbot, the author of *A Thorn in My Side*? I was calling regarding your letter, your... offer—"

"That's right... Thanks for getting back to me so quickly."

"No problem."

"One second, I want to put you on speakerphone, so that my colleagues in the... department can listen in. There we go... Can you hear me all right?"

"Yep, fine."

"Good good. Well, like I said, we are very excited about this book of yours, Mr Talbot, very excited indeed. Mmm.

Do you think that an advance in the region of a hundred thousand would be adequate for your... masterpiece?"

Jim remained silent for a second or two and thought: "What a strange way of talking, and what a bizarre tone of voice..." Then he replied:

"I think so... I mean, I don't have much experience of how these things work, and—"

"You don't have much experience. Mmm. The book is what, around 400 pages, right? So you don't think that two hundred and fifty quid per page is a good offer? Eh? Honestly. That's a fair bit above minimum wage..."

"I... I don't know," replied Jim, still more flummoxed. "Maybe we could meet to discuss—"

"Sure... sure... Let's see, let me grab my diary... let me grab my diary. Now, where are we? What day is it today?"

"It's the first, I think," said Jim, scrabbling around for a diary.

"That's right, it's the first... but what day is it?"

"It's the first, the first of April..."

"Yes, yes, the first of April... but what day *is* it?"

"Sorry, I don't—"

"It's April Fool's Day, Jimmy Boy!!!" came the shout down the phone by two chortling voices, and the line went dead.

Tom and Gautam. The bastards. Oh the bastards. No book contract, no offer, no advance. He had been April-fooled... he'd risen open-mouthed to the bait and... yum!

He crumpled the letter, threw his mobile on the bed and started packing up his clothes and books any old how. By the end of the day he would be out of here, never to come back.

* * *

Charles Randall had hardly slept for two days. He had been working day and night on the programme for his new imprint and on a profusion of grant applications, from the Arts Council to the English PEN, from the Romanian Cultural Institute to the Calouste Gulbenkian Foundation, from the Stephen Spender Memorial Trust to the European Union Special Fund for the Translation of Minority Languages. For the moment it didn't matter that he still didn't have a name for his publishing house, or that he was only in the early stages of deciding what to publish. He felt that he was on his feet again. Of course he had his moments of deep doubt and despair, when he started worrying about money, and the pointlessness of life, literature and publishing in particular. But he had always weathered similar crises: ups and downs are habitual bedfellows in a publisher's life – how many times during his thirty years at the press had he been on the verge of throwing in the towel? "I can't take this any more... What's the point, I give up..." but then an unexpected royalty cheque or a positive review had turned up, and the old enthusiasm – or at least the gritted-teeth determination to carry on – had returned.

So there he was, a happy nervous wreck, or near-wreck perhaps, a busy publisher without a publishing house or a publishing programme. His beard had now grown to an embarrassing length, his jacket was covered by a snowfall of dandruff, his shirt front was encrusted with a week-old chutney stain, and the basement flat was filled with Cimmerian pipe smog, vaguely redolent of scotch whisky. Understandably, it was with some reluctance that he went to the door when the bell rang.

He opened the door and looked out into the bright morning, seeing only a silhouette in front of him, which he struggled to put into focus.

"Dr Randall..." was announced by the stubby shadow.

He recognized the voice at once. He didn't mind being seen in those conditions by the postman or a delivery man, but one of the last people he would have liked to meet in his present state was his ex-employee, Pippa. Whatever had possessed her to come and see him unannounced at his own house at ten o'clock in the morning? How did she know where he lived? And what did she want?

"Grrnf," he snarled from the depths of his lungs – a noise which Pippa interpreted as an invitation to go inside.

Randall moved a pile of books and papers from the armchair to the floor and beckoned her to sit down. He sat opposite her on the sofa, hardly visible in the dim light of the flat, seeping through half-drawn curtains.

"Nice of you to come," Randall said gamely. "What brings you here?"

"I have left my job at the Tetragon Press," replied Pippa, slightly uncomfortable on the protruding springs of the armchair.

"Oh really."

"Yes, I left last week... I mean, I was made to leave."

"I see."

"The atmosphere had become very tense under the new management."

Randall seemed to make a sympathetic grimace.

"So what are you doing now, Dr Randall, if I may ask?"

"Well..." He took a long time over this. "I am setting up another imprint," he finally announced.

"Really?" Pippa took just as long to think about this disclosure. "That must be very exciting. What's the name of—"

"Well – grnf – I have a few ideas, but I think I am settled on... on... Vivus Press," he blurted out at last. It occurred to him that this was in fact a very good name, and an apt one. "*Vivus* means 'alive' in Latin, you know... And as I am not quite dead..."

"Vivus... That's a brilliant name, Dr Randall. Very catchy and modern... and memorable."

"Thank you." He looked very pleased with himself. "Although Jurassic Books is also a possibility... with a dinosaur as a colophon, mmm... I'll make us some, ah..."

She was left on her own in the malodorous living room while Randall disappeared to make tea. She had a good look around: everywhere paper, books, book submissions, bills, letters, contracts, photos, receipts, unopened mail, opera programmes, concert programmes, leaflets, business cards, pens, typewriter ribbons, carbon-copy paper, banana skins and junk of every description. This is exactly how she had imagined the place. She had always felt that her old boss would be a subterranean person, a man of basements.

After a long time Randall, having made a supreme effort, came back with two teacups, sugar, cream and lemon – gosh, when was the last time she had seen lemon served with tea? She took her cup and picked a brown-sugar cube.

"Thank you."

"Not at all, not at all. So," he said, sitting again on the sofa and slurping from the hot cup, with a sullen expression on his face, "what is the latest news from Tetragon Press? Before you left, I mean..."

"Well, they're talking about pulping a lot of books in the old warehouse – about eighty per cent of the—"

Randall raised one bushy eyebrow.

"Cost-cutting measures..." Pippa made an apologetic gesture. "But you must be wondering why I have come here this morning," she continued, after a long pause. "Well, it's about your desk and books."

"What about them?"

"They've been put on eBay."

"What does that mean?" Randall gave another little slurp from his cup. He was embarrassed to admit to any kind of ignorance.

"It means that they are being sold at auction online, over the Internet."

Randall narrowed his eyes and gave a soft grunt. "And who is buying them?"

"Nobody – I mean, somebody might buy them soon. I checked yesterday evening, and there were no bids on most of the items, but bidders will jump in at the last minute. The auction's ending this afternoon, so I was wondering..."

"*Yes*," he said with urgency, "I want my desk, my books. What a wonderful idea. And all my reference works, my dictionaries, my publishing directories, the *Who's Who*. What do I have to do?"

He sprang up, put the cup on a precarious pile of books on the floor and sneaked into another room. He came back two or three minutes later with a roll of banknotes. "How much do you need?"

Pippa smiled. "I don't know... But you don't use cash over the Internet. I'll pay and then you pay me back, OK?"

"Frnf. Buy everything. Especially the desk. The desk is essential. Can you do that for me? I need the desk back, even if you have to pay a thousand pounds."

"I'll get it, Dr Randall."

"Splendid. Well done, Pippa, well done. Thank you." She had never seen him so excited before, and it was the first time he had called her by her first name.

With an abrupt gesture, Randall put the money back in his pocket and stretched his three Masonic fingers. Pippa took them, gave them a little squeeze and let go with a smile. The meeting was over.

As he closed the door and waved Pippa goodbye, Randall had already started fantasizing over the desk and the books, imagining their ideal location in the flat and their position in relation to each other.

With his old desk in the right place, he would be back in business.

* * *

If anyone had told him only a week before, when he was still harbouring the highest hopes for his novel, that he would end up moving into his mother's house and sleeping under the same roof as Uncle George... There he was, thirty-seven years of age – thirty-eight in August – returning to his childhood room, full of heavy-metal posters and all sorts of embarrassing teenage paraphernalia. What a world-class loser he was. What an all-time-great underachiever. But did he have any other choice? Jim had told his mother that it would be easier for him to look after her if he stayed in Twickenham until she was back from the clinic, and possibly for the duration of her convalescence.

The lie had gone down very well, and his mum had cried her eyes out at such a show of affection. The only real problem was knobble-nosed Uncle George, who was bound to create more and more trouble the longer he stayed around.

When Jim arrived in a clapped-out rented van and started offloading his boxes and bags, Uncle George planted a foldable chair onto the front lawn and sat down emphatically, saying:

"I wouldn't miss the privilege of watching you doing some work."

And as his nephew went in and out with big long strides carrying hefty loads, George gave him the thumbs-up and commented that he would make a perfect delivery boy, or hummed *God Save Our Gracious Queen*.

That night Jim managed to dodge his mother's lethal cuisine, avoid his uncle's company and scuttle away to his room with two bottles of red wine from the corner shop. He was determined to get seriously drunk, hoping somehow that he could forget about his failures and re-emerge as a new man from the mists of a kosher hangover.

He uncorked the first bottle, filled a glass to the edge and sent its contents down his throat in one long swill, letting the warmth rise slowly to his head before breathing a deep sigh. Now he felt better. He repeated the exercise twice, and felt the alcohol rush to his brain, making him giddier and giddier. After a few minutes he emptied the bottle directly into his mouth.

He took stock of the situation: no wife, no children, no job, no place of his own, no car, no money, no status. Where did he rank in society? In the bottom three or four per cent of the population, maybe? Perhaps even lower? But whose fault was it? Certainly not *his* fault. He had been working diligently for years to fulfil his dream of becoming a writer – and all he got in return was scorn and indifference. So who was responsible for pushing him to the margins of society? He had no doubts: the finger was clearly pointing towards the impregnable citadel of the publishing world. He had tried to launch his works every which way over its ramparts, to no avail. He had been burnt by the boiling oil of rejection and had been forced to retreat many times. What could he do now apart from lick his wounds? It was clear that he could not open a breach in the walls. Not in a hundred years. But maybe he could shoot a few flaming arrows over the top and... Flaming arrows. The image caught his imagination, and he uncorked the second bottle to elaborate on it.

What could he actually do to hurt the bastards, to bring them to their knees? He could storm the offices of Faber and Faber for example? He could kidnap a famous author and demand publication of *A Thorn in My Side* as a ransom? He could demand a record-breaking seven-figure advance for his kidnapper's journal? Heh heh... He poured another glass of wine and gulped it down quickly, looking for inspiration.

Time passed, but the Muse of revenge did not come whispering to his ear. Then he heard the heavy thump and creaking noise of someone plodding up the stairs. He cocked his ear to the happy whistling and humming of his uncle as he entered the adjoining bathroom and started his meticulous gargling routine: a little slurp, followed by a two-minute burbling and a loud splash, repeated two, three, four times. Jim could hear all this as distinctly as if it were happening in his own room – and knew that Uncle George knew that he was listening on the other side of the wall. He also knew that his uncle had raised his volume a notch or two on purpose, just to annoy him. He tried to ignore him, but it was impossible to remain calm in the face of Uncle G's sustained harrumphing, spitting and – what the hell was that? – *toenail*-clipping? Did he really need to do that *now*, at eleven o'clock? He saw himself rise in the middle of the night, go into the kitchen, take a bottle of Bug Buster Extra from under the sink, sneak into his uncle's room, clamp that scarlet, crusty nose shut and then ram a dose down the gaping mouth.

It was as he fantasized over the assassination of Uncle George that a master plan for the annihilation of the whole publishing industry, the extermination of an entire generation of agents and publishers, took shape in his mind. If he could not be a new Dickens or Thackeray, at least he would be remembered as a modern-day Herostratus. What a thought! He got more excited than if he had just received the finished copies of his novel. He couldn't wait to get down to work, and let loose as many poisoned letters as he could.

As Uncle George at last returned downstairs to his room, Jim squeezed the cork down the neck of the bottle and went to bed with a light heart, and an even lighter head.

5

Charles Randall was mightily pleased. Pippa had managed to buy back his old desk and most of his reference books and dictionaries for under £400. He had found a perfect location for the desk in a small spare room that was roughly the same size as his room at the Tetragon Press and could be accessed at the end of a corridor – just like his old office. Around the walls hung the same photographs of famous authors, some of them signed, and the same comforting mess was spreading out on and around his desk – even down to the circle-stained book he used as a coffee mat. He moved a few sheets of paper to the right, readjusted the bin under his desk and checked with satisfaction the contents of the three drawers.

"That's it… I am right there… splendid…" he mumbled to himself, sucking from his pipe.

Pippa poked her head in.

"Could you come out for a second, Dr Randall?"

"Grnf. Give me a minute."

"Sure." She returned to the living room, where she had been trying to get to the bottom of an ancient pile of proofs and submissions. On the strength of her eBay triumph, she had been employed on a six-month contract as Randall's secretary-cum-cleaning lady-cum-editorial assistant, to help him sort out the chaos that had stratified over many years in the flat. It wasn't a job for the faint-hearted, but Pippa enjoyed physical work, and every now and then, amid mountains of useless junk tucked away in the most unimaginable corners and drawers, she unearthed some interesting dusty document, book or photo which made the effort seem worthwhile.

After a few moments Randall joined her. He was surprised to see how much more spacious the room had become.

"You are not throwing anything away, are you?" he muttered in a surly tone.

"I'm just making piles... just making piles, Dr Randall. This one is bills and invoices, this one is bank statements, this one's correspondence, this one submissions, this one your own poetry, this one—"

"Prnf."

"Sorry?"

"I won't be able to find anything any more. Quite upsetting."

"What is?"

"You're turning the whole place upside down... grnf."

"I'm not turning the whole place upside down, I'm just tidying up a bit. And I am not going to throw anything away unless you tell me to, after you have gone through all these..." and she pointed at about a dozen stacks of papers.

"Good. And what are you typing up on that—" he didn't know what name could be given to Pippa's laptop computer.

"I am making an inventory. I am making a list of all the important documents and books I come across. Like an archive." That was a word Randall liked, and it struck the right chord.

"Good. Good. Did you want to show me something?"

"Yes, you asked me to identify a few books that we can sell to raise some money in case we don't get any grants. Well, I found some valuable first editions... this one here, for example, signed by the author, Lindeth Wilson. It's a very rare item... I had a look on Abebooks. It's worth around twelve hundred pounds."

"Is it really?"

"Mm-mm."

"Dreadful, dreadful poet – twelve hundred pounds? Sell it. Prnf."

"Great. This one's worth about £150. Look, there's a dedication to you, it may be worth even—"

"Tsk... the grovelling bastard. I have a box full of these somewhere... Two months after the book was published he went over to Vertigo, then came back when he was dropped... haw-haw... What's that one?" he pointed at an unbound typescript tied up with string.

"Well, that's the one I wanted to ask you about. There's no title page, no author's name. Do you remember what it is and who it is by? It looks like there are some notes in your own handwriting."

"Let me have a look." Charles took the typescript, lifted his dust-speckled glasses and scrunched up his face in a succession of grimaces to put the writing into focus. "Mmm. That's an unpublished MacKenna. I thought I had lost it. Mmm. I've been looking for it for the last ten years. Where was it?"

"Here, just here, on the... do you mean MacKenna as in the *famous* MacKenna... as in the Nobel Prize-winning MacKenna?"

"Pnnf."

"Oh my God."

Charles sat down on the sofa and untied the string delicately. "It was just before he died, you know. It must be twelve, fifteen years ago, perhaps even more. He came over to London, from Ireland. He came out of a long seclusion for a special event at the Royal Society of Literature. We had been friends for many years, exchanged letters and so on. Very good man. I published his early work, a couple of plays and a short-story collection. But then he moved to a bigger publisher – didn't want to: it was his agent who forced him. Terrible woman his agent... terrible woman. Dead now, of course. Thank God. Anyway, all those years later I met him at the RSL shindig. Seemed very glad to see me. Took me to one side, started complaining about sausage factories—"

"Sausage factories?"

"Corporate publishing houses. And he pressed this little present on me." Charles hefted the typescript up and down in his hands. "He said, 'Been working on this for twenty years. It's yours. But you have to wait till I'm dead – which won't be long, with any luck. It's a very, very, very dirty book, Charles...'"

"So then... what happened to the typescript?" Pippa was pawing the ground with anticipation.

"After he died I started preparing the text for publication, writing the notes and so on. But then we ran into some financial problems and I had to put it on hold. He'd gone out of fashion by then anyway."

"There was a huge feature about him in *The Guardian* last weekend. They called him 'the most underrated literary genius of the twentieth century'."

Charles was looking increasingly thoughtful.

"Do you know – grnff – I think his centenary must be coming up either this year or next year… I'll have to check…"

"But who owns the rights to the book?"

"I do. He gave it to me. There's a letter somewhere… He left everything else to Trinity College… MacKenna had no family or children, you know."

"And what is it… what's it about?" Pippa was beside herself with excitement.

"Fictionalized autobiography, from his early years in Dublin to his life in South America and his return to Ireland. *The Great and the Damned*… Dynamite – incest and sexual abuse in it… mmm… And it talks about a mysterious Argentinian lover – quite explicitly, you know."

"The manuscript alone must be worth a fortune, and the book… this is going to be *huge*."

"We could do a lovely limited-edition hardback, on laid paper…" Randall grabbed an old book of poetry from the shelf, dated 1924.

"You can sell thousands and thousands of copies." Pippa was saying. "And translation rights, serialization rights…"

"…with nice endpapers… something like this. Mmm."

"…US rights, film rights… You can make a lot of money."

"Money?" Randall gruffed.

"Dr Randall – you can finance the rest of the programme… you won't even need to apply for grants…"

"Hm." He put the book back on the shelf and started leafing through MacKenna's typescript pensively, looking at his hardly legible notes along the margins.

"Maybe you could even buy back Tetragon Press…"

Randall's eyes shot up and fixed on Pippa's face. He sprang to his feet and gave the manuscript back to the girl.

"Good. I'll start editing it straight away. Try out a few ideas for cover mock-ups. This is going to be our launch title. September. I'll work on the blurb and the press release... I must check this centenary thing... you can, ah... we can... Trnf."

He darted back to his private study.

* * *

Just a few days before the London Book Fair, the directors of Tetragon Press had flown in from their respective countries for the monthly management meeting. This time they convened at the publisher's headquarters, located within a couple of miles of the Book Fair venue in Earls Court.

Goosen sat fully erect in the black designer chair, dictating his correspondence into a digital dictaphone in a drawly tone of voice. A courier had already been booked the day before for a 5:30 p.m. pick-up, so that the following morning, in Amsterdam, his trusted secretary of twenty years could type up dozens of letters and keep busy hundreds of people around the globe for another day or two.

Samson was not happy. Something had gone terribly wrong, something to do with shipments and bank transfers. He sat in a corner talking into three mobile phones at the same time, alternating whispers and hisses, English and Amharic, and hammering his clenched fist on his thigh from time to time.

"Do what you have to do... One million on delivery... hello, hello? One million, I said... oh shit!... Fax me the air waybill now... *now* I said, you... Yes? The transfer... nooo... nooooo... I need the money first thing tomorrow... first thing tomorrow or I'll... yes, oil for food... oil for food... hello?..."

Nick and James sat comfortably in their chairs, talking *sotto voce* and waiting for their moment with patience.

Once Goosen had finished his recordings and Samson's storm had subsided, the meeting began. The Ethiopian brought his chair over to the table and sat down with the deflated look of a beaten man, his watery eyes swimming aimlessly in their orbits as he rearranged piles of paper in front of him.

"Thank you all for coming," he started off, his mind still focused on some other place a few thousand miles away. "Mr Bain, how are you?... Nick says you are doing very well..."

"Thank you Mr Mulu. I'm doing all right, yeah... thanks."

"Could you do me a favour, Mr Bain? Could you have a look at this when you have a minute?" he pushed a slim manuscript towards Payne-Turner. "Poetry. The Minister's wife. See what you can do."

"Sure, no problem," the young publisher said with an awkward smile, giving the manuscript a cursory glance before slipping it behind his chair, on the floor.

"Where are the figures," barked Goosen, bringing everybody to attention.

"Er... these are the actuals for the first month... as well as a budget and forecast until December." James passed around a few spreadsheets and waited expectantly for the majority shareholders' reaction.

It wasn't long before Goosen growled something akin to approbation.

"Mmm. You are showing a... a—"

"Two hundred per cent turnover increase by the end of the year," intervened Nick, "and a ten per cent operating profit."

Seeing that Goosen continued nodding and was digesting the figures without the hiccup of a doubt, he added with a confident smile:

"At that point we could start looking for a buyer..."

"Mmm... very good. And how do you—"

"How we intend to achieve this? James, maybe you can explain our strategy in more detail?"

"Certainly," said Payne-Turner, straightening up in his chair and opening his laptop. "Certainly. First of all we slash the translation, editorial, production and storage costs, which have been astronomical under Randall's charity-like administration. Secondly" – and here he passed around the copy of an email from his contact within the Arts Council – "there's 120K coming our way any day now, which we'll use to develop our front list..."

"Then we have, thanks to Samson," Nick joined in, "two publishing contracts with the Ethiopian Ministry of Education, worth around 75K."

"Yes, 75K." repeated the apathetic Mulu, lifting an official document in Amharic script, full of stamps and signatures. "They'll pay by letter of guarantee."

"Very good," said Goosen. "But," he continued, pointing at a column in the spreadsheet and frowning the others into silence, "there's one thing I don't understand: why are the advances so high?"

"Well, they need to be, don't they," explained Nick with a slightly conspiratorial smile. "These days, fiction publishing is a different ball game..."

"Totally different ball game," confirmed Payne-Turner.

"It's no longer about the books or the authors: it's about psychology and *finance*."

"A case of money making money…" clarified the young publisher.

"Exactly. Now, the whole idea, when you fork out a 100K advance, is that you know already you'll be making at least twice or three times as much in foreign-rights sales."

"That's how it works. Every publisher does that."

"Mmm. Very clever," commented Goosen, with a touch of irony in his tone. "But what happens if you can't sell the book to any foreign—"

"We will," was Nick's adamant reply.

"Definitely," echoed Payne-Turner. "That's why we go to the top agents and PR companies. The secret is to create the right buzz around the book…"

"A little bit of hype and glamour…" Nick chimed in.

"…and butter up the most influential journalists…" concluded Payne-Turner with a smug expression.

"I see…" droned Samson, although in fact he could not see what the butter had to do with all this.

"It's a fantastic model," Nick added after a small pause, seeing that Goosen was still looking at the figures, unconvinced. "And there is very little risk involved…"

"But surely these big advances *are* a risk… Mmm… No, this doesn't really add up… this is… pie in the sky… you are deluded…" Goosen was now shaking his head and stroking his goatee.

"Mr Goosen, the advances are recouped before publication, and with the financial benefit from the sale of subsidiary and foreign-translation rights we can build a massive advertising and marketing campaign, be aggressive on pricing, enter the books into store promotions, get them onto radio and TV programmes…"

"It's just a matter of cash flow… of *finance*…" pointed out Payne-Turner with a faltering voice, realizing that their pitch was hitting a sticky patch.

"I want to think about it," decreed Goosen, wriggling on his chair, as if preparing to go.

James and Nick exchanged a worried look.

"How much…" muttered Samson.

Nick was quick to grab at the lifeline: "We are only talking about 250-300K… which will be paid back by April next year with a substantial interest."

Samson made a squiggle on a piece of paper.

"You sure?"

"Positive. And you know I always deliver."

The Ethiopian directed his watery eyes at Mr Goosen, who nodded imperceptibly, maintaining a poker face.

"OK, 225K," he said in a flat tone, jotting down a few more squiggles. "It will be in the company's account by the end of next week." He yawned, and silenced his vibrating mobile phone.

"Cheers," Nick said with consummate coolness, whilst James stuck his fingernails in the leather pulp of his chair.

"And what happened to Randall's papers?" Goosen suddenly remembered.

"He hasn't signed them yet."

"What?"

"Well, he's been very uncooperative. We have sent him a couple of reminders" – here Nick's nostrils dilated – "and left three or four messages on his answerphone" – he might as well go all the way with his lie – "but he hasn't got back to us yet. And in my experience he's not someone who believes in lightning response… we'll have to take a patient approach."

"Do we need to worry about him?" asked Samson in a matter-of-fact way.

"Not really… There's little he can do… I mean, in theory he could come up with a competing programme, but in practice…"

"In practice?…"

"In practice there's a number of things we can do to keep him at bay."

"Well," rasped Goosen after a short pause, "do *any* number of things to keep him at bay. And *get* those papers signed."

"No problem."

"Anything else we need to discuss?" asked Samson, as he and Mr Goosen rose to leave for their next meeting in town, a tricky negotiation involving cotton bales and castor-oil canisters. He looked at his watch, at his unsorted pile of papers, and yawned again.

"No, I think we're done for today. We'll all meet again on Monday at the Book Fair."

"Er… Do we need to talk about the actual publishing programme?" James threw in as an afterthought, just as the two businessmen were about to walk out of the room, escorted by Nick. Goosen turned around his bulk and smiled:

"Get down to work, and show me what you can do, young man."

And Payne-Turner remained alone, mulling over Goosen's nugget of wisdom, with an empty desk, a lot of money to spend and the urgent need to find a bestseller.

* * *

This is how he would do it. This is how he would shoot his flaming arrows and kill the bastards, see them drop one by one from their turrets and battlements. He would concoct a credible submission enquiry, marinate it in a fine rat-killing powder – or even anthrax, if he could get hold of it – and mail it to as many publishers and agents as possible, together with an equally poisonous self-addressed envelope. He would drop a handful of letters here, a handful there and a handful everywhere in London and Surrey, far from police stations and CCTV cameras. He was confident that the big anonymous city would offer him a safe haven. As he walked back to his mum's house from the station, carrying a Chinese takeaway in a plastic bag, he pictured his enemies wriggling on the floor and dying in the most painful ways known to man, and imagined the front-page headlines of *Bookpage* and the national newspapers: HAVOC IN THE WORLD OF BOOKS – A PUBLISHING ARMAGEDDON – HELL HATH NO FURY LIKE A WRITER SCORNED.

Having left his mum only an hour ago at the clinic, he was surprised to hear Dr Oldfield's voice when he answered his phone.

"I am afraid I have more bad news for you, Mr Talbot."

Was it only his impression or he could detect a hint of sadism in the tone of that bird of ill omen?

"More bad news? What…"

"Well, we thought we could have a local excision – a lumpectomy – but with these further investigations… almost certainly we'll have to perform a mastectomy instead."

"A…"

"A mastectomy… the removal of the left breast…"

"The removal... Oh for f—" Jim struggled to come to terms with the physical and financial horror of such a delicate operation, and remained silent as the doctor talked him through the practicalities.

On seeing his uncle's funereal face as he entered the living room, Jim realized that he must have already received the news.

"Poor Anna..." Uncle George clucked. "She'll be devastated..." There was a pause. "The only consolation is that she didn't have to do it through the NHS, thank God. She'd have had to wait for months... she could have died."

"Yeah..."

Jim trudged over to the table, sat down and started eating his takeaway in silence. He could sense Uncle George's tuberous nose directed towards him as he tried to make eye contact over the edge of his paper, and when his uncle cleared his throat Jim knew that he was gearing up to saying something, no doubt something extremely unpleasant. He tried to scarper away to the kitchen, but Uncle George caught him out as he walked past his armchair.

"I am very worried, you know."

Jim stopped with his takeaway leftovers in his hands and turned slowly to face him.

"You shouldn't be."

"Well... I doubt she'll survive the ordeal. Mentally, you know."

"She's gonna be all right."

"If she were to find out the truth, it would kill her."

"Whaddya mean? What truth? The tumour?"

"No, not the tumour. You know," Uncle George rubbed the tip of his nose, "the truth..."

"What are you talking about?"

"I had a good chat with your... your ex-landlord the other day, what's his name? Tom. He called, you know. He was after his rent. He tracked you down."

"I can explain this. He's—"

Uncle George gestured with his hand that he might as well save his breath.

"Look, son... why don't you come clean... once and for all, you know... think of your mother..."

"I..." Jim lowered his eyes onto the crumpled wrap, now reduced to a ball. "OK, OK." He sighed heavily. "This is going to be... Let me get rid of this and then we can have a chat." And he disappeared into the kitchen.

A few moments later his head popped through the kitchen door.

"Tea, coffee, Uncle G?" he asked. "I think we'll need it."

"I think we will. Coffee please. White, one sugar."

After a few minutes Jim teetered back with two fuming mugs, passed one to his uncle and sat on a chair opposite him.

"So..."

"So you're a writer, I'm told."

"Well..." Jim's face was greenish with rage.

"And what kind of books do you write?" George gave a tentative sip, but found the coffee too hot.

"All kinds of stuff... Novels, mainly."

"Novels? Really? That's peculiar. It must run in the family... I wrote a novel too, a war novel, when I was younger... I'll show it to you, maybe you can help me to get it published, mm?"

"Right."

George studied his nephew's head deliberately, meticulously, and decided that – if water was water, rock was rock and fire was fire – then this certainly wasn't a writer's head. He slurped some coffee and made a small grimace, overcoming a short choking and coughing fit. "So tell me, do you make any money out of your writing? Is someone paying you to write? How do you support yourself?"

"Well, I am not really making any money out of it at the moment, but—"

"That's what I thought. I'm only asking because Dr Oldfield's secretary has been in touch for the payment of the clinic's first invoice, you see."

"Payment? But the clinic's costs are cov—"

Again, Uncle George signalled to his nephew that all pretence was over and to no avail.

"Also, a chap from Natwest called last week – the manager of your mother's bank, no less – to check on some unauthorized overdraft…" He took a longer sip at the coffee.

Jim remained silent. His eyes darted wistfully towards his uncle's mug.

"Look, Jimmy… if you are in trouble, if you need money, just let me know, all right? But don't do anything stupid… think of your mum…"

"Right," was Jim's submissive reply.

"Now, I'm going to take care of the hospital bills, OK?… For your part, I want you to deal with Tom about your rent…"

"He's got my deposit."

"Well, whatever the situation is, you just try to find a proper job for yourself, and pay your way and your debts – and leave the rest to me. This family wants a man. Do you need any cash by the way?" Uncle George produced a twenty-pound note from his shirt pocket and waved it at his nephew. "No?"

Jim shook his head.

"Your mother doesn't need to know what you've done to her. I am glad we talked." There was a long pause. "And now, if you don't mind," the old man announced emphatically, putting the mug on the table and scrambling to his feet, "I'll go and pay a little visit to the Pope upstairs, heh heh heh…"

Once his uncle had sidled out of the room, Jim checked how much coffee was left in the mug. But just as he was hovering over it, his uncle's nose reappeared in the door frame, making him jolt back.

"By the way, don't you think it's high time you got your hair sorted out?"

6

The London Book Fair opened its doors at nine o'clock on a Monday morning at the Earls Court Exhibition Centre. A swarm of publishers, agents, scouts, booksellers, wholesalers, distributors, sales reps, consultants, PR staff, journalists, printers, designers, shippers, writers, would-be writers, translators, proofreaders, time-wasters, fraudsters, crackpots, literati, glitterati, blogerati, twitterati and other unclassifiable publishing rabble from the world over poured into the squashed-pudding-shaped building for their first appointments of the day, or to queue at the nearest coffee shop.

Nick Tinsley ambled in just after the initial rush. Strutting down the aisles lined with brightly lit stands exhibiting every imaginable kind of book – from high-brow literature to comics, from surgical-oncology monographs to crochet manuals, from *The Benefit of Farting Explained* to *0 to Bitch in 10 Seconds or Less* – he looked forward to three days of unrestrained schmoozing, partying and boozing. When he reached the Tetragon Press booth, he found Payne-Turner sitting at the table reading the book-fair edition of *Bookpage*.

"How are we doing today?"

"We're fucked," was the glum, anticlimactic reply from the young publisher.

"Why? What's up?"

Payne-Turner handed him the *Bookpage Daily*.

"Randall Makes Vivus Comeback with Unpublished MacKenna" was the main headline on the front page.

"What's this?" Nick winced.

"He's been sitting on it for the last fifteen years. It's worth millions."

"What are you talking about?"

"He's got an unpublished MacKenna."

"Where did he get it?"

"Who knows? From under his mattress, probably. Now he's starting a new list – guess what: mostly translated fiction."

"He's not."

"He is. It's written here."

Nick tried to read the article carefully, to focus on the words, but he was so angry that he ended up skimming over it, almost spitting out the most undigestable bits.

"One month after his *controversial* departure from Tetragon Press... Film rights have been pre-empted in a *six*-figure deal... 'The literary discovery of the *century*,' says Vivus marketing director Pippa Hughes... *Marketing director*? What the—"

"Stinking cow."

"How did he... I mean, what..."

"I'm telling you, we are done. The problem is that he hasn't signed the papers, and when Goosen finds out—"

"We've got to stop him, break his legs." Nick dropped his briefcase to the floor, guillotine-like.

"Yes, but how?"

After a while, Nick's face brightened up with malice.

"We'll sue him."

"For what?"

"For stealing the MacKenna manuscript from our office. It was our property. I mean, Tetragon's property."

"But it's not true…"

There was a Mephistophelean pause.

"Who's to say?" Nick hissed.

"I suppose it's our word against his."

"Exactly: we'll just muddy the waters a little bit… It'll slow him down."

"No one's going to deal with him if there's a law case pending."

"Right. And as far as I know, he hasn't got much money of his own, so he'll run out of steam in no time."

"So he'll have to sign the papers… or even give up the book…"

"…To *us*. Maybe."

"I'll write a letter to him straight away. My first appointment is at 10:30, and Holly will be here any minute to help." Payne-Turner opened up his laptop computer and hit the space bar to bring it back to life.

"No no, wait… I'll get my lawyer buddy at Hodgson & Barrymore to send him a nice little stinker. That'll smoke him out. And we'll also improve our severance offer slightly – we'll make it into a tin-plated handshake, if you know what I mean. You go and talk to your friends at *Bookpage*. I want this covered in the next print edition after the fair. And try to finalize the deal with the Arts Council girl – we don't want any surprises."

"I'll be meeting her tomorrow night at the Dorchester party."

"Good. I want to bugger that four-eyed bastard three-ways till Sund… oh, good moorning!"

Just then Samson and Goosen made their appearance at the Tetragon booth. Nick hastily chucked the magazine in his briefcase and extended his hand with an embarrassed smirk, as if he had been caught red-handed in the act of hiding a bomb.

"Nice stand," Samson commented, offloading a couple of fat folders onto the table.

Goosen sat down next to Payne-Turner, occupying two thirds of the booth's space.

"How much did it cost? It looks expensive," he said.

"It was booked by Randall before my arrival. Maybe next year—"

"Have you read the book I gave you the other day, Mr Bain?" Samson intervened.

"Which book?"

"The Minister's wife's book. The poems."

"Oh yes. Brilliant. We can print it for her. No problems. September."

"Good. Now, you see these two folders? There's an Arabic manuscript inside. Have a look." For once, Samson's face seemed animated by a certain eagerness. "Have a look. Pleeze."

James grabbed the top folder and lifted its cover to reveal the manuscript's title page, "*U. bin L.'s Terror Diaries*", followed by some Arabic words.

"I am not sure I understand..." said the young publisher after a long pause, scratching his cheek.

"You know what the U and L stand for? It's him. It's from him. It's one hundred per cent authentic. I got it through a friend. We have world rights. Get it translated quickly, I'll pay. We have funds."

"But—" Payne-Turner hesitated, leafing through the incomprehensible Arabic script.

Nick moved behind his protégé, sneaked a quick glance at the first page of the manuscript, then said with a confident voice, patting Payne-Turner's shoulder:

"That'll be fine. This will get us a lot of publicity. The journalists love this kind of stuff."

Goosen nodded his smiling condescension.

"It will sell like *Harry Potter*," concluded the Ethiopian, licking the corners of his mouth dry. "Good luck. Thank you. And let me know if you need any help with the translation. I think one of my cousins is a translator. I am not sure from which language to which language. I'll find out."

"Of course... of course," said Payne-Turner, as the spectre of the Twin Towers billowing with black smoke and crumbling down in a big cloud of dust slide-showed across his vacant field of vision.

* * *

If there was one place in the world where Charles Randall could have written a poem in a rare moment of inspiration, it would have been in his private study, his "thinking crypt". That morning he was trying to finish a short piece he had begun the night before. It was his first scrap of verse in years, and he thought it was "all right". But he just couldn't find an adequate rhyming couplet to end the poem and, as he scribbled a number of possibilities over the back of a napkin, he was distracted by an irksome babbling in the background and the sight of a stack of unopened mail from the morning post.

He sucked on his empty pipe and tried to concentrate again. He could have had "heart" and "spite" – but that was a half-rhyme, and he believed that half-rhymes were for lazy rhymesters. He could have had "smite" and "spite", but then "smite" sounded too archaic and highfalutin, and he didn't want to come across as a relic from a past century. He thought some more, scratched his brow, the tip of his nose, but there was nothing for it, so he moved the napkin away with a grunt and opened the first item of post. The babbling continued unabated.

It was a letter from one of his old Tetragon authors, who was delighted to hear that he was setting up a new imprint and took the opportunity to ask whether he would like to have a look at his latest manuscript, still unpublished. Charles let the letter fall on the floor and commented to himself: "You're being dropped." Then he grabbed a brown padded envelope – a submission by the look of it – and deposited it on a precarious pile without much ceremony. Next was the invitation to the BetnoPal-sponsored party at the Dorchester later that night, with a note from a friend who had read the *Bookpage* article the day before and dubbed him with affection "Charlie Ready Vivus". He tried to remember the last time he had been invited to a literary party, and considered that this must be evidence that he had joined again the ranks of the living. Still, he wasn't sure whether to go or not, so he folded the invitation away under his *Concise Oxford Dictionary*. The following letter stretched his mouth into an appearance of a smile. It came, unsolicited, from a UKCP registered psychotherapist, hypnotherapist and existential counsellor who argued that writers and editors, in their solitary profession, have to cope with such levels of stress (possibly self-imposed) to produce what is expected of them that they may fall prey to depression, insomnia or other manifestations of acute distress. The psychotherapist was writing on the off chance that any of Vivus's writers or editors might be needing his professional help, and had taken the liberty of attaching a small number of business cards to be passed on. "Brilliant piece of marketing," Charles thought, shaking his head in disbelief.

The babbling stopped, and Charles raised his eyes. The shadowy figure sitting across his desk gradually took the shape of the weasel-faced translator from the Hungarian. He was staring at him with a quizzical look and an air of expectation.

"Grnf. What did you say?" the publisher asked, annoyed, putting the pipe down.

"I was saying that, since there's every likelihood that the Hungarian Foundation are going to help with the printing costs, it might be an idea to create a small advertising budget for the book, to give it the push it needs – I am not saying it should be a lot of money, but I'd be happy to match any money Viva Press—"

"Vivus, trnf."

"Sorry, any money Vivus Press are prepared to put behind the promotion of the book, or even contribute a small sum on my own – I realize you are just starting up a new imprint and every penny counts, and I know how hard it is for small independent publishers these days, but I am sure it will help with the sales, and you might even consider raising the initial print run... I know there are thousands and thousands of people out there who would love to read this book: the trouble is how to reach out to them. The only way these days is publicity and—"

"Like what?"

"Sorry?"

"Grnf, what kind of publicity? The front cover of *Bookpage*? Adverts on buses and cabs? Tube posters? TV commercials? The only trouble is that there are no high-street chains specializing in unknown Hungarian poets of the twentieth century. No one's come up with that idea. Pity, trnf."

The translator revealed his yellow teeth and ventured: "But maybe a little advert in the *Hungarian Quarterly* or the *Hungarian Foundation Monthly Bulletin*... They are read by hundreds of people, all interested in Hungarian literature... And it doesn't cost very much to advertise there... Maybe we could even try the *TLS* or the *London Review of Books*, if we don't get a review there..."

"Sure, sure... why not, it might help us sell at least another ten or fifteen copies. All right, we'll do it, we'll do it, if it makes you happier and you pay for it. I believe we have finished now..."

But as Charles was helping the translator to the door, he saw something fluttering around his ankles. Charles turned around, bent down and looked on the floor.

"Trrnnf. Carpet moths," was his angry comment, as he stamped his feet on the rug.

He dashed to his desk, opened the bottom drawer and groped for a green bottle with a big orange skull-and-crossbones on the label. As soon as he started spraying the insecticide, a cloud of crazed moths flew towards the bare light bulb hanging from the ceiling. Randall ran after them and sprayed more poison around the light bulb and on the rug as the insects scattered and nose-dived all over.

"I thought they had gone," he mumbled, as he continued spraying away. "They've come back. They always do. They're a nuisance, mmm."

Once he had emptied at least half of the bottle in the windowless room and satisfied himself that no moths would survive the gassing, he switched off the light, closed the door behind him and accompanied the stupefied translator down the corridor and out of the flat.

"Nuisance," he murmured under his breath as he closed the front door – and it wasn't clear if this referred to the moths or the translator.

Pippa was about to be the bearer of bad news. The envelope she handed him – which a courier had brought in only a few minutes ago – contained such a carefully and harshly worded legal threat as to shake the most unflappable mind to its foundations.

Strangely enough, Charles's reaction – as he read the letter with puckered lips and furrowed brow – was not one of anger or deflation. On the contrary, he was glad he could at last fight his enemies in the open, after a month of nerve-racking underground warfare. He was confident he could win and knock them for six – destroy them. With a snappy gesture, he passed Hodgson & Barrymore's two-page document to his assistant.

"What is it?" said Pippa.

"They are threatening legal action."

"Who is threatening legal action?"

"Our Tetragon friends."

"For what?"

"For taking the MacKenna manuscript with me when I left the office."

"Liars! What are you going to do now?"

"Nothing." He sat on the sofa. "I suppose we'll have to find that letter. Trnf."

"Which letter?" Pippa asked after a short pause.

"The short note by MacKenna which was attached to the manuscript. I am sure it must be here somewhere," he encompassed the whole flat with a long swipe of the arm. "If we can find it, we'll be fine."

"But I've looked everywhere and I've not come across it."

"Maybe it's inside one of the books… or perhaps it's in my study, in one of my cabinets. You haven't touched anything in there, have you?"

"No," humphed Pippa. She refrained from pointing out that she wasn't allowed to do that. Randall regarded his private study as the last bulwark against order.

"Good. Good. Don't worry, it'll be all right. We'll find the letter. It's here, somewhere. I know."

"Let's start looking for it then."

"Yes, let's," said the publisher, rising to his feet. "By the way, have you got any plans for tonight? There's, ah… there's this party at the Dorchester. Seven thirty. What would you say if you were to accompany me there? We'll stay just an hour, you know… I wouldn't fancy going on my own, mmm."

"I reckon I'd say yes in a second," said Pippa with excitement.

Charles looked blankly at the girl and remained silent.

"Dr Randall?"

He had got it – he had the rhyme. The last two lines had suddenly pieced themselves together in his mind: the revelation had come in the most unlikely of moments, prompted by the most unpromising of muses. Forget about

118

"heart" and "smite" – and even "spite". The two words he wanted, the two words he had always wanted, were "reckoned" and "second". What a beautiful rhyme... what a wonderful couplet to end the poem...

"Wait a minute there, Pippa. Just a minute. We'll start our search straight away," he bellowed from the corridor, as he strode with his long, gangly legs towards the study. "One minute, grnf."

The power of words! He had forgotten about the manuscript and the legal threat. All that mattered to him now was jotting down that couplet before he forgot it. Later on he would copy the poem in fair hand into one of his time-worn poetry notebooks. Hopefully more poems would follow soon, and he'd be able to collect them in a nice edition for private circulation. A few copies would be sent to the most important libraries in the world, to be preserved for posterity. It was a comforting thought that his words, one day in the distant future, might resonate in a kindred mind and stir up living passions and thoughts.

* * *

Uncle George's digestive system had hardly been perturbed by Jim's poison-laced coffee. In the course of the following days, for good measure, he hoovered up a large doner kebab with extra chilli sauce, onion and pickled green chillies, a dodgy portion of chicken tikka masala and a family-size pack of Cajun-spiced crisps. And on the Tuesday morning, as Jim walked through the kitchen towards the front door, Uncle George was wolfing down bacon and eggs.

"A'right?" Jim mumbled with a lame smile.

"Never felt better in my life, son. Going to see your mum?"

"Maybe later – I went on Sunday. I've got to do some work at the library first."

"Work?" George stopped munching.

"Research."

"I see… Listen, ah… today we should hear from the doctors… you know, about the operation. I'm going to be out and about today, so I've asked Dr Oldfield to ring you on your mobile if that's all right…"

"Fine. See you later then."

"And, er… I'll be meeting the bank manager this afternoon… about the overdraft and the signatories on the account, you know. You may have to sign a couple of forms at some point."

"No problems."

Jim slammed the door behind him. He had been rash and foolish to pour a small dose of pest-killer in his uncle's coffee: he should have used arsenic or cyanide.

In the Twickenham library, he sat for almost an hour staring into the void. The more he thought about it, the more he realized how pathetic his plan of sending out poisoned letters was. Only a drunken madman could have come up with such a stupid idea. Flaming arrows… pah!… And how could he succeed if he was a failure at everything? It simply wasn't plausible.

He tried to think what someone like him – the wrong side of thirty, without a penny or a prospect in the world – could do with himself. For a brief moment he contemplated the possibility of starting a new book, the journal of a failed writer planning a revenge against the publishing world… then he reflected that this would be even more desperate and absurd. Hundreds of books like this must already have been written, books that lie forgotten somewhere, unread, unpublished. No one's interested in the voice of failure.

But why were his words not as good as any published author's? Why were his words destined to be written in water, to leave no mark in the world? There was no answer to these questions. And no consolation from the thought that there were millions of people like him, constantly pushed back and rejected by the system.

He had to face up to the fact that he was completely alone. The dozens of characters who peopled his books, his only friends, one might say, were made of thin air and could offer him no support. It was strange and in some ways sad that his imaginary world was so bright and exciting, while his real life was so empty and bleak, even banal. Perhaps he should do as Uncle George suggested, and give up writing altogether, find himself a proper job. Perhaps he should start seeing Helen a bit more often. He was still young enough to have a family.

He should wake up to the call of life.

As he reached this new level of awareness, Jim noticed a vaguely familiar figure walk to the borrowing desk with a pile of books by the same author. He recognized the man in a striped suit from the Fulham library. Like last time, after taking out the books on one side, he walked nonchalantly across to the check-out desk and returned the items he had only just borrowed.

"Something's going on," he thought, and followed the stranger's movements from the corner of his eye as the man started browsing the magazine carousel next to his desk. It was evident that the publication he was looking for was the one open on Jim's desk.

"Excuse me, sir," the man asked with a contrived posh accent, "are you reading *Bookpage* by any chance?"

"Uh? Oh, yes I am, actually..."

"Would it be all right if I have a quick look – I just need to double-check an address if you don't mind."

"Sure."

The man sat next to Jim and rapidly turned to the diary section, where there was a list of the most important literary parties organized during the London Book Fair.

"I wouldn't want to turn up at the wrong time or place..." he said, raising his glasses and bringing the magazine close to his face.

"Are you a writer?" Jim ventured, out of boredom.

"Who, me? Oh yes, I have written fourteen novels. Crime thrillers."

"Have you? Are they all published?"

The stranger lowered the magazine onto the desk, re-adjusted his glasses and put Jim's face into focus.

"Of course."

"Mmm... And who's your publisher? Maybe I know the name."

"Well, I've had a few publishers over the years." He gave the names of some large mass-market publishers and a couple of respected independents. "I started in the mid-Seventies, you know."

"Oh right," Jim nodded, impressed.

"Do you work in publishing?" the stranger asked, after a short pause.

"No... I am also a writer... unpublished, though."

And since there was no danger of being overheard or shushed in the empty library, Jim gave vent to his pent-up angst and recounted the story of his fifteen years as a struggling writer, perhaps in the hope of getting some tips or a word of advice from a published author.

"Well," the stranger said, at the end of Jim's tale, "all I can suggest is to hang in there as long as you can... That's my philosophy, at least. I had my breakthrough when I was only twenty-five, and I wrote half of my novels in the space of four or five years. I didn't make much money, though. They didn't pay big advances in those days. Then my editor left, I got divorced, and was dropped first by my publisher and then by my agent."

"And then?"

"Then it was a struggle all the way. After a couple of years I managed to get a new agent, a well-known one, and she placed my next four novels with some good publishers. But they didn't do very well, and my contracts were not renewed. So I ended up again without a publisher and without an agent. It took me five years to get my next novel published."

There was a long pause.

"And then?" Jim asked again.

"Then nothing for the following twenty years. The last two novels I had to pay to get printed. It's tough out there – grisly." The stranger heaved a deep sigh, raised his glasses and rubbed his left eye. Jim noticed that his fingers were shaking. "On the other hand," he continued, "I've got some good contacts in the industry, and I am still invited to all the best parties. Some of my old friends have become celebrities, internationally famous authors. I get by with the occasional review or article for the local press and—"

"It must be sad," interrupted Jim, with a growing sense of despair.

"Sad? Not really... You get used to it. I was never particularly successful, you know. I was always hoping to write a great novel, the big one, maybe win some prize and break into the A-list. But it never happened. Unfortunately, even when you are a published author, it's a lottery – there are always winners and losers... and who's to say that the winners of today won't be the losers of tomorrow, and vice versa?"

"And what happened to your novels? Are they still available in some bookshops or are they..." Jim paused before pronouncing the fatal words "...out of print?"

"No, not quite. They are not dead. They are all available on Amazon and Abebooks, as print-on-demand, and I have some stock left at home. I bought it from the publishers before they pulped it: it was very cheap – mint condition. I have a website where you can read excerpts from my novels and buy them online. Look, the address is written here." He pushed a flimsy business card towards Jim, which read "KEN TAHR, Writer", then continued: "My grandson did that – have a browse if you have five minutes. There's even a blog, which is linked to Scott Pack's one. And I do all sorts of other things to promote my books. For example, I do readings, put signed editions on eBay, write Amazon reviews of my own books, update my Wikipedia entry and keep borrowing my novels from local libraries to improve their loan rank, or—"

"You borrow your own books?" Jim gasped in disbelief: that's what the man was up to.

"It may sound absurd, but it's so competitive out there that—"

"But I mean, how can that help? No one's actually *reading* them."

"I know, but it helps at least in three ways: first, it gives the impression that they are being read by many people on a regular basis, so any potential reader won't be put off by a blank due-date slip; secondly, if any of them gets damaged or stolen, it will be replaced immediately, because of its good loan rank; and thirdly, someone's told me that I will get a few pennies' royalty each time one of them is taken out on loan. By the end of the year it will come to quite a bit, especially if you do it across ten, twelve libraries: it's a little perk… my pension is very low. As I said, my philosophy is always to hang in there…"

The man was rummaging in his inside jacket pocket. He drew out a folded leaflet and passed it to Jim.

"This is the complete order form, with a synopsis for each title, the price, etc. Let me know if you want to buy any of them, I can give you a good discount."

"I'll think about it."

"Well, now I've got to go. It was good to talk to you, Mr…"

"Talbot, Jim Talbot."

"Very good to meet you, Mr Talbot, and thanks for letting me have a look at *Bookpage*. Maybe I'll see you in there very soon, on the bestsellers' chart."

"Maybe."

"And if you fancy a glass of bubbly tonight, come along to the Dorchester party. I'll be there at around eight o'clock. I can introduce you to some of my friends."

And with that, the man left.

7

The Dorchester Hotel on Park Lane has a reputation for hosting some of the most lavish parties in London. Companies with healthy balance sheets, companies who want to appease angry shareholders after a disappointing quarter, almost-bankrupt companies who need to keep a high profile no matter what – they all organize parties at the Dorchester. These are parties where no ordinary wine is served – and no ordinary food either – where white-uniformed waiters go around with an inexhaustible supply of vintage champagne and quail eggs, where admission is strictly by invitation only, and the guest list very select.

Despite its unpromising and unromantic name, BetnoPal, a multinational enterprise employing over twelve thousand souls in a hundred and twenty-five countries, was the ideal patron of the party. As a genteel addition to its pharmaceutical and medical-supply interests, generating a turnover of just under three billion pounds a year, BetnoPal had recently extended its investments in the book industry with the takeover of an ailing literary independent and the setting-up of a new publishing house, Soror Press, devoted exclusively to "top-end-of-the-market chick-lit". The man at the helm of the two imprints, Samuel Forrester, was a notorious figure in the publishing world, and was variably described as a "genius", a "reject", a "cool operator with the Midas touch" and the "most inane biped in the Northern Hemisphere". The bald-pated, chunky-faced, flabby-chinned, queerly dressed, jelly-bellied publisher was bonhomie incarnate as he welcomed and kissed and double-kissed the guests at the entrance to the party suite, pillared by two hostile-looking bouncers.

"Hello mate, how are ya?... Hi sweetheart, so good to see you... Let me help you with a glass of champagne... Hello gorgeous..."

The party spread over a number of large rooms decorated in a sumptuously kitsch style reminiscent of a Catholic church. At seven thirty, the guests already occupied almost all available space, and a constant din resounded from wall to wall, so that people had to shout into each others' ears to make themselves heard. The talk of the party was Charles Randall's surprise comeback, and the discovery of MacKenna's unpublished manuscript.

"I thought he was dead," hollered a tall, tottering figure to his female friend.

"So did I." she replied. "They must be kicking themselves at Tetragon Books. What's the name of the guy they've appointed to replace Randall?"

"Something like Page-Turner."

The woman whinnied with laughter.

Charles made his appearance at around eight o'clock, with Pippa in tow. He was greeted by the ubiquitous Forrester with an extended hand and the most unctuous smile in his repertoire.

"Charles, so good to see you... Congratulations!"

"Hnf," grumbled Randall as he stretched his three fingers.

"Well done, it's a real coup... We should have lunch some time soon and catch—"

But Charles had already moved on to the main room and grabbed a glass of champagne. Pippa did the same.

"Cock," was his only comment as he pressed on.

They made their way through the packed room to a quieter corner, followed by a barrage of curious glances and whispers.

"Is she his lover?"

"She must be forty years younger than him."

"He can buy stockpiles of Viagra now that he's rich."

"He's always been filthy rich. He's the son of some Polish count... Jewish... he owns three or four flats here in Mayfair."

This last piece of gossip was completely unwarranted, but it quickly made the rounds of the party, and by the end of the evening had become common currency in most publishing circles.

In another corner of the suite, James Payne-Turner was trying to negotiate a complex after-party follow-up with his Arts Council friend, but she seemed strangely apathetic and unresponsive to his flirtatious overtures.

"What's wrong, Alice? Are you bored?" he asked at last, emptying his champagne glass and snatching a quail egg from a passing tray.

"No, I'm not bored, but I've just come back from Hong Kong and I am shattered. You know... this morning the Book Fair, now this party, tomorrow the Book Fair again, then another party – I want to go to bed..."

"Why don't you stay at my place tonight?" he tried. "That'll save you a long journey home. I've just moved into a new apartment on the Putney riverside. It's a ten-minute cab ride."

"Thanks, but I am staying at the Hilton round the corner," she said, continuing to avoid his glance.

Outside the hotel, under an unmerciful drizzle, Jim was standing in the shadow of a lamp-post as cab after cab delivered black-tied and evening-gowned guests. He was hoping that Ken Tahr, the eccentric writer in the striped suit, would turn up any time now and let him into what looked like a glitzy literary party. As time went on, this was becoming more and more improbable, but Jim was all right: he was happy to be so close to the movers and shakers of the publishing world and watch from a distance their smiling faces glint in the near-darkness.

After leaving the library in the morning, he had staggered back to his mum's house and, taking advantage of Uncle George's absence, had switched on the radio in his room and turned it up full blast. One after the other, he had picked his old manuscripts from the cupboard and read random bits from them, marvelling at how they seemed to have been written by a different person, not by him. They all ended up in a big box, ready to be ejected from the house and from his life. After the manuscripts came the diaries he had kept until a few years ago, full of idle observations and self-referential psychological detail. In one of them, he had jotted down the Belgian doctor's prophetic words: "Obsessive-compulsive behaviours, when accompanied by an abnormal take on reality, can only lead to depression and, ultimately, failure". The diaries were also thrown one by one into the cardboard mass grave of his past. Finally, his hands fell on the Spring 1996 catalogue of the Pink Hippopotamus Press, where on page twenty-four his face still radiated with the enthusiasm of untainted youth. He looked at the picture for a very long time. Who was that young man smiling at him from across the years? What had happened to him?

Around lunchtime, he had left his home in a kind of catalepsy, and had wandered aimlessly for a couple of hours, stopping only briefly at a cashpoint machine to withdraw some money before his debit card could be put on stop by Uncle George. The rest of the afternoon he had spent in the Kensington High Street area, where he had got himself a decent-looking pinstriped suit, a white cotton shirt complete with cufflinks, a black leather belt, a blue tie and a pair of fine Italian shoes. Then he had had his hair "sorted out". His three-year-old ponytail disappeared in a matter of minutes, replaced by a funkier hairstyle.

Having consigned the old alpaca jacket, the worn-out jeans and the red trainers to a bin near Kensington Church Street, Jim's smartly dressed double had made his way to Hyde Park, and there he spent the rest of the afternoon dawdling around and studying the reaction of joggers and passers-by to his new self. To judge by the way he was looked at, people seemed to approve, and he had to admit that he felt better himself. His stride and bearing began to take on a certain confidence and purposefulness, an air of importance and respectability – almost an authorial nimbus.

His long wait for the evening party had been interrupted only by a phone call from Dr Oldfield's secretary, informing him that the operation had been postponed until further scans and tests – some of them quite expensive – could be carried out. Since it was Uncle George who would be picking up the tab, he really didn't mind any additional costs, on the contrary... All he hoped for was that his mum would be discharged from the clinic as soon as possible, so that his interfering uncle would pack up and return to where he came from – or simply go to hell.

It was now eight-thirty, and he decided that if Ken Tahr didn't show up in the next ten minutes or so he would try to sneak in on his own, even without an invitation. The worst that could happen was that he would be rebuffed and kicked out.

Inside, the party was in full swing. A new bottle of champagne was being opened every minute. Pippa was having a chat with Alice Cameron, the Arts Council officer, while Charles was delivering a full-on rant about the decline and fall of the publishing industry to a journalist from *The Independent*.

"And they call themselves 'literary'... trhnf... gutless donkeys. They all copy each other and publish the same middle-of-the-range tripe – misery memoirs, ghost-written celebrity biographies, sensationalist junk, pulp fiction churned out by illiterate hacks – in the hope of discovering the next big thing, the next 'bestseller'. All they care about is three-for-two promotions and selling pap to the supermarkets, that's the truth. They don't give a damn about books or authors. They might as well be trafficking in pears or bananas. They are not publishers: they are more like printers."

The journalist scribbled some shorthand notes on a small pad.

"But at least printers," he continued, "or some of them, still take pride in what they do and how they do it. These so-called 'publishers' don't even know what it means to edit a book, and their books are full of horrible typos, printed on the cheapest paper, grnf..." He paused, then slurped from the glass and looked the journalist in the eyes. "Do you think I am a snob?"

"Maybe that's what people want," said the journalist, avoiding his question.

"Depressing," gruffed Charles, and he grabbed a new glass of champagne in disgust.

At the other side of the room, James Payne-Turner was in the company of a very keen, very ugly and very provocatively dressed agent. As she cackled on about a stunning debut novel by a twenty-five-year old Oxford graduate with a Master's degree in Creative Writing, he kept shooting quick, nervous glances over her shoulder to see what Pippa was up to with his Arts Council friend. They had been chattering away for the last ten minutes and – was it only his impression? – smiling from time to time and looking in his direction. He didn't like it. He was worried that Pippa might say something unpleasant about him or drop some venomous hint which could jeopardize Tetragon's funding application. He must do something about it, and now.

"By the way… she's a babe," the agent added, concluding her pitch.

"Sure. Great. Send me the manuscript, I'll have a look. Now, if you'll excuse me, there's someone that I need to talk to over there." And Payne-Turner tried to elbow his way towards Pippa and Alice.

Jim had finally managed to steel himself to cross the threshold of the Dorchester Hotel. It was now almost nine o'clock, and he was standing in a shady corner of the main lobby, watching people come and go, observing how they guffawed and barked at each other as though they owned the place. He could hear a deep humming noise from the adjoining rooms on the left, punctuated by drunken giggles and the popping corks of champagne bottles. Still wet from the drizzle, his hair was flattened down on one side and parted madly on the other, while little beads of perspiration accumulated on his brow and above his lips. He tried to collect himself and fix his hair with one hand as he peered into a giant gilt-framed mirror on the wall, but two rebel spikes kept popping up. It took him another ten minutes to muster up enough composure to try and get into the action.

In a small antechamber outside the entrance to the party, two young girls checked the names of the guests against the RSVP list, gave them their personal badges and collected their coats and bags. Jim waited for his turn with apparent nonchalance, though he was shaking inside.

"What's your name, sir?" one of the girls asked.

"Er... Tahr. Ken Tahr."

"How do you spell that?"

"T-A-H-R. Ahem. Here's my card," and he gave her the writer's business card.

The girl quickly checked against her list.

"Mmm... Doesn't look like it's in here... have you RSVP'd?"

"Sure... couple of weeks ago..."

The girl checked again for a very long time. Jim's collar suddenly felt sticky and tight against his throbbing neck. His fingers itched to loosen it a bit.

"Oh, hang on..." the girl said at last, producing a smile. "There it is, my mistake: I was looking under TH. Here's your tag, sir. Enjoy the evening."

"Sure."

And a few seconds later, he was in.

It is difficult to describe Jim's feelings as he entered that room full of publishing heavyweights and picked up his first glass of champagne. It wasn't exactly awe or excitement, but rather a strange sense of calm, bliss, hope, the feeling of somebody who has been trudging along for years on the lower slopes of Purgatory and is offered a quick glimpse of what's going on in the highest sphere of Paradise.

He looked around for a while, then he pushed his way through the guests, stopping only to leave his now empty glass on a small round table in a corner and pick up a full one from a waiter's tray. He moved on to the second room and stationed himself near a foreign-looking couple who were talking and gesticulating with more animation than those around them.

"But you must have seen the article in *The Observer* yesterday?" asked the man, who had the impudence to wear a black T-shirt under his jacket, and no tie. "In this country alone, a hundred and twenty thousand titles are published each year... a hundred and twenty thousand! And only ten per cent sell more than a thousand copies over twelve months. Half of them sell thirty copies or less. Makes you wonder..."

"Too many books are published," said the woman, betraying a slight French accent.

"Too many books are *written*," continued the man, with a deep sigh. "Everybody has a computer at home – and because they know how to tip-tap words on it, they believe they can write a book, get it published and become famous. If it wasn't so easy to commit your thoughts to a silicon chip or a piece of paper, you wouldn't get so many words written down. That's why Caesar or Tacitus were so concise:

try scratching your ideas into hundreds of expensive waxed tablets... We have Bill Gates to thank for being submerged in all this rubbish every day."

"And J.K. Rowling for spreading the myth of the millionaire writer... this Cinderella story, this idea that anybody can write and make a fortune out of it. That's why there are all these creative-writing courses and writing master classes. It all comes from America, doesn't it. As if you can teach how to write literature."

"Quite. But what's really scary is that there may be hundreds, even thousands of genuinely talented writers whose voices are drowned out by the white noise that surrounds them. More and more publishers won't even consider unsolicited or unagented manuscripts any more."

"Or if they do, they get some work-experience novice to go through them and send out a standard rejection letter."

"Do you remember that hoax organized by *The Times*? They submitted the work of Jane Austen and some Nobel Prize winners under a different name to agents and publishers, and got rejection slips..."

"But, honestly, how can one read hundreds and hundreds of unsolicited proposals? It is simply impossible. And some of that stuff really is atrocious – a total waste of time. You can't imagine how many nutters write or call us every day – and we are a small publisher. Thank God there are agents who go through all that stuff..."

"I think you are wrong there: agents rarely pick up anything from the slush pile on its own merits – maybe one submission in a thousand, if that. What they do is package a particular kind of author for the publishing circus. They only take on and promote writers who are perceived as an easy and safe commercial proposition. The rest will be shredded into oblivion, good or bad."

Jim listened with spellbound interest, lapping up each word of their exchange. He was about to venture a comment himself, but the conversation moved on to something else, and he lost his opportunity. He grabbed another glass of champagne – his third of the night – and when he turned back the couple had gone.

Payne-Turner was pushing his way towards Pippa and Alice, but wave after wave of incoming people kept knocking him back. When Pippa realized that her ex-boss was edging in their direction, she found a quick excuse and left Alice on her own, joining Randall's group a few yards away.

"How is it going?" James asked Alice, with an uneasy smile on his face.

"All right."

"I've seen you were talking to Pippa Hughes." He jerked his head to one side. "She worked with us until recently."

"She was telling me."

"Oh yeah? I hope she hasn't been bad-mouthing me." He laughed nervously. "Things got a bit nasty towards the end, you know? Envy... unfair dealings... missing documents..."

"Right."

"Listen Alice, er, I was wondering whether you had a chance to sign off our application, because—"

"I don't think this is the right place to talk about this."

"Certainly not. Sure. But you see, we—"

"And I don't think it's the right time, either. I told you I am knackered, and the last thing I want to do is to talk about work. I'm going to leave in two minutes."

"Sure. Sure. When do you think we could—"

Alice gave him a silencing glance.

"OK, OK. I understand. I'll catch up with you later then, all right? No problems. I'll give you a call," and he slunk off with one hand in his pocket and his tail between his legs.

The trouble with vintage champagne is that it tends to go to the head pretty quickly, especially on an empty stomach. Jim had gulped down a dozen glasses in rapid succession, and eaten only a handful of quail eggs since morning. His movements had become relaxed, his head twitchy, his tongue furry. He was smiling at anybody who made eye contact with him, chatting with complete strangers, crashing into people's conversations without any restraint. Once, he offered to fetch a drink for someone who worked for a publisher that had turned down many of his novels and, hiding round a corner, he spat into the glass. Drifting along from one room to the next, he grabbed random fragments of conversation, casual snippets, which hardly registered with him.

"He's got some real Christmas crackers."

"It bombed like Hiroshima."

"It's a bookgasmic experience..."

"We've just exchanged contracts – on Second Life."

"There's no great price tag attached... he's been turned down many times."

"She's the queen of schmuck... the queen of schmooze."

He approached a knot of people who formed a semicircle around a Rabelaisian figure wearing black-framed glasses and a thin goatee beard.

"It's genius, pure genius," bawled the man at the centre of the group, William Gascoigne-Pees, the head of a successful imprint belonging to a huge conglomerate. "It debunks the whole genre... it's gripping, cinematic, full of pizzazz and chutzpah."

"What you talking about?" Jim slurred from behind.

The man turned slowly and had a long look at him.

"Do I know you?" he asked.

Jim shook his head.

The man turned back, shrugging, and continued to rhapso-
dize over this book he had just bought for a "substantial six-
figure advance after a hotly contested auction", a book by a
twenty-four-year Chinese blogger who had been raped for
years by her stepfather and had turned to prostitution from
a very young age. This was her bare-all, no-holds-barred,
uncensored memoir, a special Richard and Judy selection
and a soon-to-be-filmed Hollywood blockbuster.

"What's your initial print run?" asked a young fellow on
his left.

"A hundred and fifty thousand copies," the publisher answered coolly, swilling down the content of his glass.

"I have got a similar book," Jim butted in. "Only it's
better. It's the diary of an eighteen-year-old nymphomaniac
prostitute who's had underage sex with politicians and heads
of state all over the world."

There was a long silence, as Gascoigne-Pees turned again
to look at him.

"And you are?..."

"Jack Lawson, Jim Talbot Agency."

"Never heard of it. Have you got a table at the Rights
Centre?"

Jim didn't have the faintest idea what the man was talking
about.

"We are a very small agency... relatively new. We work
on the Internet. We receive thousands of submissions –
from Russia, India, Africa – we keep an eye on blogs, small

creative-writing courses, and when we come across an interesting writer, we—"

"Jack Lawson of the Jim Talbot Agency?" intervened a tipsy Irish agent, coming to Jim's rescue. "Didn't we meet at the Sceptre party a couple of years ago?"

"Maybe?... My recollections of that night are a bit hazy..."

"Well, I'd had a few too many of everything myself..." quipped the Irishman.

A ripple of laughter ran through the semicircle.

"I thought you looked vaguely familiar," the ursine publisher added, as he tugged at his goatee. "So, this book you've got... what's the title?"

"The working title is... *Tart à la Carte: Confessions of a Teenage Nympho.*"

There was a pause.

"Mmm... I like the sound of it. And... is it possible to have a look at the manuscript?"

"Well..." Jim took some time over this. "You know, it needs a little bit of work... polishing..."

"You are showing it to someone else, eh?... Who is it? Picador? Chatto? Faber? Cape?"

"I can't really get into, er... and anyway the author," Jim said, "the author is very young, you know. And all the high-profile people she mentions in the book... we've got to be very careful from a legal point of view. We don't wanna get burnt, if you know what I mean."

"Course not. Do you have a card?"

"A card?" Jim rummaged in his pockets. "I think I... I think I may have run out of cards, actually. It's been a long evening... Anyway, my email address is easy to remember:

talbot123@yahoo.com. Just drop me a line and I'll send you the synopsis and a sample."

"Sure. Let me write it down – I have a very bad memory," and he winked at Jim. As the publisher's clumsy fingers punched the keys of his BlackBerry, at least three other people – including Payne-Turner, who was right behind the Irish agent, bringing to a close a promising conversation with a good-looking blonde – made a note of the address.

In another room, Charles Randall's tirade had grown in virulence and incoherence, as a small group of white-haired, purple-nosed guests had gathered around him.

"Literary prizes... trnf... it's a racket... Reviewers... they're all friends of friends, trough-snouters... what's the point... grnf. Depressing."

"Dr Randall," Pippa whispered, tugging gently at his elbow. "Dr Randall, I think it's time we went."

"Grnf. Give me another glass of champagne."

"I really think we should go."

"In a minute. In a minute. Grnf. Where's the champagne?... A minute, I said! Listen to this: a compost salesman becomes a book buyer, a book buyer becomes a publisher, a publisher becomes an agent, an agent becomes a writer, a writer becomes a journalist... Trnf... Then the journalist reviews the books of his writer friends, who've asked their agent friends to place their books with their publisher friends, who've managed to get their crappy little books into each single bookshop thanks to their book-buyer friends... Depressing."

"What about the compost salesman?" observed a captious person, probably a lawyer. "How does he fit in?"

"Hnnf. Pippa, let's go." And he strode off towards the exit.

Having nearly passed out in the lavatory, Jim staggered back into the party and made his way towards the group he had left a few minutes before. As he advanced, he noticed a man at the further end of the room who was moving around nervously, as if looking for someone. He rubbed his eyes. It was Ken Tahr... His face seemed angry and determined, bent on revenge. Jim ducked out towards the wall and walked a long circuitous route to avoid him.

"We're off to my club for a night cap," boomed Gascoigne-Pees when Jim reappeared. "You coming along?"

"Sure."

Just then Ken Tahr walked past, but failed to recognize him. Jim's knees wobbled under the fear of discovery.

"Are you all right, man?" asked the Irish agent.

"Drunk as hell, but I'm fine. Perfectly fine. Let's hit the road."

Outside the Dorchester, the rat race for a West End-bound taxi was fierce. Gascoigne-Pees tottered up Park Lane and made an imperious gesture that brought to a halt not just one, but two black cabs. These were rapidly filled by the group of revellers. Before jumping in and closing the door, Jim looked back at the entrance of the Dorchester Hotel and saw Tahr standing there, under the drizzling rain, looking in his direction.

8

The following day, Jim woke up at two o'clock in the afternoon, dragged himself to the shower and remained under the pouring water for more than half an hour. As he stumbled out of the glass cubicle, he tried to remember exactly where he had gone and what he had done after the party. He had vague memories of lights, high ceilings, billiards, cigars, vodka. Lapdancing? Lapdancing. He could see himself vomiting twice – once down a toilet and once in the street. The second time, he'd thought he was checking out for good. He also recalled talking at length about the nympho book and giving vivid descriptions of it, with such conviction and enthusiasm as to make everybody want it. He wished he had written down some notes.

He double-shaved, gelled his hair up and slipped into his smart suit again, then went downstairs to see if there was anything to eat in the fridge, all the way massaging his temples to appease a head-splitting hangover.

As he cut through the living room, he found Uncle George sitting in Father's easy chair, with his face buried in *The Daily Mail*.

"Sir," he croaked, lifting his nose from the page, "this is private property. Make yourself known, or I shall call the police."

"Ha, ha… very funny," Jim said as he walked past him and entered the kitchen.

Uncle George rose to his feet and followed him there.

"Mmm, nice, especially the hair... Honestly, son, in that suit I'd offer you a job tomorrow."

Jim grabbed a piece of cheddar and two carrots from the fridge, put them on a plate and went back into the living room, without deigning to reply. Uncle George followed him out.

"And, by the way, thanks for letting me know about the operation yesterday," he said as his nephew drew up a chair to the table and sat down. "I had to call the clinic myself."

"I was busy."

"Yes, you were busy. I know. And didn't have time to go and see your mum or give me a call."

"Look, Uncle G," Jim sighed, "let's not have another fight, all right? I'll go and see Mum today. Yesterday I had some important meetings. I had an appointment with a couple of publishers who are very interested in my work, OK?"

"Oh did you? And I suppose that's why you came back home at five o'clock in the morning, eh? Are they a sort of nightclub publishers?"

"What's your problem?" Jim's head was about to explode.

"My problem? My problem is that you don't seem to wake up and smell the coffee – that's my problem." Uncle George rapped his forefinger on the table. "Your mum is dying of cancer and you don't give a damn: you still go round chasing butterflies—"

"Chasing butterflies..." Jim scoffed, biting off half a carrot.

"—and still taking out money from your mum's account without authorization..."

"What was I supposed to do," Jim interjected with a full mouth, squeezing his temples with one hand, "go to those meetings in jeans or pyjamas?"

"Well, you could have asked *me*, first. I thought I had been clear the other day. But it's all over now, sonny Jim," his finger kept rapping on the table, "it's all over: you won't be able to withdraw a single penny from your mum's bank account any more... You'll have to find yourself a new—"

Jim sprang to his feet as if to assault his uncle, who started back and instinctively raised his arm to protect himself.

"OK," said Jim, letting out a geiser-like sigh. "OK, Uncle G – got your message, loud and clear. Thank you. Now leave me alone and read your bloody paper – and don't pile more shit on me." He sat down again and continued to eat.

"Splendid. You do seem to have got the message loud and clear."

Jim gave him the finger, without lifting his eyes from the plate.

"Nice. Very sophisticated. Classy. I suppose this is the sort of education—"

"Fuck – off."

"Sure, sure." Uncle George walked round the table and, with a laborious manoeuvre, sank into Father's armchair again. "Keep your head in the sand, son. Carry on like this. Carry on."

Jim raised his head and looked at his uncle with spite.

"I'll tell you one last thing, Uncle G. When you die, don't expect even a plastic flower from me... you'll be lucky if I come and piss on your grave."

"I doubt it. I'm getting cremated."

"Whatever. Shut up."

After a long, tense pause Uncle George cleared his throat and added:

"By the way, would you mind checking your phone? It's been ringing like mad all morning. It could be someone from the clinic."

"Where is it?" Jim patted his pockets.

"On the small table near the front door, together with your keys."

Jim rose with a loud snort, galumphed to the entrance hall, picked up his mobile phone and saw that there were a number of unanswered calls and unread text messages. As he scrolled through the list of calls and read the messages, his expression quickly changed from sulky malevolence to disbelief.

"I knew it would happen... I knew it..." he murmured, then grabbed the keys and dashed out of the door.

* * *

Charles Randall was on a roll. As soon as he had stepped into his flat the night before, he had started bashing out poem after poem. They just kept coming, and there was no way of stopping them. Were they good? Were they bad? Who could tell? After all, "fanatics have their dreams", as Keats said, and the final verdict on whether his dreams were a poet's or a fanatic's would be pronounced only after his death. But did it matter, this ever-looming judgement of posterity? Would it make any difference if his words were lost to oblivion and remained unread by the legions of the unborn? It was the act of writing in itself that gave him pleasure beyond anything else in life. "All things fall and are built again," said another of his favourite poets, "and those that build them again are gay." When he experienced his moments of revelation, of epiphany, when he felt he was a step closer to truth and had the impression he could capture a semblance of beauty with his words – then he didn't care about being unremembered as if he had never lived. He was ready to descend into Orcus without his lyre.

"Trnf."

The only person he had ever shown his poetry to was Patricia, the auburn-haired flame of his youth and his companion into middle age, who had left him ten years ago. He used to read his verse aloud to her on a Sunday morning, before breakfast, while still in bed. She didn't seem particularly impressed with his poetical creations, and accepted them with a polite smile, occasionally muttering a courteous word or sound of approval. He never had the courage to ask her what she really thought of them, but he suspected that she didn't rate them as the work of a talented writer – rather the sort of stuff a sixth-former could come up with in an idle moment between school sessions. But that didn't matter, either. What mattered was that he was writing again – and that made him happier than he had been for a very long time.

A gentle knocking startled him.

"Come in!"

Pippa entered with a long sheet of paper.

"Have you found it?" asked Charles, with a vein of hope in his voice.

"I'm afraid not. I have looked absolutely everywhere now, in every possible box, cupboard and drawer, between the pages of every single book…"

"I'm sure it's here in this flat, somewhere… mmm…"

"Timothy Thorpe from *Bookpage* called a few minutes ago. They are going to run the story of Tetragon's legal challenge in this week's issue. He wanted to know if you were available for comment... I said no."

"Good."

"And someone from *The Daily Telegraph* wants to write a feature about the MacKenna manuscript. I have asked him to call again next week."

"Good."

"Do you think we'll have to cancel the book?"

"I don't think so."

"It would be a real shame."

"We'll be all right, don't worry. What do you have there?"

"Oh, this? This is a fax that has just arrived for you. It's from Trinity College, Dublin, from the... curator of the MacKenna archive."

"Hnf. They probably want to make some claim too. Give it to me."

"Maybe they want to buy the manuscript..." Pippa said as she handed the sheet.

"Maybe."

Charles dropped the document on his desk, and a gloomy silence fell in the darkening room.

"Pippa?"

"Yes?"

"What do you think of this?" He gave her a scrap of paper with some words on it in his own handwriting. "In all honesty."

"What is it? A poem?"

"Yes."

"You wrote it?"

"Grnf. Tell me what you think."

Pippa read and reread the short composition, then raised her face and smiled.

"I am not a poetry expert… but I think it's good."

That smile again! That polite, uneasy smile – just like Pat's! His poems must be really terrible… or perhaps people saw him as a publisher, an editor, and could not take him seriously as a writer – in their eyes he was a brick-layer rather than an architect of books.

"Thank you."

"Are you getting your poems published?"

"Maybe."

"If you are, I'd love to buy a copy."

"Trnf."

When Pippa left, he cast around a despondent look, picked up his pipe and started fiddling with it. True, the creative act gives you an immense feeling of joy, but this joy is sapped dry by the prospect of not being able to share it with someone else. Just like visiting a museum on your own. Only by making it available to your fellow human beings can your joy be fulfilling, can your joy be complete.

* * *

Payne-Turner had been holding for about twenty minutes on the line. Every now and then, from the submarine depths or satellite heights of his intercontinental communication, emerged the faint rustling of Samson's echoing voice.

"Hello? Hello, Mr Bain?"

"Yes, I'm still here."

"Hold on pleeze."

For the past two days, since he had been back in the office after the London Book Fair, James had been trying to find out from the Ethiopian whether the promised £225K transfer had been made. There was a worrying pile of unpaid invoices stacking up on his otherwise immaculate desk, and the company's bank account was well into the red. If the money didn't arrive in time, he would not be able to pay his own salary at the end of the month, and consequently the rent on his luxury riverside flat.

The problem with Samson was that he was virtually impossible to pin down, as he didn't use email like normal human beings. The only way to communicate with him was by telephone, but his mobile was often engaged, and on the rare occasions when James had managed to get hold of him, Samson was busy on one or two other calls already. This time James decided to hold on for as long as it took.

"Hello Mr Bain?"

"Yes, I'm here."

"OK, tell me."

Payne-Turner swung his feet off the desk and sat up.

"Sorry to trouble you, Mr Mulu. I just wanted to check if the transfer... you know, what we had agreed with Mr Goosen... We have a few payments to make and—"

"It's been done. It's in your bank."

"Well, I checked half an hour ago – nothing has come through."

"Then it will arrive on Monday. If it's not there on Monday, let me know."

"Sure. Thanks, Mr Mulu."

"No problems. How is it going with the book?"

There was a short silence.

"You mean the Minister's wife's poems? It's at the printers, I think."

"No, the other one..."

"Oh, the *Terror Diaries*? It's going great… I'm really excited. I am getting a few translation samples done."

"I see. And when will it be published?"

"Oh, I don't know, it's a bit early to—"

"What about the Ministry of Education tender? Hold on, hold on… Hello? Hello? Hi… how are you? Mr Bain, can I call you back?" The line went dead.

A few minutes later, Nick Tinsley sauntered into the room, holding a copy of *Bookpage* open at the News section on page fourteen.

"Ta-ra!" he grinned. "A master stroke – word-perfect, my boy, word-perfect!"

He slapped the magazine on the table and slunk down into a chair.

"That's gonna hurt," he added. "They're gonna shit long, thorny logs. They're dead. So how are you? Did you have a good time at the party? Sorry I couldn't come. I bumped into Holly in a pub near the Fair – she's a beer monster. By the end of the night, I was too pissed to make it to bed. What about you?"

"Well, I—"

"By the way, who's that cutie who opened the door?"

"Oh, she's some work-placement girl. Will be here a month or two…"

"Good for you… so… what are we discussing today?"

"Well, I thought I'd run through some of the proposals with you, so that I can start commissioning."

"All right," said Nick, fishing a biro and a brand-new note-pad from his briefcase. "I'm all ears."

Payne-Turner cleared his throat and got to his feet.

"OK. Basically, we have some very commercial submissions."

"Good. From agents?"

"Only from agents. Trouble is, it's pretty expensive stuff."

"Hit me hard."

"OK. There's this blog by a Chinese refugee—"

"A *blog*?" Nick scoffed.

"All right, let's rewind. What about this: I've got a biography of a very famous Chelsea player with a history of alcoholism and mental illness…"

"That sounds better. Written by?"

"His daughter. She lives in Spain – a nervous wreck. She's divorced from Ricky Burns, the darts champion, the one with six fingers on his hand? They've got two small children, one slightly handicapped. That's good for the press. Of course, we could get the book ghost-written."

"Mmm… maybe. What else?"

"Well, there's this novel about mutant turtles. Great film potential. The writer's black, dyslexic, poor and has been in prison, so it could be cool from a PC point of view. And we could get subsidies."

Nick shook his head. "Turtles? Can't see it working."

James raked his hand through his hair.

"Well, then there's this young Oxford graduate with a Master's degree in Creative Writing… And she's got nice boobs."

"What has she written?"

"I think it's a '*Bridget Jones's Diary* meets *The Tenderness of Wolves*' kind of thing – you know, a debut – but I'm not a hundred per cent sure. There's a good endorsement from Will Self. We should be able to get it for ten or fifteen grand."

"Probably not for us…"

"OK… Then I've got a *History of Orgasm and Mastur—*"

"Nah, that market's shot its bolt…"

"There's also this Colombian—"

"What?… Are we competing with Randall?"

Payne-Turner slumped down into his chair, defeated.

"Is that all?" Nick raised his eyes from the notepad. "All right… well, not bad… not bad as a starting point… it's OK but…" He scratched his cheek, sniffed, then added: "But there's nothing… nothing that bowls me over, you know… nothing that immediately grabs my attention… You've got to go for the jugular, give me a good kick in the balls… find something really special…"

There was a long silence, then Payne-Turner had an idea.

"Well, there's this dirty schoolgirl memoir they were talking about at the party, *Tart à la Carte*, but…"

"What's that?"

James delivered such a pithy description of the book that he himself was surprised at how commercial it sounded. The Shark stared at the young publisher with an earnest look.

"Now you've got my attention. You see? This is exactly the kind of thing we need. How can we… get hold of…"

"Well, from this geezer I saw at the party, Jack Lawson, from the Jim Talbot Agency… The only problem is that Gascoigne-Pees – you know, Gascoigne-the-Vulture-Pees – is also interested in the book. People say he's got two kinds of chequebooks: one pre-printed with four zeros and one with five. We can't compete with him."

"Don't be so negative…"

Payne-Turner rolled his eyes and turned his face to the window.

"What? What's wrong now?"

"How can I see off Gascoigne-Pees when we don't even have enough money to pay the bills?" He pointed at the pile of papers on his desk and explained that the promised transfer had not materialized. "How can I be positive if we don't even have a single title on our programme, apart from Randall's Third World crap? The reps presented the Christmas titles to Waterstone's and Smith's over a month ago... soon they'll be talking about 2009 and 2010 titles: we'll need a Houdini trick to deliver a two hundred per cent turnover increase by the end of the year..."

"Look," Nick said, after drawing a deep breath. "All we need is one good book – right? And you forget something: we are a smaller company and can be very nimble." He jutted his paunch out. "Get that Lawson guy out for lunch somewhere posh early next week. He's not a teetotaller, is he? Then get him blind drunk and try to secure some sort of verbal agreement. That's how it works, right? And don't worry about the money: I'm sure the transfer will be in next week – I'll give Samson a call on Sunday morning to remind him... Now, you can go up to twenty or thirty grand if necessary, even fifty if you can get world rights... but make sure you don't get carried away, and start as low as possible: chances are you can bag this book for ten grand or less if you move quickly enough."

"Sure, but..."

"But what?"

"Well, suppose that Gascoigne-Pees or someone else has already made an offer... suppose we are gazumped... what shall I—"

"Well, tell the agent that we are not a big company and... yes, maybe our advance is on the low side, but we can punch above our weight and compensate with our enthusiasm, our personal touch, higher royalties… the usual stuff, you know. Bullshit him. Christ, tell him that we're going to take on more of his authors." His hand gestured a Pinocchio nose. "And if you do need to raise your offer above fifty grand, just give me a call or send me a text – we'll sort something out. I'm a bit busy this weekend, but I'll make myself available as much as I can. Anyway," he added after a short pause, "looks like we've finally got a publishing programme for the autumn, eh?"

"A publishing programme?"

"The dirty memoir in September, the MacKenna book in October and bin Laden's diaries for Christmas… from chick-lit to sheikh-lit… what a cracking line-up… If just one of them takes off and becomes a bestseller, we'll be rolling in cash by next spring."

"Don't you think we should—"

"You've read my mind, James, you've read my mind. We've done enough work for the week. Let's go to the pub and celebrate in style."

* * *

Jim parked his bicycle outside the café on the North End Road and marched in with a swift, purposeful, businesslike stride. At first, Helen and Sarah struggled to recognize him as he queued by the counter – then, as his turn approached, they started exchanging significant glances and venturing a few curious peeks at Jim's haircut and new attire. What had happened to his ponytail? Where were his trademark red trainers? Had the philosopher got a new job in the City?

"Hi Jim," said Helen with a smile. "What can I get you? A cappuccino?"

"Sure, thanks. Can I talk to you for just a second?"

Helen darted a quick look at her sister, took off her apron and followed Jim to his favourite table near the window.

"Hem. Sorry to bother you, Helen," he began as he sat down, with a shaky voice. "You see, I've got a bit of a situation at the moment, and... I need somebody to help me out."

The sorry truth was that he had nowhere to go. A number of publishers had been hounding him with text and email messages for the past two days, asking for the manuscript of *Tart à la Carte* with increasing urgency. They wanted to see at least a few chapters, a synopsis – and he had somehow managed to stave them off saying that he was travelling abroad and promising that he would show them something as soon as he'd be back on Monday. He had agreed to go and see the most enthusiastic and persistent among them, William Gascoigne-Pees, "straight from the airport".

He had not had a chance to visit or call his mum, and had slept only three or four troublesome hours at night in the Twickenham house amid the all-pervading snores of Uncle George from his room downstairs. During the day, he ran around trying to get someone to set up a website for him as cheaply and as quickly as possible – sat in shabby Internet cafés in a vain attempt to research into the world of underage nympho prostitutes – stared for hours on end at a blank page, racked by a growing sense of despair as the initial excitement turned into panic.

"My mother's dying," he said, without a hint of emotion in his tone. "Cancer. She's been terminally ill for a long time, and it was left to me to look after her. She's got no one else in the world to help, and the NHS... well, you know what it's like these days."

"I'm sorry..."

"I am not complaining, you know: it's given me the courage... the motivation... the discipline to... you know... even while I'm looking after her... carry on and remain focused on my goal... on my writing career..."

Helen nodded sympathetically as her sister brought Jim's cappuccino.

"The thing is..." he continued, recoiling from a premature sip, "the thing is that we've spent a fortune on private healthcare... we've no money left in the bank... even after remortgaging our family house. So I've been forced to put my literary work on hold and take on some more commercial commissions..."

"You abandoned your novel?"

"Had to." He straightened up and gave her a stoical look. "Now, I've just had an offer to write a... a slightly different kind of book... more on the mass-market side, you know... The money's just too good to say no. Do you think... do you think you can help me? With all this stuff going on, it's difficult for me to concentrate... I used to be so prolific... now I think I may have developed a bit of a writing block... Or perhaps I am too literary for this kind of thing."

"Well, maybe... What's the book called?"

He told her, and she gave a nervous laugh.

"What? This is a joke, right?..." She tried to nail down his shifty eyes. "It's not a joke. Oookay..." She reflected for a few seconds. "But who'd pay you for something like that? It's trash. A men's magazine? A tabloid? How much are they offering you? What is it that you want me to do, exactly? I used to keep a diary when I was at school, and I've been to a few creative-writing classes... but since we opened the café the longest thing I've written is a cheque..."

"You don't need to be George Sand to write this kind of thing."

"Well, OK, but... I'm not a tart and... well, I'm past my teens, that's for sure..."

"But you're a woman," Jim dropped in.

"Oh I see," Helen snapped. "I see... So are you suggesting that, deep inside, every woman—"

"Oh no no no no... What I mean is that you have a different sensibility from us guys... that you would know the way a woman thinks or feels about these things... that's all. I swear to God I have no hidden agenda: you're my best female friend, Helen, and I just need a little bit of advice and support to write this book... or at least get it off the ground, set the right tone, find the right voice, come up with ideas... You see, it's not the sort of thing I can ask my dying mum to help me with..."

"I don't know," Helen said, rising to her feet. "I don't know. Give me a call on Monday, when we are closed... now I've got to get back... it's very busy. Call me in the morning..." And she joined her sister again behind the counter, leaving Jim to his frothy cappuccino and a gathering crowd of Machiavellian thoughts.

9

There had been very little time for thumb-twiddling for Jim during the weekend. He had squeezed together a synopsis and drafted three short chapters of *Tart à la Carte* by plundering material from various websites, such as NymphoGirl or The Over-Educated Nympho. His agency website was now up and running, and he had even received a couple of early-bird submissions during his first day of trading. He was as ready as he could be for his meeting on Monday.

On the Sunday afternoon, he turned up at his mother's clinic with a bouquet of roses and a get-well card. But her bed was empty, and a familiar voice croaked from the far corner of the room:

"Looking for a head transplant, boy? Second door on the left." Uncle George became absorbed again in his paper.

"Where's Mum?"

No response.

"Where's Mum, Uncle G?"

"As if you care..." George hissed, as he continued reading.

"Where's Mum?" Jim asked again, this time in a curt tone.

George looked him in the eye and exhaled a garrotted man's sigh.

"In the operating theatre, you brain-dead moron."

Jim's tongue curled into a nasty curse, then relaxed back into its watery bed.

"When did she go in?"

"Couple of hours ago. They gave her the anaesthetic at around twelve thirty."

Jim dropped his bag on the floor, put the card and the flowers on the table and flumped down on a chair.

"Is it going to take long?" he asked, half an hour later.

"Yes."

"What did the doctors say?"

"About what?"

"About the operation, you know… Is Mum going to be all right?"

"Hope so. I think it's fifty-fifty. Weak heart, high blood pressure…"

"Fifty-fifty…" Jim considered for a while, thinking about the Twickenham house, a loft conversion and an interior-designed studio, where he could see himself sitting in total silence and jabbing away with his index fingers at his computer keyboard.

Another full hour passed before Anna, corpse-like and still unconscious, was wheeled in on a stretcher and eased onto the bed. It took more than three hours before the anaesthetic wore off completely and she could recognize her son. It was eight o'clock in the evening.

"Jim…" she wheezed with a feeble voice.

"Mum?"

"Thanks for coming, Jim… Don't worry about me… I'll be all right. You and Uncle George can go home now… go… don't trouble yourself…" Then she fell asleep.

Uncle George shuffled away at around ten, but Jim didn't

go. He stayed overnight and kept a long vigil by her mother's bedside, making sure the nurses replaced the various drips the minute they were empty.

In the morning, at around eight, Uncle George came back and brought a black coffee for his nephew. Jim didn't wait for the doctors' first visit, but planted a kiss on his mother's sleeping head, waved at his uncle and scuttled out of the clinic, pumped up for the important day ahead.

* * *

Pippa had left for work bright and early on that Monday morning, after a weekend in Paris with one of her best friends. As she entered the Vivus headquarters, she called out "Dr Randall?" and noticed that one of the windows was open and all the lights were off. Papers and books lay scattered on the floor. Had someone broken in over the weekend? As she tiptoed down the corridor and peered into the empty rooms, she called Randall once more, this time louder, but again there was no reply. It was very uncharacteristic of him to be out this early. Had something happened?

She tidied up the room and sat at her desk with a growing sense of anxiety. She answered a handful of emails, wrote a blurb, picked up a few calls, read an alarming fax from their lawyer – but her mind kept wrangling over the possible reasons for Charles's absence. Had he found the MacKenna letter in some secret drawer and dashed out to tell the whole world?

She checked whether Randall had left a message on his desk, but there was nothing there apart from more papers and more books. She picked up a semi-crumpled document at the top of the heap, a letter from his bank manager dated only a few days ago. With the short-winded elocution of bureaucratese, it regretted to advise that – although his thirty-five-year custom was very much valued – due to stringent directives resulting from the global credit crisis, his application for a business loan had been declined. As the possible repercussions of that refusal sank in, Pippa grew even more depressed.

She cast a dejected look around, drew a cavernous sigh and started pulling book after book from the sloping shelves, leafing through them with frantic fingers and the mad desperation of someone determined to find the proverbial needle in a haystack. After she had gone through the lower shelves, she jumped on a chair and analysed the upper reaches of Randall's personal library. At the far corner, shelved away from the rest of the books, there was a row of strangely sized leather-bound notebooks. She took one out, bearing the inscription "1975".

"His diaries," Pippa said aloud.

She climbed down from the chair and sat at Charles's desk with her booty. The paper was blotted and tawny with age. On one page there was a crossed-out fragment that read:

Am I a God or a dog?
Am I a God or a dog?
God, dog –
God, dog –
Woof!

On another page, a peculiar list could be found:

Dante	Genius
Dostoevsky and Balzac	Great
Shakespeare	All right
Joyce	Twat

The diary was also filled with scraps of paper, opera and theatre tickets, photos of Charles's younger, bearded self and other long-haired people of his generation. But there was nothing noteworthy, no annotations like "on such and such a day I met such and such a person and did such and such a thing" – only the occasional squiggled note. It looked more like a scrapbook for aborted ideas and intentions, a shelf-sized skip for intellectual residua. She climbed onto the chair again and had a look at the other diaries. They were all similar, and didn't seem to go beyond 1979, way too early for Charles's meeting with Mackenna.

The front door creaked open, and Pippa froze in mid-air. The door was quickly shut and heavy footsteps could be heard advancing towards Randall's study. Pippa put back as many volumes as possible on the shelves and scrambled down, but there were still piles on the floor when Charles entered the room.

"Cleaning up again, Pippa?" He didn't seem particularly annoyed, and he wore an unusual smile on his face.

"Oh… well, I was looking for that letter… this is the only room I haven't checked properly, and I thought—"

"I went through all the books myself on Friday, when you were away… couldn't find anything…"

Pippa followed him in silence as he went round to his desk and sat down. She thought he smelt funny.

"It's over, then," she said.

"Oh, no… we'll be all right." He sat down, picked up his pipe and shoved the bank's letter into the bin. "We'll be all right," he repeated, and lit up. "We'll fight on. I used to be pretty good in the scrum, you know, at college…" He puffed out a vast cloud of smoke.

She remained silent for a few moments and tried to breathalyse him with a piercing look and dilated nostrils. It was not even twelve-thirty and he seemed well above the limit. Maybe he had resorted to the bottle in despair… She suddenly remembered something.

"We've received a fax from your lawyers this morning. I'll go and get it."

She returned half a minute later.

"What does it say?" asked Randall with a relaxed tone.

"It says that we may face legal action."

"Legal action?"

"Well, Tetragon will claim that the book is theirs, not ours. They're pursuing the line that MacKenna's book was given to you in your role as publisher and director of Tetragon Press, not to you as an individual, and that therefore they should have control over it. They'll probably seek an injuction to stop the publication of the book."

"Will they? Mmm. Let them try… They can be my guest." He kept puffing away with a devil-may-care expression on his face.

"But the litigation costs—"

"That book is *mine*, Pippa: they're not going to get their dirty paws on it."

"But you have no contract, Charles."

"I don't need a contract. MacKenna gave it to me, personally, in a gentlemen's agreement – and that'll be it."

"I don't understand," continued Pippa, frustrated and close to cracking point, "you've been a publisher for over thirty years, and you should know the importance of the written word over verbal agreements…"

"*Scripta volant, verba manent…*"

"Exactly. Contracts are—"

"A pile of rubbish – that's what they are. Hnf. They don't count, Pippa. Only the goodwill counts. Without the goodwill, they don't mean anything. That's why a gentleman's word is worth a hundred contracts. Learn from me."

"A gentleman's word won't stand in a court of law, though."

"Oh yes it will…"

"Well, Charles, I don't want to keep contradicting you, but if that's your opinion, I think we are heading for disaster."

"We'll be all right, Pippa, we'll be all right… as it happens, the written authority is also on our side in this case, not just my fading memory of some gentleman ghost's word… You see those diaries on that shelf?" As he pointed towards the top-left corner of his library, Pippa's face went bright red. "Diaries are very useful things," he continued between puffs, without noticing the girl's embarrassment. "They record events. Do you keep a diary, Pippa?"

She shook her head.

"Well, I used to, you know. I used to. I stopped a long time ago. I prefer to keep it all in here now." He tapped his forehead. "I felt I was wasting enough paper as it was… mmm… Well, MacKenna kept a detailed diary all his life, and a bunch of Trinity College dons have been publishing it volume after volume… they say it'll fill up over forty tomes… it'll keep them busy for some time to come… That's why the archive's curator wanted to talk to me…"

165

"What did he say?..."

"Well, he just wanted to etch my name onto a footnote of history... my rightful place, I suppose."

"I don't understand."

"Maybe it'll be clearer if you read this," he took a photocopy from his pocket and handed it over to her. "I got it from the British Library this morning. It's written black on white – page 534 of volume twenty-three, published a couple of years ago. Trnf. They'll add a little dagger and a footnote in future editions... *requiescat in pace*..."

Pippa scanned the document with avid eyes.

Sept: 15, 1994 (*Th.*): Trip to London for the RSL do. Finished two poems on the train. Read about fifty pages of WBY's *A Vision*—waste of time. Went for a long walk to Regent's Park in the afternoon. Entered the Zoo almost by accident. Too many tourists. Written another half poem on a concrete bench near the lions' cages. Total crap. I let the mangy lions have it. Feeling glum and rather peevish. Had a couple of drinks in a pub. Maybe three or four. Youth's easy—middle age is tricky—old age is torture. It'd be good if I'd been dead three hundred years already. Party at the RSL in the evening. Too many lights and mammarazzi. Too many complete strangers shaking my hand. SWC is tailgating me all the time—pompous ass. CR was there too. Good man. Honest chap. I have given him *G&D*. I've asked him to take care of it when I'm pushing up daisies. He'll know whether to make it public or not. He'll look after it, he's a good man. If I keep it a bit longer, I'll end up burning it. Got drunk by the end of the night. Wrote a funny poem in the hotel, which I threw down the toilet in the morning. One of the best I have written.

Pippa lifted her eyes with a smile.

"Interesting, eh?" Randall said, still sucking at the pipe with gusto. "The curator was delighted to hear about the manuscript. They'd been scratching their heads over this passage for years... mmm."

"So we can go ahead as planned? I can confirm the interviews and the features?"

Charles nodded, unfazed.

"I told you we would be all right," he added after a pause, taking out his glasses and placing them on his desk. "I told you everything would be all right in the end."

* * *

"There's always hope... there's always hope..." Helen repeated to herself when she woke up at nine o'clock on a Monday morning and saw her fat, dishevelled sister sitting in a corner of the room, smoking a cigarette and chuckling away as she instant-messaged some stranger met in a chat room. As depressing as this and their flat and their humdrum London life seemed, she still hoped that things, after all, would take a turn for the good one day. What was worrying though, apart from the splitting headaches that besieged her when she tried to break from her routine during her rare days off, were the uncontrollable words and images that kept bouncing around in her head. The words "hard-boiled banana", for example, or the mental picture of an arrow's trajectory from a non-existent bow to an ever-shifting target, followed by a thud, were special favourites of her mind. Where did these intruders come from? Was there an explanation? Did she need to see a psychiatrist? She turned towards the wall and had a quiet cry.

When, an hour later, Jim called her and she agreed to see him the following day in central London, a sardonic smile crept over her sister's face.

"What's your problem, Sarah?" she said after hanging up.

"You're not going out again with that tosser, are ya?"

"Excuse me? That's none of your business. I never make any comments on the people you date or sleep with."

"I'm just worried about you, that's all."

"What?"

"He's a bit of weirdo, ain't he? Looks like a pervert. He's got pervert eyes. And only perverts wear red shoes."

"No he *doesn't*. And he's not bad-looking either, especially with the new haircut."

"Suit yourself. Just be careful when you meet him. My suggestion: open spaces with lots of people, crowded pubs. And if he asks you to do anything strange—"

"Sarah, I've had enough of this. Please. I know how to look after myself. He's just asked me to help him out with his new book."

"You watch yourself, girl. He's gonna try to have sex with you."

"Sarah!"

"I'm sure he's got something kinky in mind."

Helen stormed out of the room, but not before her sister could shout after her:

"And don't forget to take *War and Peace* with you this time round."

* * *

A chilly wind swept across Vauxhall Bridge as Jim crossed to the north side of the river. He was glad, a few minutes later, to enter the warm hall of a tall building in Pimlico, the cathedral-like headquarters of Vanitas Books. The floor and the ceiling were panelled with slabs of pure granite, and so were the side walls, in which two enormous glass bookcases were enshrined. The first editions of hundreds of famous bestsellers – some over fifty years old – were displayed face up in long parallel rows, surrounded by an otherworldly halo. It was a breathtaking, awe-inspiring sight. The peroxide receptionist at the farther end of the hall was one big flossed smile.

"How may I help you sir?"

"I'm here to see William Gascoigne-Pees. Jack Lawson, Jim Talbot Agency."

"Sure, would you care to sign here, sir?... Here's your tag. Through security, on the left. Seventh floor."

A silent lift took him up in no time. He reached another reception area, a smaller room with wooden bookcases all around, full of more recent bestselling titles.

"Jack Lawson. I have a meeting with Mr Gascoigne-Pees," he announced to the young receptionist on this floor.

"Please take a seat. I'll let his assistant know." And after a few seconds she murmured something into the microphone of her headset.

Five minutes passed, then ten, then fifteen, then twenty. The receptionist directed the odd call and kept examining her painted fingernails as if he didn't exist. He harrumphed twice, but made no impression. At around half-past eleven, a slim, twelve-year-old-faced girl came up to escort him inside.

"I'm Melissa – Will's assistant."

"Right."

They proceeded through a maze of corridors which seemed to go round and round. On the window side, a series of rooms opened up, inhabited by motionless, glum-looking, bespectacled literary folk, intent on staring at their computer screens, whispering on the phone or doing nothing.

"Executives," Jim thought.

On the other side, an open-plan beehive of cubicled mini-offices – each equipped with a person, a computer and a phone – buzzed with the frenzied touch-typing activity of hundreds of invisible fingers. No spoken words could be heard across the whole of the floor.

At length they stopped in front of what promised to be a particularly large room. Melissa gave a cautious knock and opened the door.

"Can I offer you something, Mr Lawson?"

"Some water would be lovely, thanks."

Gascoigne-Pees was on the phone. He gestured Jim to sit down in the room's only armchair, then signalled that he would only be another minute. Melissa brought a small bottle of water and eased the door shut.

"Yeah... yeah... I've read about it, and Chris told me... busy fools..." Gascoigne-Pees was saying. "They pooped in their pants, heh heh heh... I know... I know... idiots... they've been credit-crunched... no one's gonna pick up the shards now... no... no... we're not gonna bid... no... not worth it... no... All they've got is mid-list flotsam... yeah... Good old Jerry is in big trouble... won't be able to bluff his way out this time... he'll be lucky if he lands a job at Tongue-Twister Press, heh heh heh... Listen, pal, I've got to go... I've got someone in my office... all right... all right... catch you la'er... bye."

He hung up and extended his big fat hand across the table, smiling.

"How're you doing Jack? Had a good time in Spain?"

"Oh yes. It was great..." Jim replied, leaning forwards to squeeze the publisher's hand. "Only too short..." He had a long sip of water.

"You look a bit tired."

"Didn't sleep much last night, to be honest. Had to catch a very early plane."

"Well, glad you came to see me... So... where's the stuff?"

"Sure. Here's the first three chapters and a synopsis... hem."

"How long is the book?"

"Well, the entire manuscript is... around 120,000 words."

Gascoigne-Pees grabbed the papers and sat down. He flicked through the sheets a couple of times, stopping to read bits in an apparently random fashion, grinning, puckering his lips, stroking his goatee in fierce concentration. After four or five minutes he declared, tapping his fingers on the manuscript:

"This is good. It's rude, dirty, zeitgeisty... it's got potential. 'It gave me such a kick to host two Members of Parliament in my upper and lower Houses that when a third member demanded a chamber in which to...' Very subtle. Is she dropping any big names later on?"

"Well, under disguise, you know... we've got to be careful..."

"Sure... I like it, Jack. I like it. Good stuff. What shall we do about it? Have you gone out with it yet?"

"Not really." Jim had another sip. "Three other publishers have heard about it and want to see it – that's it."

"Who are they?"

Jim told him, and Gascoigne-Pees burst out laughing.

"Don't waste your time, mate," he said, grimacing. "They're Mickey Mouse operations... We can make this big. Launch a Juggernaut media campaign. *Huge* marketing budget. PR company. Get the author on radio and TV. Secure interviews in *The Observer* and *The Daily Mail*. Serialization in *The Express*. Features in *The Telegraph* and *The Evening Standard*. Talks and festival appearances. Dozens of reviews in the dailies and women's magazines. We can ease it onto the shortlist of some prize. Sell translation rights to fifteen-twenty countries. Get it optioned for a movie... Will you consider a pre-empt?"

"A pre-empt?" Jim didn't understand. "Maybe. I suppose it depends..."

"Look, I'll make it easy for you. See that white door? You can walk out of it this morning with an offer. How do you like that?"

"I like it very much." Jim smiled and gulped down the last mouthful of water. "Hem...What kind of figure were you thinking?"

"Something on the low side... After all it is a first-time author, always risky. You'll want to see the details of the contract of course, but in terms of the advance..." There was a short pause, during which Gascoigne-Pees seemed to roll an internal dice. "Say... £250K?"

"Mm-mm..."

"OK, OK. Three hundred. But—" Gascoigne-Pees raised a finger.

"But?"

"I must have the finished manuscript by the end of the month, or the deal's off."

"Why's that?"

"One of our authors was supposed to deliver in March, but he's cracked up."

"Cracked up…"

"Had a mental breakdown. A total burn-out. We had a shedload riding on that book, so we need something really big to take its place…"

Jim nodded, one eyebrow higher than the other.

"We can publish the book in October, but I need the finished manuscript by the end of April, otherwise it'll miss the Christmas cycle and it's not gonna work for us any more."

"I see. Complete manuscript by… end of month," Jim squiggled on a notepad and cast a glance at his watch. "No problem. A week on Wednesday. Perfectly feasible. We're just going through the final draft." He wiped the sweat off his brow and under his nose.

"So… do we have an understanding?

"I think we do…"

They shook hands.

"Good man. Then I'll email you a draft contract today."

Jim stopped listening at that point. As the publisher gossiped about some of his competitors and showed him the high points of his career at Vanitas – books that had won prizes or sold hundreds of thousands of copies – Jim was lost in his own tangle of thoughts and intrigues, from which he was roused only by Gascoigne-Pees asking:

"I don't want to sound pushy, Jack… but I'd love to meet the author."

10

As he looked outside the window, Payne-Turner reflected that this had been by far the blackest day of his publishing life.

At ten, he had walked into a silent, empty office. Holly had called in sick again, and the cutie had sent a text message saying that she'd been offered a paid job somewhere else. At ten thirty, after piling more invoices and statements on his desk, he had phoned the bank. Obviously, the money was not in. He tried calling Samson and Nick for over an hour, but their phones just kept ringing and ringing. Then an email came from Jack Lawson at the Jim Talbot Agency. As he had feared, Gascoigne-Pees had made an offer for *Tart à la Carte*. He read the first three chapters of the book and immediately sent a message to Lawson, promising to submit Tetragon's offer by the end of the week.

With no secretarial screening to defend him, he was at the receiving end of a number of unwanted calls from angry creditors, not to mention sales people from India. He coped as best he could, but getting anything done that day was out of the question. He grew more and more frustrated, and started worrying about the mortgage. If he didn't pay himself a salary by the end of the month, he would go into an unauthorized overdraft – simple as that. And his riverside flat would be repossessed. He was tempted to ram himself head first into the wall.

He paced up and down the long corridor, talking to himself. He had not commissioned a single book, had no staff, no money... He considered handing in his resignation there and then – but to whom? Maybe he could just leave a letter on his desk and pull off a disappearing act? No, that wouldn't work... and it would take him some time to find a new job anyway. He needed to sort this out *now*.

He returned to his desk and composed a frenzied email to Nick, flagging it up as super-urgent. Then, just as he was about to click on the "Send" button, the phone rang again.

"Hello?"

"Can I speak to Mr Payne-Turner, please?"

"Speaking."

"Hi, this is Sam Barnett from Reuters. I am calling regarding this new book you'll be publishing shortly..."

James jumped up from his chair.

"Yes?"

"I understand it's all quite confidential... I'll keep it very short. I just wanted to find out a little bit more about it... is that all right?"

"Of course, of course. Please go ahead."

"First of all I wanted to ask you if you think there is any doubt about its authorship."

"Absolutely not."

"How can you be so sure?"

"We had the text checked by experts. They confirmed it's authentic."

"And are you confident you can go ahead with the publication without facing any legal consequences?"

"That's all been sorted out. Our lawyers have looked carefully into it, and have given us the green light."

"Can you tell me what the book is about?"

"I'm afraid I can't – the material is embargoed until we finalize serialization..."

"But if you had to describe the book in two lines, what would you say?"

"That it's one of the most important publishing events of the century, and a defining moment for Tetragon Press."

"Well, it certainly is a big coup for you... and you'll sell a few copies, no doubt. But don't you think that people might accuse you of cynicism?"

"Why cynical? Because we are publishing in September, on the anniversary of... no, I don't think you can call this 'cynical'. Relevant is what it is."

"So is it about freedom of speech?"

"It's about publishing a very important work by one of the most influential men in recent history."

"And what do you think the international reception will be?"

"I am sure that the book will be read by millions and translated into every foreign language. We have already been inundated with requests."

"One final question: who will you be paying the royalties to?"

"The author isn't exactly in a position to issue any specific instructions, so they'll probably be donated to some charitable organization..."

"OK, perfect. That's all I need for now, Mr Payne-Turner... thanks very much for your help. We'll run the story in the next ten or fifteen minutes, so it should make it into tonight's news programmes and tomorrow's papers. I'll give you a call if I have any other questions... bye for now."

"Bye-bye."

When he hung up, James felt slightly better. He was pleased with the interview: he had sounded confident, businesslike, and had come up with at least a couple of quotable sound bites. Now the problem was to try and snatch MacKenna's book out of Randall's clutches. He looked at the computer screen and decided to delete the email he was about to send to Nick. Better talk to him on the phone.

He had punched half the number when the fax started ringing. A couple of minutes later, an ectoplasmic swirl of paper rolled out of the fax machine, followed by a loud beep. James tore off the long sheet, folded it twice and tried to decipher the faded transmission. The phone rang.

"Hello?" he said.

"Hello?" a distant voice echoed after a pause.

"Hello? Mr Mulu?"

"Hello? Hello? Mr Bain? Hello?... Hello?..."

"Hello?"

"Hello Mr Bain? Hold on pleeze." There was a long, muffled argument in a semitic-sounding language, then Samson continued: "Mr Bain?"

"Mr Mulu?"

"I've got very good news for you. You received my fax?"

"I was just trying to read it: it's a bit faint..."

"It's the copy of the transfer. 150K will be in your bank tomorrow morning. There was a problem with the bank in Valletta. It was a holiday there."

"I see."

"Did you also get copy of the letter of guarantee?"

"I can't read it really, but—"

"Good. 75K. Delivery in three weeks."

"Sorry, delivery of what?"

"Did the Reuters journalist call? I gave him your number."

"You gave him my number?"

"He's very keen on the *Terror Diaries*. Talk to him. Explain. Find out. He went to university with my cousin's husband. He's a friend."

"He's a friend? The *Terror Diaries*? I mean... do you mean... you... do you..."

"Sorry Mr Bain... Hello?... I have another call. Give me a ring later."

"But can you—"

"Later, later... Good luck."

The line went dead, and James kept the phone's receiver to his ear for a few seconds as if it were a seashell. His pink tie heaved on his red shirt like a long dog's tongue. With a shaky hand he put the receiver down and looked into the distance, out of the window.

Yes, that was definitely the worst day of his publishing life. And there was nothing he could do: the media wheels were in motion, and he'd be crushed in their cogs. He gave another quick look at the fax: at least the money was coming in. But it was too late now... far too late. But maybe... He punched the remaining half of Nick's number and waited for the ringing tone.

* * *

When the phone rang at the other end of the line, Nick was naked in the bathroom of a suite in a Paris hotel. He was grabbing at the fat overflowing from the sides of his belly and trying to peer over at his manhood, thinking: "How on earth am I going to lose all this weight?"

"Shall I take it?" shouted a shrill woman's voice behind the door.

Nick growled and wrapped around his abdomen a towel two sizes too small, then tiptoed into the room and snapped the phone from the table. He frowned at the display, and turned with an apologetic expression to the woman who lay on the bed with a glass of champagne in her hand.

"It's from the office."

He sat on the edge of the bed and, summoning a baritone voice, answered:

"Nick Tinsley."

"Oh, hello Nick," James said with relief. "Is this a good time to talk? We have a bit of a problem."

Nick listened in silence as the young publisher went on and on complaining about the recent mishap.

"I thought he was talking about the MacKenna novel," he concluded. "And the interview didn't last more than a minute. He caught me off guard."

"Oh well," said Nick with a sigh, turning on the TV. "Shit happens, you know... Look... you are already on CNN," he teased him, as a group of playful polar bears appeared on the screen. "Breaking news: British Publisher to release the alleged diaries of Osama bin Laden. Great. Well, you know what they say: 'No publicity is bad publicity'. It could turn out to be a stroke of luck. Maybe Samson was right: it could be our bestseller... I wouldn't worry too much about it... it'll blow over. Everything blows over... We'll sort it out. Take it easy man... Go home. I'll see you in the morning. Bye."

He hung up and turned to woman on the bed, who was staring at him with a curious smile.

"You see, Holly," he said, with an unusually benevolent smirk, "little Jamie still can't toddle without a baby walker. We'll have to go back to London tonight."

"You must be joking," she screeched, placing the glass on the bed stand and switching the light off. "Not now that we've started to have fun…"

* * *

On the way back to his mum's house in Twickenham, Jim made a rare visit to Waitrose and bought a whole sea bass, a bag of organic spinach and two expensive bottles of Riesling. Pushing his credit cards to the limit, he also purchased another suit and a couple of gold earrings, as well as a striped bobble hat for more casual outings.

Uncle George was not at home yet, so he quickly boiled the spinach, shoved the fish into the oven and sat at the kitchen table with a generous glass of wine to his left and the fourteen-page contract from Gascoigne-Pees in front of him. He read and reread it: it was too good to be true. The only slight problem was the delivery date. However, that was only a small detail. A hundred and twenty thousand words in nine days… that would be… what? Around thirteen thousand words a day? Perfectly feasible… D.H. Lawrence could write more than five thousand words a day, long-hand… and James Patterson and Alexander McCall Smith seemed to write at least half a dozen novels a year… Robert Ludlum could even write novels while being dead…

He helped himself to another glass of wine and reflected: "If you do this, you'll be rich and famous ever after. You can do it. You *must* do it." He clenched his fists and gritted his teeth. "You can dictate into a tape recorder... use speech-recognition software... or, even better, you can dictate to a typist... like Dostoyevsky, when he wrote *The Gambler* in less than a month... All you need is some first-hand material to make it sound more authentic... you can't just take it off the Internet... too dangerous... someone could find out..."

The bell rang. Jim lazily rose to his feet and, scratching the back of his head, went to see who it was. He expected to see the pockmarked asperities of his uncle's nose; instead, when he opened the door, the receding light of the day revealed the craggy profile of Tom, his ex-landlord, barely contained within the door frame.

"Hello Jimmy... long time no see..."

"You all right?" Jim tried.

"Yeah, I'm all right." Tom made a step forwards, to prevent the door being closed. Jim made a step backwards.

"Have you come to give me your wedding invitation?" Jim said with a smile, trying to sound cool.

"Where's my money?" the other retorted.

"What money? You've got my deposit, mate. We're all square."

"I don't think so."

"Well look... I left on the first of April, so I owe you nothing, right?"

"Wrong. You must give a month's notice."

"OK, I must give a month's notice. I left on the first of April, and that was when I gave my notice. Today's what? the twenty-first. You've got two months' deposit from me, so it all works out fine... one month for the notice, one month for the redecoration of the—"

"Listen, Cockzilla..." Tom grabbed Jim's shirt near the shoulder and shook it firmly. "We spent more than twelve hundred pounds repairing and redecorating your room. It was a pigsty. If I don't have my money by the thirtieth of April, I'll give your arse a free waxing and wear your cojones as a bow tie. Here's the statement and the receipts, with the bank details." Again, he turned to leave.

"So I guess I'm not invited to your wedding, eh?"

Tom turned back with a livid face.

"We ain't getting married any more. We've split up. Janet's gone back to Ireland."

"Oh, sorry to hear that..." Jim said with a grimacing smile. "I suppose it's the wheel of fortune... some go up, some go down... that's life. Guess what: I've just got a book contract for three hundred grand... and that's just for one novel..."

"Good for you, Jimmy, good for you..." He pinched Jim's cheek as he said this. "If you don't pay by the end of the month, I'll kill ya."

* * *

Charles's laughter, the following morning, could be heard from out in the street. Pippa went down the steps to the basement flat and opened the door with caution. A few seconds later, as she hung up her coat, Randall bounded into the living room and gave her a bundle of newspapers.

"Have a look," he said with spirited eyes under his glasses. "My favourite one is the piece in *The Times*. Brnf."

Pippa sat at her desk and started reading the article in question. A smile started to creep over her face, and then she read aloud: "The moral integrity of the new management at prestigious literary independent Tetragon Press has been brought into question... documentary evidence shows that their claim to the recently unearthed manuscript by Tom MacKenna is totally unfounded... Many eyebrows were also raised at yesterday's announcement that Tetragon Press intends to publish the purported *Terror Diaries* of Osama bin Laden, which Tetragon's publisher James Payne-Turner has described as 'a pivotal work by the most influential man in history'. This has attracted much scepticism and a torrent of snide remarks from the publishing community. A British publisher is reported to have said: 'I doubt this will win the Nobel Prize for Literature, or the one for Peace.'" Pippa riffled through the other papers and looked up at Charles in amazement. "It couldn't be much better if we had made it up... they've pressed the self-destruct button."

"I know."

The phone didn't stop ringing for the next couple of hours. Every newspaper, radio and TV journalist in the country and abroad wanted to know more, demanded a comment or a quote. Randall replied that justice had been done and greed had been punished, and said that "this was nothing less, nothing more than what I expected of the bunch of cowboys who forced me out". He asked not to be quoted, but he secretly hoped that some journalist would ignore his request and put his words into print, even make them into a headline.

Around noon, as he poured over the typescript of MacKenna's *The Great and the Damned*, Pippa gave a gentle tap on the door and entered his study with an interested look on her face.

"Trnf."

"There's someone for you, Charles."

"I'm not seeing anybody. I'm busy."

"A woman… she says she's come from abroad."

"What's her name?"

"Patricia."

The old publisher goggled his eyes and seemed flustered.

"Patricia? Hrr-humf." He stood up and looked around. "What does she look like?"

"Oh, she's a nice-looking lady… long red hair… big white hat… elegantly dressed… tall… leather boots… painted nails… late fifties, maybe?"

"Frrnf. It's her." He moved things around on his desk, as if tidying up.

"Who is she?"

"It doesn't matter. It doesn't matter. What does she want? Did she tell you?"

"Not really: she just said she's here to see you. I thought she had an appointment."

"Tell her I'll be there in a minute… and take your lunch break. Please."

"All right."

When Pippa left the room, Randall sat down again, propping his head up on one hand and resting his elbow on his thigh. A couple of minutes passed, then he heard the front door closing. Cautiously, he tiptoed down the corridor and, when he reached the living room, popped his head around the corner, turtle-like. There she was, with the same fierce expression as on that grey February morning in 1998, when she had turned away with a curt goodbye, boarding a train for France and disappearing from his life. She was standing by the window, reading a book – or pretending to: it was always difficult to know what was going on in her mind. He cleared his throat and stepped into the room.

"Oh, there you are, Charles," the woman exclaimed, placing the book on Pippa's desk and giving him the once-over. "You've grown so old. You look terrible. Your hair's all white. Look at your clothes. Gravy stains on your shirt. And you're so thin. Have you become a breatharian? Still living in this awful place? There's a bad smell in here. You still smoke? Open the windows. So you've left Tetragon? They made you leave? Must have been horrible. What's this story about MacKenna? I may be moving back to London. How are you keeping?"

Randall stood motionless in front of her, his lifeless arms dangling by his sides. She was talking to him as if they had not seen each other only for a couple of days, as if the deep gorges furrowed by time could easily be bridged across.

"I'm doing…" He cleared his throat again, almost choking. "Excuse me. Grnf. I'm doing… all right."

"Glad to hear that. Have you married? Are you seeing someone? I have left Jean-Philippe. He's a dirty pig. All Frenchmen are. They only think about one thing. Who's that girl who was here? The cleaner? Your secretary? She's very pale. I like her earrings though. Are you busy? Shall I come back another time? Do you still go to concerts? To the opera? Museums? Nothing? Only books?"

"I…" Charles replied, with a weakening voice. "I write poems…"

"Oh, I remember your poems. So you carry on writing them? At your age? Poetry's no business for old people. You should do gardening. Go on cruises. Watch golf on TV." She looked around. "Where can I sit down in this place?"

"Hem. What... why have you come to see me, Pat?"

"Oh, for old times' sake, you know. I still care about you. I read you were in trouble. The MacKenna affair. I thought I could help. I can testify. I was there that night with you. You remember? We celebrated that night in my flat. I bet you don't remember."

"I do remember."

"Well, that was a long time ago. You might have forgotten. People forget. Especially old people. Look how thin you are. Your cheeks are hollow. You don't look good with that beard. It's unkempt. And those glasses are awful. I've seen some that might suit you. In Venice, last month. Are you doing all right, Charles? Do you need any money? Can I help you with anything?"

"I'm doing fine," Charles said with a confident voice. "And I need no help, thank you... I need no help. The MacKenna dispute has been sorted out... they've lost... it's in the papers today." He pointed at the open pages of *The Times*. "But thank you for caring, Pat... for remembering me..." Then he mumbled, after an awkward pause: "I thought you had forgotten me... that all the world had forgotten me..."

"Oh don't be so tragic. We're all destined to be forgotten one day. You haven't changed a bit. Always gloomy, always melodramatic. You've read too many books. Let's go out. Let's get some fresh air. And stop writing poems. Are you free for lunch? I have booked a table at Lucio's. I'm sure they can add a chair. I'll order a *fiorentina* for you. *Al sangue*. Then we can have a drink somewhere. If you are not busy. And talk about old times. Or about the future. You've got the keys on you?"

She had already stepped outside, and was almost dragging him out. Charles threw a wistful look back to the empty flat, as the door closed behind him.

"Brnf."

* * *

"What now?" Payne-Turner was asking Nick, who sat opposite him with a dark expression on his face, as the phones kept ringing unanswered. "Where does this leave us?"

After a long deliberation, the Shark replied, scratching his cheek with a pained movement of the finger:

"Up shit creek without a paddle – that's where it leaves us… This is bad. Very bad."

He was looking at a fax from the Arts Council, which informed them that Tetragon's funding application had been rejected and that they could not be associated with any company or organization that risked lending credence and support to terrorist groupings.

"We've been crucified by the press… and the phone lines have been burning up… we've even received some death threats…"

Nick shook his head.

"And the money from Samson has not arrived," the publisher continued in a panic-stricken voice. "I've rung the bank three times today. What's going on?"

"I wouldn't worry about that…"

"You wouldn't worry? But how are we going to pay our wages? How are we going to pay the bills? Look at these letters from debt-recovery agents. We'll receive a court summons one of these days… Soon the bailiffs will come knocking at our door…"

"Money is not the issue. I'm sure Samson's transfer will come through any time now. And if there's a problem, I can make some funds available from my own account. So stop fretting about that…" There was a long pause, then Nick added: "You really think we shouldn't just go ahead and publish these *Terror Diaries*? With all the publicity going on, it'll sell like hot cakes…"

"Are you kidding?… I have received the sample translations back now, and it's gibberish… completely unpublishable… The translator thinks it's a fake: he says that there's a lot of Algerian slang words in it… it was certainly not written by someone from the Gulf…"

"Who cares? I mean, people will buy it anyway. Let critics and journalists pour gallons of ink over it. What? Why are you shaking your head?"

"No one will stock that book, Nick. Just look how quickly the Arts Council has booted us into touch… And even if you sell a lot of copies, it would be a scorched-earth strategy… nobody will want to deal with us any more…"

"What shall we do then? The MacKenna novel has also gone… well, maybe I could… mmm…" Nick rubbed his brow as if he was sweating. "What's happening with the dirty memoir?"

"Oh yes, I forgot to tell you… I've read it, and it's good… but that's pretty much gone too: Gascoigne-Pees has made an offer on it."

"And?"

"Well, I told the agent we'd make our offer by the end of the week… but with no money in the bank…"

"Make an offer."

"What?"

"I said make an offer – now."

"Are you sure?"

"Positive."

"And what happens if it's accepted?"

"Then we go ahead with the publication."

"No, I mean: how are we going to pay?"

"I told you not to worry about the money. Just make sure that we get that book."

"And how much should I offer? I'm sure Vulture-Pees's used his five-zero chequebook."

"Offer a hundred thousand."

"A hundred thousand?"

"A hundred thousand. We need to make a big splash. We must have that book."

Payne-Turner straightened up and drew a long breath, as the phones kept ringing.

"OK, I'll offer a hundred thousand pounds… Cool. Maybe with a bit of luck—"

"It's our chance to turn defeat into victory. Don't screw it up, James."

"I'll send an email right away."

"Good. Holly!" Nick shouted, opening the door and sticking his head out. "You can answer the phone now. Just take messages – no one's available for comments." Then he turned to James again: "It'll blow over. Trust me… it'll blow over. And Randall will pay for all this."

* * *

Later that evening, in another part of town, Jim and Helen were walking along together in silence, just like they had done two years before. Jim was wearing his new bobble hat and gold earrings, which made Helen terribly uncomfortable. She got the distinct impression that even in the teeming streets of Piccadilly and Soho, where people are used to seeing the most bizarre things, passers-by were sneaking sideways glances at him. To her relief, this time he was not listening to his walkman.

"Shall we get a coffee?" Jim said, as they passed by a café on the Shaftesbury Avenue.

When they sat down at the table with their cappuccinos, Jim produced from his bag a copy of Gascoigne-Pees's draft contract. Before printing it, he had cunningly deleted a zero from the advance clause.

"Thirty grand... It's a lot of money, Helen," he said, smiling. "But I'd be happy to share part of it with you – say twenty, thirty per cent – if you can help me write the book by the deadline."

"The thirtieth of April?"

"Yeah."

"It's impossible. I don't have enough experience... surely it takes a year or more to write a whole book?"

"Not these days. Not with all the new technology. Have you ever heard of 'instant books'? They turn up after some massive event, like 9/11, or the sudden death of some footballer or rock star? They're turned round in a few days."

"But you don't even have a story here: all you have is a title and two or three short chapters."

"We'll build the book around the title. All we need to do is gather some first-hand material, to give the story a touch of authenticity, then we can bash it out quickly..." He took a long sip of his cappuccino and wiped his lips with a napkin.

"I think it's unrealistic," Helen said after a pause, shaking her head. "Anyway, I can't just take ten days off like that. My sister wouldn't be able to cope on her own."

"I tell you what," Jim said in a decisive tone, going through some bits of speech that he had prepared in advance and played out many times in his mind, "why don't we turn this into a team effort and involve your sister too? You can close your café for a few days... like a holiday. And I'll give you fifty per cent: fifteen thousand pounds. How about that?"

Helen reflected in silence. She could definitely use some time off from the deadening work at the café. And the money was tempting... She could take a long holiday. Go on a trip abroad. Move out of her sister's flat... As to involving Sarah in this project, she wasn't too keen... although it's true that Sarah could type faster than her, had a computer and much greater knowledge and practical experience of the facts of life.

"OK, I'll ask her," she said, lifting her eyes.

"Excellent. Thank you so much, Helen. Much appreciated."

They left the café and crossed into what used to be London's red-light district, now a curious amalgam of cheap restaurants, reeking pubs and dodgy tourist shops. Jim stopped in front of a doorless opening that gave access to a narrow staircase disappearing from view after the first landing. It was lit up by a string of red lights running along the walls and a crude neon sign flashing the words "MODELS UPSTAIRS".

"This is where I have arranged the first interview."

"Interview?"

"Yeah, I've picked up a few cards from a phone box this afternoon and made bookings with a couple of professionals.

Just to have a chat, you know?... What's that face for? You are not thinking that I... Look, I've never been to a place like this... I swear to God... And now I'm not going to... It's just to get some real-life stories... factual information... a sense of the milieu... You can call the police if I am not back in ten minutes, heh heh..."

He tentatively walked up the staircase; then, as he reached the first landing, he turned and made a feeble attempt at waving goodbye before disappearing beyond the wall.

"Tosser," Helen mouthed, as she stepped to the other side of the street and drew a book out of her bag.

At the top of the stairs, Jim entered a tiny lobby with an empty reception desk.

"Hello?" he ventured, after pressing the desk bell.

A short, sturdy middle-aged woman with a white dress and a pink wig appeared from a door behind the desk. Her hands were busy counting money.

"What do you want?" she asked, stopping the count.

Jim was slightly taken aback when her Gorgon-like features came into full view under the strong red light overhead.

"I'm... I'm the writer... the journalist... I called earlier on and made an appointment to see Candy..."

"All our girls are called Candy, darling," she pointed out with a mastiff's grin.

"Well, I've called this number." He showed her the card, where a curvy topless blonde wearing black gloves and garters stood in a provocative pose, next to a list detailing all the services offered.

"Oh, that one... Down the corridor, third door on the left."

Jim moved off a couple of steps, but the brothel-keeper called him back.

"I need some form of ID, and full payment in advance. It's a hundred pounds for an hour."

"I'm only going to be here ten minutes."

"Sorry. Minimum charge."

Jim handed over the notes and one of his credit cards. When the woman was satisfied with everything, he took his credit card back and proceeded to the designated room with a jittery feeling in his stomach.

The corridor was hellishly dark: there were only three dim security lights hanging from the ceiling. Jim groped his way forwards as best he could. He counted one, two, and at the third door gave a gentle knock. No one replied. He knocked again and opened the door with great circumspection. The room was almost as dark as the corridor outside, but some vague forms could be recognized: a low bed with a mattress on it, a chair, a small bedside table with an unlit lamp and, at the far corner, a strangely shaped cupboard with a phosphorescent wig on top. A weak funereal light penetrated through a chink in the curtains.

"Is anybody here?" Jim called out faintly, as he stepped inside.

The cupboard teetered and turned, revealing under the fluorescent wig a twenty-five-stone, treble-chinned white woman, with rolls of fat spilling all over her body and two udder-like boobs hanging over blubbery Louis XIV-style legs.

"Come here!" the prostitute bellowed.

"I'm... I'm the writer, madam..." Jim wheezed, recoiling. "I don't know if your colleague passed on the message..."

"Where do you want to do me?"

"Well, I can sit on the bed if you want, or on that chair."

"No. Too uncomfortable. Come over here. And remember – I don't like bad language in my room."

"Hang on a sec, there's a slight misunderstanding. I've not come here to… you know… I'm just here to interview you."

"What's that supposed to mean?"

"Just a quick chat about your experiences as a… you know… sex worker… just five minutes, a few questions, and I'll be gone. I'm a writer, a journalist, not a client."

"Is this an excuse? You were expecting the girl on the tart card?"

"Pardon?" gasped Jim.

"Is this just an excuse because you don't find me attractive?"

"No!" Jim shook his head with violence in the dim light. "I don't believe this." He had just paid a hundred quid to be harangued by a colossal whore with low self-esteem. "It's nothing to do with you being attractive or not. Can we just switch the light on and talk about your background, your—"

"You think I'm fat and ugly… and you're chickening out." Candy had stepped across the room and was now looming over a terrorized Jim.

"That's not the point. My point is—"

"Well, if you don't think I'm repulsive, come here and give me a big hug." She clutched him in a suffocating embrace, pressing his head against one of her giant breasts. Jim managed to tear himself away with difficulty.

"Leave me alone! Don't touch me!" He tried to open the door behind him, but a vicious blow felled him.

"I knew it was just an excuse," she said, landing another big wallop on Jim's head.

"You fucking bitch…"

A third blow knocked him almost senseless. "I said no bad language."

Jim found enough strength to rise on all fours and scarper out of the room. The prostitute was close at his heels, and continued to deliver deadly blows with both hands any old how, shouting abuse all the way.

"Help! Help!" was Jim's desperate cry as he scuttled along the corridor and into the reception area. He rose to his feet and lurched down the stairs, the pink-wigged brothel hostess looking on without curiosity, but in the rush he tripped over one of the steps and fell down awkwardly, head first.

When she heard the commotion, Helen closed her book and rushed across the street, just in time to see Jim's head spin round and bang against the wooden panelling of the first landing.

"Oh my God!" she cried, leaping up the stairs.

With a slow, painful movement, Jim turned his face towards her.

"Call the ambulance, Helen... I think I've broken my leg."

11

The following morning Pippa was surprised to find a dishevelled Charles sitting on the steps leading to his basement flat. On seeing her, the old publisher jumped to his feet and looked her in the face with feverish eyes.

"Pippa... Pippa." He cleared his throat. "Pippa..." He grabbed her arm and gave it a little squeeze. "Tell me that it was you who took it..."

"Took what?"

"The manuscript... The MacKenna..."

Pippa's face went blank: things started swimming around her. Her silence and her confusion gave him the answer he didn't want.

"Trnf..."

He dragged her in by the arm, through the living room, down the corridor and into his private study. Books, papers and various objects lay scattered on the floor, as if someone had been rampaging around the flat all night. Charles levelled a shaky finger at his desk and shouted:

"It was there! I left it there when I went out! You didn't take it, did you? Brnf. Did you make a copy of it? Do we have a copy somewhere? Did you type it up? Photocopy it?"

Pippa was about to burst into tears, and could hardly speak or make sense of what she said.

"Where... what... when do you think..." she mumbled.

"I don't know! I don't know! Grnf." He let himself fall heavily on his chair and grabbed his pipe, trying to compose himself.

"You think someone might have taken it? Stolen it?…" she asked. "But who? Maybe you're just being paranoid, Charles… you might have misplaced it… it's happened before."

"I've been searching for four hours. Nothing. It was right here, on my desk, next to my poems. I had almost finished editing it. I went out with Pat ten minutes after you, then we had lunch at Lucio's… it must have been one o'clock… then we had a few drinks in a hotel near South Kensington, around two, two thirty… then we went to some other place and had a couple more drinks… then… then I think I jumped into a cab and…" He stopped abruptly and remained silent.

"And?"

"Trnf. I don't remember."

"You don't remember?"

"I don't remember what happened after that. What I did, what I didn't do… a gaping hole… I suppose I came back home. Trnf. Wait a minute: I had a dream… but that was last night… you know, one of those nightmares you have years after finishing university, when you imagine you've got an exam and you're not prepared for it… I was in this room, and this horrible little man – bald, red eyes, a long white beard – was taking all the books off my shelves and throwing them into a big shredder, pulping them all, one by one… He was laughing, like a demon… I woke up in a sweat… it was five o'clock in the morning, and the manuscript had gone from my desk. It was right here… right here… hrnf."

"Do you remember seeing the manuscript when you came back last night?"

"No."

"Do you think it's possible your friend has taken it?"

"I don't think so."

"Can you call her and check?"

"I don't have her number."

"Do you have her address?"

"No. But she wouldn't have taken it. She doesn't care about books and manuscripts. Grnf." He squeezed his temples with one hand and muttered: "That woman's brought nothing but trouble and misfortune in my life…"

"OK… So who else could it have been? You're not thinking that Tetragon Press…"

"Well, maybe… he's capable of anything, Nick Tinsley… Or perhaps someone's read the articles in the papers and…"

"But I locked the doors and shut the windows before going… I left around five, and no one entered the office in the afternoon… it can't have vaporized… let's have another look around together… shall we start with this room?"

"Don't bother, Pippa… don't bother. I looked everywhere. I give up. It's all over."

"What shall we do then? Issue a press release? Cancel the interviews? Call the police?"

"I think you'd be better off calling the undertakers."

* * *

The sun shone high in the sky, flashing a rare smile on the dark-grey rooftops of London. Payne-Turner strode on with renewed optimism, pep-talking himself with an assured mental tone:

"Go for it, man. Go for it. You can do it."

That morning, he felt at the top of his game. He felt he had graduated to the world of high-flying publishing. He had made his offer for *Tart à la Carte* and, whether it was successful or not, his hundred-thousand-pound offer would leave an indelible trail of gossip. People would talk. People would know about it, and start taking him seriously. He would be on the map now. And since publishing was all about perception, all about psychology, that six-figure offer would stand out on his CV more conspicuously than ten years' editorial experience.

As he turned into the short cul-de-sac leading to the Tetragon headquarters, he was startled to see a large crowd amassed in front of his office building. There were people holding long-necked microphones, TV vans with huge discs on their roofs and yellow-jacketed police officers. James's first thought was that someone had been killed, or that some major burglary had taken place. He didn't think it could be anything to do with him or Tetragon Press, but he realized he was being observed as he made his way to the entrance of the building.

When he reached the thick of the crowd, an indistinct murmur rose around him. Microphones were promptly thrust into his face, and a salvo of questions exploded in quick succession.

"Is it true you'll also be publishing bin Laden's political manifesto, as reported on an Islamic group's website last night?"

"Where are you going to print the book, Mr Turner?"

"What's MI6's position on the book?"

"Has the author been in touch with you directly?"

"How many experts have checked the manuscript?"

"Has Charles Randall left Tetragon because he refused to publish this title?"

"Can you confirm that the Arts Council has rejected your company's funding application?"

Waving his arms about as if to shoo away a persistent insect, James cut through the questioning mob and reached the door. He fumbled for the right key while the din sounded around him, and just about managed to slot it into the lock with a shaking hand. A couple of moments later he was safe inside.

"Bloody hell!" he whispered, his back pushing against the door.

He drew a deep breath and ran upstairs, climbing two or three steps at a time. The phone lines were ringing wildly, almost in unison, in the empty office. He cautiously walked down the corridor and craned his head forwards to look through the window down into the street.

"Jesus Christ!" he said to himself. "This is it… I quit. I quit. I'll give my notice today… right now." He dialled Nick's number from his mobile and got through to him at once. "Nick? Hi, it's James here. Listen, we've got a very big problem… what did you say? Where are you? What? Nick? I can't hear you… bad signal. Nick? Shit." He tried to ring him again, but it went straight to his voicemail.

"Where the hell's Holly?" he shouted, banging his fist on the wall, as the phones didn't stop ringing. "Doctor's appointment", said a note on her desk. He walked to his room and sat in front of his laptop. He went online and checked the company's bank account for a resuscitating transfer – but the balance was still well into the red. His inbox was equally disappointing, delivering him only a few otiose Google alerts and a couple of spam messages. There was no response from the Jim Talbot Agency to his offer.

"I'll call Goosen," he said aloud, with a shaky voice.

But between saying this and actually speaking to his boss fifteen long minutes passed. He waited for one of the lines to be available and dialled the main number of Goosen's head offices in Holland. The receptionist, confused, put him through to Goosen's secretary. Goosen's secretary, even more befuddled, put him on hold for what felt like an eternity. Then, seemingly from outer space, the Dutchman's voice boomed out:

"Who is it?"

"Mr Goosen... it's James Payne-Turner here, Tetragon Press, from London..."

There was a long silence, then Goosen snarled:

"Who gave you permission to call me? Only Nick and Samson are authorized to contact me directly. This is totally unacceptable."

"Mr Goosen... I'm sorry... I can't get through to Nick, and Samson—"

A loud whistle sounded at the other end of the line.

"Fuck Goosen," James hissed, putting down the receiver.

He stormed back to the front door and picked up the entry phone.

"Hey, you! Journalists!" he shouted. The hubbub outside subsided. "You hear me? I'll make a statement about the book... OK?... In half an hour."

And he hung up.

* * *

Uncle George couldn't stop his raucous laughter as he sat down in front of Father's easy chair, in which Jim lay immobilized with his left leg, right arm and collarbone in plaster or all bandaged up.

"What's so funny?" the younger man asked, sneering at his uncle.

"What's so funny?" George repeated, between chortles. "First of all, you look like a Picasso painting. And secondly," – here he guffawed again – "I've just read a very interesting article in *The Richmond and Twickenham Observer*..."

"I can explain everything."

"Yes, I know," George said with condescension, "you can always explain everything. So, Jimmy, let me see... it's in their 'Caught in the Act' column... where is it? Ah, there we go..." He brought a folded newspaper close to his glasses. "'According to a police report, yesterday evening at around 18:30 a man in his late thirties, by the name of Jim Roderick Talbot, of Twickenham, Middlesex, wearing blue jeans, white trainers, a striped bobble hat, two golden earrings and a black T-shirt bearing the words DANGER: MAN AT WORK' – heh heh, I'm joking, it doesn't say all that – 'entered a well-known massage parlour in Berwick Street, Soho...'"

"It wasn't a massage parlour."

"All right, all right... be patient... let me read on. 'Berwick Street, Soho... The man, who described himself as a writer and a journalist' – heh heh heh – 'paid one hundred pounds in cash to parlour manager Becky Davies of Lambeth, South London, and demanded to see one of the models, by the name of Candy, aka Jenny Daniels, of no fixed address. What ensued was—'"

"That's enough. It's not funny, Uncle G." He jerked his neck inside his surgical collar and twisted it left and right. "I was just doing research, I told you already."

"You were doing research, eh? So you don't know about these things yet? Oh boy. Well, know this for a fact, son: I'm sick and tired of your antics."

"Look, I was doing research for a book I'm writing. I've got a contract. It's in my bag over there: take it out."

George fished out the contract and perused it with a wrinkled nose and a sceptical expression on his face.

"Tart... aa... laa... caarte... Is that French?"

"That's right."

"What's it about?"

"Well, it's an academic study of prostitutes and their environment."

"Won't sell very much then, will it?"

"I'm getting paid for it. Thirty grand."

"Thirty grand?! For a book on whores? Cor, the world has gone mad." He examined the contract for a little longer and threw it on the table with scorn. "It's not even signed: I could have written that. Could be like your mother's health policy."

"Sorry to disappoint you, Uncle G, but it's all legit, and I'll get the money as soon as I deliver the book."

"Which is when exactly?"

"All being well, a week today."

"Perfect." George scratched his ruddy nose and gave a wry smile. "Your mum's getting out of the clinic in a week or so, so you should be able to pay all the hospital bills yourself. Super."

"Hang on a sec: you said you'd take care of all the clinic's expenses. You're not thinking of reneging on your promise now, are you?"

"Well, I had to help because I knew you had no money of your own, but now it looks as if you're going to be all right..."

"Come on, Uncle G, you're not being serious, are you? Don't you appreciate the situation I'm in?" Jim was fidgeting so painfully inside the plaster casts that they seemed about to burst open.

"Oh, I appreciate it son, I do appreciate it. And I think this will be good for you. It'll give you a little bit more incentive... help you concentrate."

Jim shot a basilisk's gaze at him, but said nothing.

"Now," George continued, after an excruciating pause, "you remember I told you I'd written a sort of patriotic war novel when I was younger – forty, forty-five years ago? Well, I've still got it, can you believe it? It's entitled *Little Short of a Hero*, and it's all written in longhand... nine hundred pages... there were no computers in the good old days, you know. I haven't touched it since then... it may need a little bit of work... I asked my neighbour to post it to me... she waters my plants when I'm away, you see. Do you think we can come to some sort of arrangement about it?"

"What do you mean?" Jim humphed.

"Well, you know, after you've finished with your tart book, maybe you can help me get my novel typed up, clean it up a bit and send it to a few of your publishing friends... Then perhaps we could look again at the hospital bills and so on, do you understand?... What do you think? Is that a deal?... Do you mind if I read you a few chapters? You tell me what you think, OK?"

From a plastic bag, he produced a brownish heap of scribbled-over squared paper and placed it on the table.

He started to read without waiting for a blink or grunt of approval from his nephew:

"'It was a dark and stormy night when our sergeant told us to get ready for the attack...'"

* * *

In the studio flat above their café on the North End Road, Helen and Sarah were typing away at a feverish speed on separate computers. Helen was sitting on her bed with her back against the wall and a pile of books on either side of her slick new laptop. From time to time she stopped typing, picked up one of the books seemingly at random, opened it, read a bit, closed it and started typing again. Sarah was sitting at her small desk, and by eleven thirty in the morning she had already gone through five mugfuls of coffee and half a pack of cigarettes. She was having a whale of a time.

"I could write a million pages of this stuff. No problem at all. Actually, you know what? I'm enjoying it. Are you sure we're gonna get paid by Mr Jerkoff?"

"Concentrate."

"What?"

"I said *concentrate*. We're never going to make the deadline if you keep interrupting. Have you finished with your chapter?"

"Yes, I'm finished, I'm finished... Why do you want to go over my stuff?"

"To sort out the grammar and make it a bit more literary. And make it all tie up. Let me see..." Helen went over and sat on Sarah's chair. "God... this is really gross, Sarah... how can you come up with such filth?"

"Well, it's all true. I've heard it from some of my girl-friends... Or done it myself." She winked. "How are you finding the books you're cribbing from?"

"I can't believe the library stocks this stuff. They're all bestsellers though."

"*The Diary of a Brazilian Call Girl...* mm, sounds interesting... what's this one? *Girl with a One-Track Mind: Confessions of the Seductress Next Door...* I think I've seen a poster of it on the tube... *How to Make Love Like a Porn Star...* that's a classic, I read it years ago... and this? *The Intimate Adventures of a London Call Girl...* hang on, isn't this the one they are doing on TV?"

"Yep."

"Maybe we should watch it. We could get some good ideas."

"We don't have time. Let me get on with this."

After a pause, Sarah added with a mischievous tone, as she lit another cigarette and opened the window:

"I told you that guy had something kinky in mind... It's all part of his plan to have sex with you."

"Oh Sarah, let's not get started again. Please."

"All right, all right... There's one thing I don't understand, though: if he's got a contract to write this book – right? – why does he want *you* to go and meet the publisher on Monday?"

"Because he told the publisher that the book has been written by a *real* prostitute, and that he's acting as a sort of agent."

"I see. Well, that makes sense. So you are the prostitute, eh? Both of us are, in fact."

"I suppose..."

"And you reckon it's fair that we bust a gut doing all the work and he gets half the money, like a pimp? I think we should rewrite the first couple of chapters – which are rubbish anyway – change the title, give the book a slightly different angle and try and get a contract directly with the publisher. That's what I'd do. But since you've taken a shine to that loser…"

"I haven't taken a shine to anybody, but it doesn't seem right to leave him in the lurch like that, Sarah… all in plaster and with a dying mother. This could be his big chance…"

"Wake up, sweetheart. You're still dotting the 'i's with tiny little hearts… Can't you see he's only using you?… He doesn't give a damn about you or his mother."

"OK, now let me read and get on with this." Helen gestured her sister away.

"It could be *our* big chance…" Sarah added after her last puff.

"Shut up."

Helen was neither listening to her sister nor reading the words on the screen. For some moments her mind was too crowded with fragments of music, meaningless words and the mental picture of an arrow tracing a vast arc in the sky and hitting a sinking target with a violent thud.

"Just shut up," she said again, although her sister had not breathed a word.

* * *

The radio interview had been a terrible mistake. Pippa had persuaded him, against his better judgement, to go live on Front Row and answer all the questions as if the manuscript had not been lost, claiming that it was too late to cancel the interview and too premature to announce its disappearance. The journalist had subjected him to a cunning interrogation, resorting to the wiliest tricks of his trade to elicit as much detail as possible about the contents of the novel and its miraculous "rediscovery". Charles had acquitted himself as best he could, in the most confident and enthusiastic tones he was able to muster under the circumstances, although he knew that each answer was, if not an outright lie, at least a half-truth. Deep down, he felt he had made a complete fool of himself, and that the whole interview had been nothing but an exercise in futility. Once the news of the missing manuscript was out, there was little doubt that he'd be pilloried by the press and his rivals in the publishing world as a doddering fool or a mad fantasist.

Leaving the BBC building behind, he went down Regent Street and ended up in a grotty pub near the Liberty store, populated by young media types on their lunch break. He sat at an empty table, as far as possible from the flat TV screens hanging at the corners. After the first two glasses of red wine, he started talking and laughing to himself. At the third glass, he drew out a notebook and, with an uncertain hand, jotted down a few illegible words, which he hastened to cross out and rewrite. He finished off the wine, shook his head and tore up the sheet of paper, crumpling it in his hand. He realized how pathetic his poetical stammerings were. Pat was right: poetry is no business for old people. It was an unpleasant truth, but he had to swallow it. He had already said what he had to say to the world, and if that amounted to very little, then that was his destiny. And MacKenna was right too: old age is torture. Better to have been dead already three hundred or five hundred years than live through this long, barren decline and obfuscation of the mind.

He looked up at one of the TV screens, where the four members of a rock band were twisting and twirling around their microphones or strumming away at their instruments in front of a sea of waving arms. Who were those puppets, those papier-mâché idols worshipped by the masses across the world? Were they the new poets, the bards of our modern age, with their easy, cheesy lyrics?

He ordered a fourth glass of wine and then a fifth, and was pretty much drunk when he staggered out of the pub towards Piccadilly Circus underground station. He managed to squeeze into the first westbound train, and a young lady offered him her seat with a compassionate look. As he sat down, his head began to spin, and the smell of his own breath almost sent him into a fit of nausea. He looked around and puckered his lips, as the wine kept sloshing about in his stomach with each jolt of the carriage.

Most passengers, especially the younger ones, were wearing earphones connected to a small plastic rectangle attached to their shirts or nested in their hands. Many were reading one of the commuters' newspapers or some fat mass-market paperback with a dark or pinkish cover. Others were fiddling with their mobile phones, videogames or laptops. Only the tourists were talking to each other.

He lowered his eyelids wearily and slipped into a sort of pictureless reverie, where he could only hear the murmur of his own voice.

"How could you lose that manuscript? What did you do with it? Have you thrown it in the bin? You don't remember? You fool. Why do you drink so much? What are you trying to escape from? Put an end to all this. And stop writing poetry. Stop escaping. Live your life... die your death."

When the train slowed down for the next stop, he came to and opened his eyes momentarily. A few passengers stood up and made towards the nearest exit, some of them still reading or toying with their hand-held appliances. He closed his eyes again as the train tore away from the platform.

"We're all locked up in our prisons... each dreaming of the key... Why do people read? Escapism... like TV, music, sport, cinema, computers, alcohol... virtual realities... Words don't inspire any more... they go through our brain and... are forgotten... without leaving a mark... Literature is dead... poetry is dead... the word is dead... and books... books have become only... a cheap, momentary distraction from the daily grind... depressing... All this printed paper, all these felled trees are just... fish-and-chip wrapping... martyrs of pies and relics of the bum... No point in writing, publishing, reading... Waste of time... my life... MacKenna's... tales told by an idiot... Destroy your poems... pulp... let the curtain fall... and universal darkness bury all..."

The train screeched to an abrupt halt, shaking the old publisher awake.

"Grnf."

He adjusted his spectacles, turned his head left and right, bounced to his feet and in a split second was out through the closing doors.

12

"I do not fucking believe it!" shouted Nick, pounding his fist on the table. "How could he... Oh fuck! What did he make that statement for? And why did he announce his resignation to the press? To the whole world? Knuckle-shuffling git! Let's just hope the news doesn't reach Goosen or Samson..."

Holly was standing in front of him and said nothing.

"If I lay my hands on him, I'll make him shit blood. Where is he now? Where's the computer that was on this desk?"

"It was his own laptop... he must have taken it away, like he did every evening."

"Did he leave any handover notes? Any details about the offer he made to that agent?"

Holly shook his head.

"You know where he lives, don't you? Maybe we should get a cab and try to catch him there?"

"I've been calling his home number all morning, and there's no reply. His mobile is switched off. He left no message. Maybe he'll be in touch."

"Sneaky little bastard. Keep trying. What the fuck does he think he's doing? Leaving us in this shit, with piles of crap to be sorted out..."

"Do you think it's something to do with us?"

"What do you mean?"

"Maybe he's found out about you and me?"

"Fat chance." Nick made a dismissive gesture. "He's just a lily-livered coward. He doesn't give a toss if I'm boning you or a three-humped camel."

Holly raised one eyebrow and turned to leave.

"Hey! What? Where're you going? It's just a figure of speech. Siddown. Let's talk."

The girl reluctantly turned round and sat opposite him.

"We'll be all right, don't worry. I just need to take a more 'hands-on' role in the company, that's all. And we need a new publishing director, urgently…"

"I wouldn't mind a little promotion and pay rise… Don't forget I have an MA in Publishing…"

"I meant a *male* publishing director. Goosen and Samson wouldn't approve."

"Oh I see… the old 'men only' club… Helloo? When was the last time you went into a bookshop?"

"Well, I don't—"

"Go and check out the kind of books piled on front-of-store tables. Have a look at the covers. Read the blurb and a few pages. They are tailored for female readers. It's the girls who buy the books, not the boys. And most people who work in publishing are women. Men only think about beer, cars and football."

"And sex. All right, but I don't see the point of—"

"The point is," Holly interrupted him, with a forceful tone, "the point is that this publishing company, if you want my opinion, is far too old-fashioned and male-centric. Look at the covers for example: they're all dark and gloomy. And if you go through the entire list, you'll be lucky if you find three or four women writers out of four hundred authors.

Randall was an anachronism even thirty years ago, let alone today. I would know how to turn things round, how to bring this company into the twenty-first century."

"Right... Tell me then: what would you do?"

"First of all, I'd revamp our website, which looks a bit like Space Invaders. Make it transactional, blog-friendly. Then I'd create a Tetragon profile on MySpace, FaceBook, YouTube, add podcasts... that sort of thing, to encourage word of mouth and networking, you know. Then I'd link up with all the best literary blogs and magazines, review and author sites, and so on... And then, I'd turn most of the backlist digital. What's the point of keeping all those musty old books in the warehouse when they're only selling one or two copies a year?"

"What is the point?"

"There isn't one. Just make everything digital. Haven't you read about those espresso-like book machines they're installing in Blackwell's? You walk in, order a book and bang – they print it for you in five minutes. That's the future. Print-on-demand, web-to-print, e-books, that kind of thing. We should follow the example of House of Stratus and The Friday Project."

"They both went bust," pointed out Nick.

"If they went bust it's only because they wanted to grow too fast too soon, and because they were too far ahead of their times. The important thing is to commission books by young women for the female market. I know someone who runs a creative-writing course for post-grad students in London, and I could ask her to put me in touch with the most talented girls. Alternatively, a couple of boozy lunches with some good agents should do the trick. I am sure we can put together a commercial list very quickly, without having to fork out huge advances. Let me have a go."

"So you reckon we shouldn't go for that dirty memoir? It sounded the right kind of thing for us... I think I've got the agent's name somewhere on my pad, let me see..."

"I'm not saying we shouldn't go for it if it comes our way, but I wouldn't pay a hundred grand for it – that's what James offered, isn't it?... It's a lot of money for just one book, Nick, and there's millions of books out there that could be as good. What we need to do is change the focus of the list – make it more mass-markety, more girly..."

"All right, all right – power to the girls... let's see what you can do... But do something quickly, and show me the money. I'll tell Goosen that I'm the acting managing and publishing director, but I'll let you run the show for a while. If things go well, I'll give you the promotion and the pay rise, all right? Now let me do a little bit of fire-fighting and call the bank to remove gonzo boy as a signatory. What are those letters over there?"

"Today's post. I picked it up on the way up."

Nick sifted through the envelopes until he found one that seemed vaguely important, and ripped it open with a pen.

"Uhmm..." he groaned half in disgust, half in disbelief as he glanced over it.

"Bad news?"

"Sort of. Looks like Randall might sue us for libel and unfair dismissal."

* * *

When Jim rang Gascoigne-Pees to let him know that two signed copies of the contract were in the post, a voicemail message informed him that the publisher would be away until the following Monday – the day on which Helen was supposed to meet Gascoigne-Pees in Pimlico. His frustration, over the past couple of days, had been mounting dangerously. He found it impossible to move around the house without having to ask his uncle for help, and he had no easy way of logging onto the Internet or checking his email for any important messages.

With very little to do and a great deal of time on his hands, he couldn't resist the temptation to exhume his old manuscripts from the cardboard box in his room. "The way British publishing works," he had read somewhere, "is that you go from not being published no matter how good you are to being published no matter how bad you are." For that reason, he was confident that once he'd had his big break, he could publish all his other novels.

His favourite work remained *A Thorn in My Side*. Yes, perhaps it required a little bit of editing, as it had been written in a relative rush over the past few months, but it had some fantastic set pieces and bristled with vigour and enthusiasm. His other novels had some great stuff in them too: the second part of *The Woman with Three Faces*, for example, was as good as anything written by Ian Rankin or Ruth Rendell, and the historical background to *The Warrior of Kiev* was meticulously researched and full of convincing detail. Not a new *Name of the Rose*, admittedly, but in the same league. It was galling that he couldn't be recognized on his own merits and had to resort to devious manoeuvres to get into print.

He tried to work out which books should be published next, and at what intervals. He started reading bits out loud, making little cuts and corrections, picking up the oldest manuscripts with a certain apprehension. As the day drew on, a sense of loneliness and dejection swept over him, such as he had not experienced for some time. Just as he threw the manuscripts back into the cardboard box, Helen rang.

"Hiya! How are you doing?"

"Fine, fine," Helen replied, with a worn-out voice. "I think we're on target."

"Excellent. That's what I want to hear. And how many words…"

"Maybe about… ninety thousand to—"

"Ninety thousand!? Really? You've written that much? Then you're almost there! That's amazing… fantastic… well done!"

There was a short pause.

"Ninety thousand left, Jim… to go… I'm not Agatha Christie, you know. We've been working flat out since Tuesday night, with hardly any break other than for a bit of sleep, and we've managed to clock up twenty-six, twenty-seven thousand words. To be perfectly honest, I can't guarantee we're going to make it. We're exhausted."

"Oh, I'm sure you'll be all right. Keep up the good work, eh! Hem. And… do you think it's possible to have a look at what you've done so far?"

"Why?" Helen asked curtly.

"Just in case Gascoigne-Pees rings me up and starts asking questions… I don't want to sound stupid, that's all…"

"I can ask Sarah to send you a few chapters by email."

"I don't have access to email at the moment… my old modem's gone."

218

"Well, our printer's not working, it's run out of ink or something... so I'm afraid you'll have to be patient."

"Maybe you could read me a couple of chapters on the phone, so that I can get the gist of it?"

"We haven't got *time*." Her tone was getting tetchy. "If you want us to deliver by the thirtieth, then you'll have to let us get on with it. Sorry."

"OK, OK... forget it... I'll read it when you've finished it, OK? Don't get angry with me... I'm just... frustrated that I can't help, that's all, and..."

Jim's voice seemed to give that croaky sound that precedes tears. Helen relented.

"Don't worry, we'll do our best... Hopefully we'll make it..."

"Thank you," Jim said, after a long pause, then added almost as an afterthought: "Will you give me a call on Monday, before you go to your meeting?"

"Sure."

"Just for a quick rehearsal, you know... what to say, what not to say... Gascoigne-Pees is a very tricky animal..."

"Is he?"

"Oh yes. You'll have to be on your guard all the time. And mind each word you say. What are you going to wear, by the way?"

"Pardon?"

"I mean for the meeting. Were you thinking of wearing, like, a miniskirt, fishnet stockings, that sort of stuff?"

"What are you talking about?"

"Well, he's expecting a professional prostitute, so I thought you might want to dress up a little bit, act the part..."

"And wear heavy lipstick and high heels?"

"Maybe?"

"What else? You want me to give him a quickie too? Is that what you've fixed up with him? Is it part of the contract?"

"Come on, Helen, it was only an idea... just to give the whole thing an air of authenticity."

"How can you give a farce an air of authenticity? It's like sending a real cop chasing after Charlie Chaplin. I am not a prostitute, I'm not an actor, and I'm not a professional writer – and frankly, I've had enough already of this pathetic charade. Now let me get back to my work."

"Helen?"

There was a receiver-replacing clack.

"Helen?" Jim repeated hopefully, but there was no reply at the other end.

* * *

The "thinking crypt" was at its gloomiest, with no light other than the pale glow around the edges of a curtained window – and right in the middle of the room, enthroned in his chair, Charles sat at his desk holding his head in both hands, looking down at a blank piece of paper, thinking of nothing. His face seemed to have transformed from the previous day: his bony cheeks had grown more sallow, more hollow, almost as if rigor mortis had started setting in.

The morning papers, with the news of Payne-Turner's public retraction and resignation, had offered him only momentary solace: if Athens cried, Sparta was certainly not laughing. Despite hours and hours of searching in the most improbable nooks and crannies – including under the publisher's pillow and mattress – the manuscript had refused to turn up. Features were being run in the newspapers, serialization and translation rights requests kept flooding in, interviews were scheduled to take place, and the abyss in front of him seemed only to be widening and deepening by the minute.

When Pippa gave a gentle rap on the door and entered the room, Randall didn't even bother to raise his head.

"Charles, I've got some good news."

"You've found it?" he asked, with the hint of a sparkle in his voice, still without looking up.

"No... I wish. But we've received a letter from the Arts Council, saying that they've accepted our funding application. For the whole programme. Isn't that great? We can do the Naruszewicz book after all... Did you hear me?"

"Good," was the publisher's answer, after a long pause. "Is that all?"

"Well, Pat called a few minutes ago... she's on her way to see you. I've asked her about the manuscript. She doesn't know anything about it."

"I told you, mmm," he muttered, plunging back into silence.

"Are you all right, Charles?" Pippa asked, now seriously worried.

"I'm all right, yes."

"Would you like a coffee or something?"

"Grnf."

She tiptoed out of the room, closed the door and disappeared down the corridor. When Pat finally arrived and stormed into Randall's study, not even her shrill voice and intense body language managed to shake him out of his catalepsy. She talked and talked, and pricked and prodded him, but Charles remained motionless and didn't respond, like an old boxer at the ropes, too proud to collapse, too winded to react.

"Maybe you've got dementia," she said. "Alzheimer. A friend of mine suffered from it. He'd shine his shoes with toothpaste. Anyway, it's a wake-up call. Or some kind of message. Bad karma. I wouldn't sleep on it. I'd take action, do something. Why do you sit there doing nothing? You're not thinking up one of your poems, are you? Say something. I hate that kind of head-in-the-sand attitude. Why don't we go out for a walk or a cup of coffee? It'll blow the cobwebs away. It might help you remember. Have you been drinking today? I can smell alcohol in here. You're not hiding a hip flask? That would explain the amnesia. But I think it's to do with old age. It's what the French call *gâtisme*. Or a combination of alcohol and senility…"

"This long hangover, my life…" Randall mumbled, almost inaudibly.

"What did you say? Was that one of your witticisms? You're making fun of me?… I think there's something wrong with your head."

"There's always been something wrong with my head."

"Not to the extent of blanking out for hours… losing manuscripts."

"I've always lost manuscripts. It's the story of my life."

"Oh, shut up! There's no rhyme or reason in what you're doing or saying…"

"No reason maybe, but as to rhyming… trnf."

"Come on, Charles, get out of this smelly place… get out of this country. Leave your world of words. Come with me. Let's move abroad. There's a life waiting for you elsewhere. Sunshine. Cruises. Concerts, exhibitions. Give me your hand. Let's go."

Randall looked up and smiled.

"I can't," he said, after a while. "I've got some unfinished business here. And I'm not an ostrich. I haven't stuck my head into the sand. I haven't lost my mind, either. It's just that... it's just that, in life, there are people who fight and people who desert. And I'm a fighter... I cannot help that... I'm probably destined to be killed in action..."

"You're an old fool, that's what you are. Always high tragedy. Always melodrama."

"Woman!"

"You'll never change. You're beyond help. I'm leaving. Maybe it's wrong to try and drag you out of here. Maybe you don't want a new life. Here's my number, in case you change your mind. Goodbye."

The door of the study was slammed shut, echoed a few seconds later by the front door. Charles rose from his chair and wandered around the room for a few minutes, picking up an old book at random from the shelves, or a piece of paper from the floor. He lifted his glasses and wiped his eyes, shaking his head in silence, then he made his way to the living room, where Pippa was struggling to concentrate on a hefty set of proofs.

"How is it going?" he asked from behind her desk. "Is this the Hungarian poet? Yes? It's a very good book. Mmm. We should get a few reviews. I'll start working on the Naruszewicz book. I've already written the blurb... I have a couple of ideas for the cover. Good news about the Arts Council grant... sorry I... ah..."

He tried to rush back to his study, but before reaching the corridor he was already blubbing like a child.

13

How do you get from Twickenham to Pimlico with a leg in plaster, a heavily bandaged arm, a surgical collar around your neck, an inimical uncle and no money? Certainly not by train, cab or bike. Your only possibility is to purloin the electric wheelchair provided by the clinic ahead of your mother's discharge, pray that your old Oyster card still has enough credit on it, and joystick your way to the nearest bus station on the Heath Road. From there on, you need to take an almost mystical leap of faith in the accessibility of London's public transport. In more empirical terms, you'll have to hope that the buses you want to board are equipped with disabled-friendly ramps and that there are no prams or idiots obstructing the wheelchair area. If you are lucky and leave around ten-past seven in the morning – changing in Richmond for the 337 to Clapham Junction, and from there taking the 344 or 156 to Vauxhall – then the chances are you'll have covered the fifteen miles to your destination by around eleven o'clock.

But on that particular Monday morning, traffic happened to be pretty bad on the South Circular London-bound. It grew worse between Putney and Wandsworth, due to an accident; it became solid between Wandsworth and Clapham, and was absolutely chocka between Clapham and Vauxhall.

At a quarter to twelve, Jim rolled off the bus in a state of throbbing delirium. Helen's meeting with Gascoigne-Pees was scheduled for twelve, so he drove the wheelchair manically along the pavements, careering across the bridge with his orthogonal white leg sticking out and garnering pitying looks from occasional passers-by. Helen had broken her promise to ring him, and his repeated attempts to get in touch with her during the past few days had met with a wall of silence. What was going on? Why wasn't she accepting calls or contacting him? Was she still angry with him? Was she offended? He had to find out.

When he arrived in front of Vanitas's office building, he was breathless and drenched in sweat. Just then, a girl answering Helen's description, but dressed in the interview attire of knee-length skirt, tailored blouse and severe jacket, was marching towards the entrance of the building on the other side of the street. Jim let out a sub-human howl:

"He-e-e-len!"

Two red double-decker buses crawled past just at that time, and as they moved off the girl had already disappeared.

Jim crossed the street and kept driving his wheelchair up and down in front of the building's entrance, stopping at times to throw furtive glances into its granite cavities. He wondered how the meeting was going, whether Helen was managing to sound convincing, whether Gascoigne-Pees was buying into her story, whether she had written more of the novel, and whether what she had written was remotely passable from a publisher's point of view.

Just as he was about to roll away in despair, thinking that it couldn't have been Helen he'd seen, he caught sight of a couple emerging from the main entrance of the building, side by side. The man was laughing out loud and gesticulating, while the girl followed in silence, with a subdued smile on her face. They descended the few steps to the pavement.

"Helen! William!"

The couple stopped and turned round. Helen's face went crimson.

"What the hell is he doing here?" Gascoigne-Pees stared at Helen in disbelief, then moved slowly towards Jim, frowning.

"I just wanted to check on things…"

"How did you get here?" Helen whispered, as the blush spread across her face. "You should be in bed. You look really ill. Your leg…"

"How's everything going?" Jim asked in a dry, reedy voice, feigning a smile. "You had a good meeting?"

"Look, Jack – or shall I call you Jim?" Gascoigne-Pees rasped, bending the upper half of his towering bulk towards the wheelchair-bound man. "Why don't you get the fuck out of here, and sharpish? What did you think you were doing, playing with other people's lives and careers? Do you think this is a joke? Just sod off. Fucking loser. Just pray I'm not gonna sue your sorry arse off. Wheel yourself away. And don't show your fucking face anywhere near here. Ever." He turned to some passers-by who had stopped to see what was going on. "Don't think he deserves pity just because he's in a wheelchair. This man is a cheat. He's a fake. A crook."

"So how did it go, Helen?" Jim tried again – a very long shot, admittedly.

Gascoigne-Pees gave him a push on his unhurt shoulder.

"It's none of your business, pal. You've wasted enough of our time. And now, if you'll excuse us, we'd like to go to lunch."

"But we've got a contract. I've sent you two signed copies."

"What contract? I haven't seen a contract. Have you, Helen? There was never a contract. There was never a book. And you never existed. Bye-bye."

"Hang on a second," Jim said, scrabbling at the publisher's jacket. "Helen... what's all this? Why are you doing this to me?"

The girl remained silent, and turned to look at the roaring traffic, as a hubbub of images and sounds whirled around in her mind.

"Go back to where you belong," continued Gascoigne-Pees, "the big empty space, heh heh. You're a nullity, a non-entity. Worse than that: a gravitational zero."

"Do you really need to..." Helen murmured in embarrassment.

"And let me tell you this: you're a pervert, a wacko, a fantasist – and more bent than a roll of toilet paper. You're the scum of the earth, you're dross, filth, chaff, vermin, knotweed, leprosy, landfill waste... but probably I don't need to remind you..."

"I think we'd better go," Helen said decisively.

"What happens to our contract?" Jim stammered out.

Gascoigne-Pees didn't reply but, as he turned to leave, his hand seemed to slip down to his bottom and make an arse-wiping gesture.

"Would you like to see the finished manuscript? Can I send it to you?" Jim shouted at the couple's receding backs.

"Sure," a voice roared from a distance. "And don't forget to include a self-addressed envelope and sufficient postage."

* * *

Nick had got out of bed at 4:30 that morning. After a quick shower and coffee, he had driven to the Tetragon office and started tackling the mountain of invoices, bills and correspondence accumulated on James's desk. Just before the weekend, he had tried to contact Goosen and Samson, but was told that they were travelling abroad, due back only later the following week, and unavailable till then. Samson's transfer had yet to materialize, and the bank, for some reason, couldn't track it down, though a copy of Samson's signed and stamped form had been faxed to the bank's customer services in the morning. In Nick's long experience of dealing with Goosen and Samson, bank transfers could at times be delayed by unpredictable administrative problems, but would inevitably hit the recipient's account at some point. For expediency's sake, on Friday afternoon he had decided to transfer a hundred thousand pounds of his own personal funds into Tetragon's ailing account, as an unofficial bridging loan, with the idea of getting the money back with interest once Samson's transfer arrived.

By nine o'clock he had gone through all outstanding bills and salaries, making arrangements to pay by BACS or cheque. The digested pile of papers had been chucked into an enormous Jiffy bag and biked over to Roger, the accountant, for processing. Nick felt like a roaring lion.

Since a balance of around twenty-five thousand pounds was still available, he thought that this could be used for commissioning the front-list programme. Holly had scheduled meetings with a handful of literary agents that day. She had been given a budget of fifteen thousand pounds, and her mission was to come back – no matter what – with three or four publishable manuscripts, preferably by young British female authors. She was confident she could do it.

After a quick round of calls to creditors and suppliers to reassure them of the imminent payment and update them on upcoming projects, Nick set down to work on the two books for the Ethiopian Ministry of Culture. Payne-Turner – or "that tit", as he now called him – seemed to have done nothing about it so far. According to the letter of credit faxed by Samson, delivery was expected in less than three weeks' time, so they really needed to speed things up if they didn't want to let slip such a good opportunity. With a series of calls, emails and faxes, and despite Samson's absence, he managed to get copies of the texts in question, and sent them to a hack copywriter he used from time to time for his own presentations – who would put them into proper English and sort them out.

Next, he dealt with Randall's legal threat. His impulse was to fight him and even sue him back, but his "lawyer buddy" at Hodgson & Barrymore took a more dispassionate view and advised him to offer the disgruntled publisher a higher settlement, as it would cost more in legal fees to pursue this further through the courts. Nick reluctantly agreed, but that didn't stop him thinking up the most extravagant plans for a cold-served revenge.

After the volcanic activity of the previous week, the phone lines had gone remarkably quiet, except for a couple of sales calls and a scheduled interview with Timothy Thorpe of *Bookpage* for a piece on Tetragon Press. He had prepared his answers with care over the weekend, as the company could hardly afford another media gaffe. His angle, in explaining the recent management turmoil at Tetragon Press, was that "James Payne-Turner had resigned to pursue other business opportunities". He wanted to "thank James for his contribution to Tetragon over the past two months and wish him all the best for his future career". He added that he would take responsibility for the management of the company until a replacement was hired, and that, notwithstanding the current economic gloom and the near-terminal crisis within some traditional book businesses, he had faith that Tetragon would soon become one of the major players in the UK literary arena. To Tom's question as to whether he would maintain Tetragon's focus on literary translation, Nick didn't reply directly, but declared – glancing at his notes – that he was looking to "increase the company's top line through higher revenues, protect its profitability and improve its gross margin".

After lunch, he felt so drowsy that he dozed off in his chair. He was only awakened an hour later by the stubborn ringing of the phone.

"Tetragon Press," he said with a husky voice, rubbing his eyes with two fingers.

"Oh hello," the caller chirped at the other end, "this is Jack Lawson, from the Jim Talbot Agency."

There was a long silence, during which Jim expected to be recognized and Nick struggled to regain consciousness and focus his mind.

"Jack Lawson of the Jim Talbot Agency?" he finally said. "Do you have a meeting with Holly?"

"Er, no… Would it be possible to have a word with Mr Payne-Turner, if he's around?…"

"He no longer works here. What's it about?"

"Oh... I've been away a few days, and I've only checked my email today. James sent me an offer last Tuesday for one of the books I represent..."

"Oh yes? I think he mentioned it to me."

"Oh, good. I was just ringing to say that the offer is accepted."

"The offer is accepted? Really? And was this for that memoir..."

"*Tart à la Carte*."

"*Tart à la Carte*, that's right. The teenage nympho..." Nick frowned as he decided what to do. "Well, Jack... I'm afraid we might have to pass on your excellent script and withdraw our offer."

"What—"

"Things have changed in the last few days, and we have to tighten our belts."

"But what do you mean 'withdraw your offer'?" Jim asked, with a hint of panic in his voice. "I've turned down many other offers in order to accept yours."

"I'm sorry to hear that. We simply don't have enough cash. Unless you're prepared to negotiate."

"Negotiate?"

"Come down on the advance. Substantially. We cannot afford six-figure advances any more – that's the truth of it. We have some tough times ahead of us, and we must keep an eye on the bottom line."

"So... how much would you be prepared to offer?" Jim asked, after a short pause.

"Well now... five thousand ideally but—"

"Five thousand?!"

"...but I can stretch to ten."

"Ten thousand? But that's a tenth of what your colleague offered last week…"

"It's still a very good advance for a small publisher."

"But how can I go back to the author and tell her that your offer has been reduced to ten thousand pounds?"

"I understand. I'm sorry. I'm afraid that's the new reality of this situation. Of course we could just call the whole thing off…"

"But James said you were really keen on this book and wanted to make it your lead title for the autumn…"

"Ten thousand – half on signature and half on publication."

"I'd be very happy to consider something in the region of seventy, seventy-five thousand, but ten thousand is—"

"Ten thousand."

"This is an extremely commercial book… It's got all the ingredients of a bestseller, and the author is young, good-looking, full of promise…"

"Ten thousand."

"Let's meet halfway, at least. What about fifty thousand?"

"Ten thousand."

"OK, let's make it twenty-five thousand then."

"Ten thousand. Deal or no deal."

There was the longest pause.

"I'll send you a draft contract by email this afternoon."

As Nick replaced the receiver, he felt a surge of joy and pride welling in his chest. He was such a good manager, such a tough negotiator, such a natural-born leader… In less than twelve hours, he had managed to do what Payne-Turner had not been able to do in six weeks and what Randall had not been able to do in thirty years: put Tetragon Press back on track as a company on the way to success.

* * *

Even in the pits of despair, the thought of committing suicide had never crossed Randall's mind, but on that particular morning he would have welcomed the arrival of the Grim Reaper.

During the weekend, he had searched his flat again and again, from top to bottom, inch by inch. A lot of insignificant items had cropped up, including a few embarrassing photos which he thought he had lost, but the MacKenna manuscript was still nowhere to be found. Despite his lack of success, he had managed to stay totally dry and keep his wits about him for over forty-eight hours – an incredible achievement in itself. But in the early hours of Monday morning depression had set in again.

After Pippa's arrival, in an attempt to alleviate his queasy feelings, he had made the unwise decision to go to the London Library to continue some long-running research on a couple of forgotten authors – and there, in the narrow alleyways of the gloomy reference rooms, among rows and rows of identical-looking shelves tightly packed with old volumes, he had heard his breath come short and fast. He had staggered out of the library and slumped onto the marble steps of a building nearby, where he rested for a long time.

In the afternoon, he rang the office to check if there were any messages for him.

"Your solicitor's secretary called," Pippa said, "to confirm your appointment. He'll be expecting you in his office at three."

When he hung up, he leafed through his pocket diary and looked at the relevant page: it was blank. He thought the appointment must be some sort of cock-up, so he called the solicitor's office, but the secretary confirmed that he had an appointment with Mr Gregson in little more than half an hour. Gregson was with another client, so it was not possible to enquire about the reason of their meeting. He decided to go and see him.

Gregson & Partners occupied the top floor of a plush building near Tower Bridge, with great views across the city of London. Charles had been a loyal client of the firm for a very long time, and had used its services for a couple of tricky libel cases in the mid-Eighties, getting out of them more or less unscathed. Daniel Gregson, the chief partner, was a physically unimpressive-looking man of the most diminutive appearance, with a sparse white beard, thick glasses and a hunchback's posture. When Charles entered his room, Gregson was sitting in his leather chair, signing some documents with long, methodical hand strokes.

"So…" the lawyer began with a gentleman's drawl, without interrupting his signing routine, "how is the MacKenna book coming along? I heard your interview on Radio Four. You must be terribly excited."

Randall uttered some unintelligible words of assent.

"I haven't read any of his books personally, but my wife is a great fan of his work… she's very much looking forward to the new novel… what's the title? *The Great and the Damned*… Anyway, you'll be pleased to hear that we received a fax this morning in response to our letter…"

"What letter?" Charles mumbled, in utter confusion.

"The letter you asked me to write the other day in relation to your settlement with Tetragon Press."

"The other day? Oh, *that* letter. Of course. Trnf." Charles hadn't a clue what the lawyer was talking about – his recent troubles seemed to have wiped out half his memory – but was too ashamed to admit it.

"Well, here's their reply." Gregson handed him a sheet of paper. "If you would care to read it carefully and let me know what you think…"

Randall examined the document in puzzlement. He lifted his eyes and gave a weak smile, while the lawyer kept looking at him with an enquiring gaze.

"This…" he managed at last. "I'm not sure I…"

"I think it's a fairly decent settlement," Gregson intervened.

"Is it?" Randall still had no idea what this was all about.

"If you ask my personal opinion – not as a partner of this practice but as a friend – I think you should take up their offer. It's the easy way out. You may still feel a bit emotional about it, but there's not much to be gained in looking back. You have your own company now, your own office. You are your own boss. And you have a potentially successful book in the pipeline. The last thing you want to do now is get embroiled in a long legal battle… be dragged through the mud. You never know how these things will go, and it could turn very nasty. You'd probably win, but even if you did you'd end up paying a heavy personal toll, what with stress, anxieties… So my advice is: take the money and run."

Charles examined the letter again, and little by little the pieces of the jigsaw started falling into place. He remembered now. Not everything, and not exactly, but he could see himself jumping out of a cab and taking the lift to the top floor of this same building a few days before. It was the day when he had gone out for lunch with Pat, returning home in the late afternoon in a rather intoxicated state. At odds with himself, with life and the whole world, he had decided to throw down the gauntlet to his enemies, to raise his middle finger to them once and for all in a liberating gesture. It seemed to have worked. Their reply was aggressive, but grovelling at the same time... hostile, but submissive too. He had scared them. They'd had to eat humble pie. He had brought them down. He had brought Nick down. He had humiliated him... the squirming little worm... He had forced him to cough up the money he wanted. That was victory enough for him.

"Go ahead. I'll accept the settlement."

"I think this is a very sensible decision."

"But tell them I want the money before the end of the month, or I'll take them to court."

"I'll ask my secretary to write a letter straight away. We can probably still catch the post."

Gregson pressed a button on his phone and called his secretary in. A minute later, a young woman carrying three big folders entered the room. She placed the folders on Gregson's desk, right in front of him, and waited for instructions.

"Oh yes," the solicitor said, lifting the flap of the top folder. "The most important thing. Here are your two copies."

"My two copies?" Randall repeated, groping for a meaning.

"Yes, not just one. Remember the other day? You were joking about it. You said you'd descended into such a bad mood that you might have destroyed this and all your other books... I thought: better not take a chance, it's been lost once already... so we made a copy for our files too."

"Extraordinary," Charles whispered, and the last missing images of that hazy afternoon ran through his head in quick succession. He remembered going back to his place – it must have been around five twenty, five thirty: Pippa had already left for the day. Pat, and alcohol, and mortality, and all his recent troubles had plunged him into the strangest, blackest, most misanthropic and anarchic mood of his life. The flat was empty, the silence was unbearable. He tried to find shelter in his private study, but the silence was even more oppressive there. He read some of his poems aloud, then bits from MacKenna's book – that's when he felt the sudden, irrational urge to shred the two manuscripts into a million pieces. And he would have done it, too, if an ambulance hadn't hurtled past at that moment, its siren searing through the silence and his momentary psychosis. Frightened by his own potential for self-destruction, he had decided to get some fresh air, and on the way out he happened to see a document on the floor. It was the redundancy offer Nick Tinsley had given him the day he was sacked. When Charles remembered the unceremonious, humiliating way in which Tetragon's new owners had dismissed him and the despicable accusations they had spread about the theft of the MacKenna manuscript, he boiled with rage. He went back to his desk and called Gregson for an impromptu meeting in half an hour. On impulse, he took *The Great and the Damned* with him, to get it copied and keep it out of harm's way. His poems, on the other hand, he left behind: the world wouldn't be much poorer if they were lost or destroyed.

"Quite extraordinary," Charles repeated, almost to himself.

"What's so extraordinary about making photocopies?" Gregson said, smiling through his beard and exchanging an amused look with his secretary. "Anyway, here are your copies."

"Can I use the phone in the other room, while you dictate your letter?" Charles asked, getting to his feet and grabbing the two folders with avid hands. "It's urgent."

Before Gregson could reply, Randall had already disappeared through the door.

14

Jim raised his head an inch or two in the darkness, then let it fall down gently onto the pillow. Someone was knocking at the door behind him, at regular intervals, with a certain urgency. He tried to open his eyes, but one of them seemed to be stuck, and he couldn't pry it open.

"Who is it?" he barked at last.

Rather than get a reply, he saw the door opening slowly, letting an elongated triangle of light into the room. A second later, Uncle George's bulbous nose appeared just above the door's handle.

"Are you all right, son? Is it OK if I switch on the lights?"

"No, don't."

But it was too late, and a nuclear flash forced Jim to hide his face in the pillow.

"What did you do that for?" was his muffled scream.

"Sorry. You're right. What did I do that for? It's broad daylight outside." George pulled the curtains open and switched off the lights. "It's eleven o'clock, to be precise. And I wanted to go to Tesco to buy some food before your mother arrives. The ambulance will be here any minute now."

Jim slowly re-emerged from the pillow, still half-covering his eyes, and sat up on the bed.

"Eleven o'clock?" he repeated in a daze.

"That's right. Sorry to wake you up, Jimbo. I know you were up till all hours last night... I went for a pee at about three thirty, and I saw the light on under your door. Mmm. I've been wondering what you were up to so late... Good Lord... What's happened to your eye? It looks like a poached egg. You should put some eye drops in it."

"I've been writing all night... I've got a deadline."

To be absolutely literal about it, this wasn't quite accurate. He had not been *writing* all night: he had been *trying* to write all night. The problem was that words just wouldn't come. The cursor had kept blinking aimlessly, the page had remained blank. A few words had appeared from time to time, like a sudden spurt of water in the desert, only to dry up and evaporate the next minute.

"I see. Well, if you can finish your book with one hand, one leg and one eye, I think you can get into the *Guinness Book of Records*, and perhaps make some good money too. That would be the day... I'm off now. If I'm not back before your mum arrives, sort her out, will you?"

A few minutes later, Jim grabbed his crutches and limped out of the room and down the stairs, ouching at every step. Before even washing his face, he went to check if the post had arrived. To his joy and relief, he found what he had been hoping for – what he had been chasing by phone, letter and email over the past three days: two signed copies of the contract and the advance cheque from Tetragon Press, which had been conveniently made payable to Jim Talbot. Just as he was squeezing the cheque in his hand in a mute gesture of victory, the bell rang. He reached forwards to open the door, expecting to see his mother, flanked by nurses in white overalls, but what was standing on the threshold was the ominous bulk of his ex-landlord.

"Someone's been here before me, apparently," Tom said, with a voracious grin, looking him up and down.

"I had an accident," Jim explained, recoiling.

"An accident? Sure. Where's my money?"

"Your money?" Jim repeated, after a little hesitation. "I sent you a cheque the other day... no, wait a minute, it was yesterday. Yesterday."

"First or second class?"

"I think it was first. Yeah, it was first. You didn't get it? Strange. Well, the Royal Mail isn't what it used to be... You should complain to your employer."

"I don't work there any more. They made me redundant last week, me and another five of us, including Gautam."

"Really? That's disgraceful, mate. I'm very sorry to hear that. That's why a first-class letter takes so long these days... staff shortages..."

"I want that money. Now."

"Look, like I said, I sent the cheque first class yesterday, so you should get it tomorrow or on Monday. Well, hopefully."

"Show me the cheque stub."

"I don't have the chequebook here with me now, and—"

Tom lurched forwards and grabbed Jim by the collar.

"Listen, pal. If you're lying to me... if I don't get your cheque in the next couple of days, or if it bounces, you'd better relocate to Papua New Guinea." He let go of his grasp and took a step back. "I don't like to be messed about, understand?"

"No probs. The cheque's in—"

The slamming door drowned out his last words. Jim wiped the sweat off his forehead with the back of his hand, then looked at the cheque, almost reduced to a crumpled ball, and pulled it delicately at the edges to smooth out the creases.

Not long after, Uncle George returned with three bags full of canned food and items on special offer, followed a little later by the ambulance carrying the discharged patient. Anna was visibly shaken – especially when she saw her young son on crutches and with a leg in plaster – and although she put on a brave face and a vague smile at first, she burst out crying when the nurses eased her into her wheelchair, and declared that it would have been better for everybody if she had died.

Jim listened to his mum's wailing and to the ensuing protestations by her brother with an absent mind, biting his fingers in silence and darting quick glances out of the window from time to time. At around two o'clock, after Uncle George had served a bunker-style meal, Anna went for a lie down. Only then could Jim sneak out of the house without giving the impression of being a callous, uncaring son.

He first went to his bank to deposit the Tetragon cheque. When the cashier pronounced the fateful words "All done", a big smile appeared on his face, and he hopped out of the building in elation. Then he stopped at the Post Office on King Street and mailed a cheque for just over seven hundred pounds to Tom. He finally popped by the library to read the latest news from the publishing industry, and was appalled to see a big article in *Bookpage* about Gascoigne-Pees's latest acquisition, entitled 'VANITAS SNAPS UP DEBUT SISTER ACT'.

A heated auction between three UK publishers has resulted in Vanitas Books publishing director William Gascoigne-Pees securing world rights to a debut novel by Scottish sisters Helen and Sarah Douglas for a "colossal" six-figure deal negotiated directly with the authors. *I Want to Be Lily Allen*, to be published in Vanitas' erotica imprint XXXpress in October 2008, follows the steamy sexual adventures of two young sisters from Glasgow who are prepared to do anything to become successful popstars. After an initial pact to help each other, they become fierce rivals and vow to destroy each other once they've achieved success. Gascoigne-Pees said: "The minute I read the first few lines of the manuscript, I knew this was one of those rare books that only lands on your desk every fifteen or twenty years. I was spellbound all the way through. This is a classic of the future, a book that will be read and revered by generation after generation long after all of us are dead. This is going to be one of our strongest submissions for the Booker and the Orange." In a separate deal, Vanitas has acquired world rights to the next three books by Helen and Sarah Douglas.

Jim studied Helen's picture for a long time. She seemed to have already shaken off her barmaid looks, and had something intellectual about her, which made her even more attractive. He read the article again and again, shaking his head in frustration, with a mounting dismay inside. Life was so unfair: he had spent fifteen years and the best part of his youth serving the cause of literature with no reward, and those two casual dabblers, who had no real writing experience or literary ambition, found themselves with a lucrative contract and the opportunity to become bestselling authors almost overnight. His mouth went dry, and he closed the magazine in disgust. But at least he had his own book to look forward to, if he could only overcome this momentary creative impasse. As he rose to go and check his email on one of the library's public computers, he felt a bony hand on his shoulder, near his collar. He snapped around and saw Ken Tahr, the thriller author in the striped suit, standing behind his chair. The older writer was carrying a stack of old mass-market paperbacks with his name on their spines.

"Hello," the man said, placing the books on the adjoining desk.

Jim squinted his eyes, not sure how he should reply. Tahr didn't seem to be angry with him in the least.

"You're Jim Talbot, aren't you? We met here a couple of weeks ago, you remember?"

"Of course. Of course," Jim said, mustering a smile and sitting down again.

"You had a bad fall?"

"Just a little accident at home..."

"Well I hope you'll recover soon. How is it going with your writing? I have just finished two new novels, and one of them has been short-listed for an important Internet prize out of more than ten thousand entries from self-published authors. That should give it some publicity. Oh, by the way, last time I forgot to tell you that I've started a reading group at my place, and I'm looking for new members. If you want to join, there are details on the noticeboard near the entrance. Next week we'll be reading and discussing my first novel, which was published in 1975. I've managed to bring together a dozen people, all locals, a few friends. If this works, I am planning to organize more readings across London, in bookshops, small theatres, public libraries and possibly even some creative-writing courses..."

The man went on feeding his monomania and talking about himself, his books and other ways to promote them, to keep them alive. Nothing else existed for him: life didn't seem to have any other joys or attractions. Jim kept nodding absent-mindedly, and thought that he really didn't have time to waste. He must go back home, chain himself to his desk and finish his own book. He was about to rise to his feet again, when Tahr seemed to say his name.

"Sorry?" Jim said by reflex.

"I was asking if you knew or were in any way related to this Jim Talbot Agency in Twickenham. There's an article in *Bookpage*, in the News section. Have you read it?"

Jim flipped through the pages and spotted the article, a half-page piece on Tetragon Press, which detailed the latest misadventures of the literary imprint and included an interview with its new managing director Nick Tinsley, ending with an upbeat mention of "a strong six-figure deal through the Jim Talbot Agency of Twickenham for *Tart à la Carte*, the most sexually explicit memoir ever to be published, and an inevitable number-one bestseller".

"Never heard of them," Jim muttered. "Just a coincidence."

"I thought so," Tahr said, picking up his pile of books. "Anyway, I'm going to look them up. I don't think I've ever tried them. Might be worth sending a speculative letter and a couple of my recent novels. By the way, here's my new card. It's got a blurb from my latest book on the back. Good idea, eh? Well, nice to see you, Jim."

The man went to the lending counter, topped up his private book pension scheme and disappeared. Jim remained seated at his desk and read the end of the article time and time again, with one thought looping through his mind:

"A number-one bestseller... a number-one bestseller... a number-one bestseller..."

* * *

As Nick walked into the Tetragon offices, he heard a distant whirring sound coming from Holly's room. He proceeded down the corridor gingerly, and stopped in front of the girl, who was sitting on a low stool and feeding sheet after sheet into Payne-Turner's state-of-the-art shredder.

"What's this?" he asked.

Holly raised her head slowly and turned to look at him.

"They are here," she whispered.

"Who?" Nick asked, knitting his brows. For a second he thought she meant the police.

"Goosen and Samson. They're waiting for you in the other room. With some other guy."

"Goosen and Samson? Are you serious? What are they doing here?"

"They've asked me to shred all these." She pointed at half a dozen piles of paper in front of her. "Do you think we can have a word later?"

Without replying, Nick stepped over to his room and opened the door. There, sitting around his desk, were a young corporate type that he remembered seeing somewhere, Goosen – who was whispering something into his dictaphone – and Samson, who was installed in Nick's leather chair and talking to someone on the phone in a foreign language.

"Good *moorning*. How are we today? What a nice surprise," Nick said, trying to sound jovial, although he was peeved by the unannounced intrusion.

His entrance was acknowledged only by the younger man, who stood up and shook his hand in silence, while Samson and Goosen continued with their own things as if he wasn't there.

He took a seat between the Dutchman and the Ethiopian, and waited until Samson's conversation was over and Goosen's dictaphone was switched off and placed on the glass desktop.

"So," Nick commenced with a cheerful tone at the first available pause. "To what do I owe the pleasure of your visit?"

Goosen immediately made it clear that this wasn't going to be a pleasant meeting.

"The situation is totally unacceptable, Nick," he roared. "Out of control. Who authorized that man to go on TV and talk about our business? Who—"

"Well I…" Nick tried to chip a word in.

"Did someone ask you to speak?" Goosen interrupted him brutally. "You've fucked everything up. Randall couldn't have done worse than you. And he's doing fine now, isn't he? With rediscovered manuscripts which could have been our own. And with our own money." He placed a copy of Tetragon's settlement offer in front of Nick. "We should have kept him… we shouldn't have listened to your advice."

Nick drew a long breath and placed a hand over his face, covering his mouth.

"It was you who brought in that man… Payne-Turner," Goosen continued, "that walking disaster. He was in this office for two months twiddling his thumbs, and then the minute he *did* something we had the entire world turning against us. We cannot afford that, Nick. We cannot afford anyone sticking their noses in our businesses."

"The British Government has launched an inquiry into our group of companies," Samson explained in his habitual singsong voice, muting his ringing mobile. "They've frozen the last transfer... money-laundering checks, they said... antiterrorism laws. But it's OK... I can sort it out..."

"You see?" Goosen snarled. "You see, Nick? We have no time for inquiries... or for sorting out other people's blunders. This is why we asked you to keep an eye on this company. But you haven't done it. You were too busy sleeping with this girl next door... Congratulations, by the way..."

"What?" Nick exploded, looking left and right.

"She told us everything," the Dutchman continued, this time in a calmer, even patient tone. "Including that you were in Paris with her when Payne-Turner was making his grand announcements to the world on satellite TV. And I don't think anyone authorized you to take a member of staff on a personal trip to Paris on a weekday."

"Well, I cannot deny we went... but this doesn't mean—"

"Listening is certainly not your forte any more, Nick." Goosen shook his head in disapproval. "You used to be better, much better. We're not talking about a little escapade here... we are talking about gross misconduct. Not only have you wasted a great amount of our time and money, but you have potentially got us into trouble. For this reason, your services are no longer required. You are dismissed."

"Well, I wouldn't—" he tried to retort, but was struck dumb by Goosen's fulminating look.

"And to draw a line under all this and move on, we have decided to sell Tetragon Press to the Croesus Publishing Group. This is Geoff Dyson, Croesus' Vice President of Acquisitions and Development, and Tetragon's new

Managing Director. Now, Nick, if you could just sign the usual papers and make it as quick as possible... you should be familiar with the procedure..."

Samson pushed a bunch of forms and letters towards Nick.

"Do you have a pen?" he asked, in the tense silence that ensued.

Nick frowned and shifted in his chair, wiping sweat off his face.

"Look, I don't have a problem with this," he finally said. "It's your business, and you can do whatever you like with it. The only issue I've got is that I recently injected some of my own money into the company to make a few payments, so before I sign anything I'd like some assurances that..."

"This is not something that we authorized," barked Goosen, "and it has no relevance to the matter in hand. Please sign the papers. I have a plane to catch."

"Wait wait wait," Nick said, getting agitated and throwing quick glances around. "This *is* relevant." He tried to smile. "I'm not talking about two or three hundred quid here: I'm talking about a hundred thousand pounds of my hard-earned money. A hundred thousand pounds. I need some sort of guarantee that I'll get—"

"Give him a pen, Samson."

"Sorry, Mr Goosen, with all due respect, I'm not gonna sign any of these unless—"

"Nick. We know where you live..." Samson threw in, with an expressionless face and drooping eyes.

He riffled through the papers a couple of times, wiped more sweat off his brow and grabbed the pen offered to him by Samson.

"OK, I'll sign. But I'd really appreciate it if you could sort something out about that money…"

"We'll see," Goosen said with a benevolent smile, which clearly meant the exact opposite.

One by one, the documents were signed and passed to Goosen, who in his turn passed them on to Geoff Dyson for checking. At the end of this process, drops of sweat could be seen beading the glass surface of the desk.

"You may go now," announced the Dutchman.

Nick got to his feet and with an embarrassed smile extended his clammy hand first towards Samson and then towards Goosen, who returned his squeeze limply.

"I'm going then," Nick said, negotiating his way between the wall and the ponderous chairs towards the door. Then he seemed to have a sudden thought and stopped. "Do you mind if I have a quick look in the bottom drawer of the desk? I think I may have left some papers there."

Geoff Dyson shook his head, and said in a robotic tone:

"You are required to leave the premises immediately."

"I see. All right. See you la'er, then."

"Not a problem," Dyson replied, deadpan, while Goosen gave him an almost imperceptible nod and Samson, busy with his mobile phone, totally ignored him.

As he stepped out, Nick sneaked into the small toilet next door and washed his face. He looked at himself in the mirror. It wasn't the first time he had been fired. It had happened once before, about forty years ago. He had been a lank, pimpled shop assistant then, and his boss had caught him munching a Mars bar pilfered from a box behind the counter. He had forgotten how horrible and mortifying an experience it was, although he had himself inflicted it on countless people over the years. Now he understood why Randall was seeking revenge with such dogged determination.

He pulled the plastic seat down and sat on the toilet, then hastened to call the bank to see if he could stop any payments and transfer some money back into his own account. After fighting his way through a phalanx of automated options, he managed to speak to someone in customer service, a very helpful Indian lady whose spoken English was almost unintelligible and whose comprehension of English bore a close relation to what she could read on the screen.

"T–I–N–S–L–E–Y... that's right, Tinsley..." he whispered into the phone. "Yes I am the main account holder... no, I haven't set a security password on this account... You what? You need to identify me? All right then, gw'on... I said *go on*... proceed, continue, advance... What was that?... OK... three... 19th February 1950... BT... Good, now, could you give me the available balance and read out every transaction from Monday 28th?" As the woman ran through the various cheques and amounts charged to the account, he made notes on a small piece of paper. Randall's payment had already gone through, and there was no way of stopping it, as it had been made by BACS. The only significant sum that had yet to be debited was the signature advance for *Tart à la Carte*, so he put an immediate stop on that cheque and a couple of smaller ones. He got out of the toilet with a sense of relief, having just salvaged around nine thousand pounds.

On his way out of the office, he stopped to talk to Holly.

"How did it go?" the girl whispered, feeding more sheets into the shredder.

"All right."

"Have they sacked you?"

"Well, they've asked me to go. Give me a call me later, will you?"

"They sacked you?"

"Practically, yes."

"They tried to do the same with me, but I made them change their mind."

"Really? How did you do that?"

"I caught them by surprise... and you won't expect this either..." There was a long, fateful pause, then she added with a wicked smile: "I'm pregnant..."

* * *

In just a few days, Vivus's headquarters had been transformed, gradually taking the shape and look of a proper office. Gone were all the books – gone was the furniture, the junk and the clutter – gone too was Randall's beloved desk. A team of builders, carpenters and decorators had been busy round the clock doing up the flat and making space for the two new members of staff who were soon to be employed.

On that sunny morning, a torrent of light and fresh air was flooding through the open windows, such as the basement had never been exposed to in ten years. Pippa was sitting at her desk and divided her time between giving directions to the builders and keeping the momentum going in the run-up to the publication of *The Great and the Damned*. Randall had delegated the entire management of the company to her. He had decided to take a step back and devote more time to reading, writing and travelling. He would still help and remain involved, that was for sure, but he was happy – after thirty years of publishing – to leave the day-to-day running of his business, with all its associated chores and drudgery, to the younger generation. He would soon be relocating to Paris with Pat, to her roof-top flat in the Latin Quarter, travelling back to England as and when necessary.

Another remarkable change was the disappearance of Randall's beard and glasses. As he sat reading *The Times* on a chair near the front door with his one piece of luggage, waiting for Pat to come and pick him up by cab, he seemed to have shaken off ten or fifteen years. He also looked more relaxed, more in control of himself.

"Are you sure you don't want to take a copy of the proofs of MacKenna's book?" Pippa asked.

"You take care of everything," Randall replied in a half-absent tone. "I have seen enough proofs for my sins. Just send me the finished copies when they are available."

"What about your poems?"

"I'll send you the final typescript from Paris. That will be my last book. My swan song. Or perhaps my crow squawk, mmm... I've published too many books, Pippa. I have said too much in thirty years of publishing."

He again became absorbed in his reading, until a car's honking was heard outside.

"It must be Pat."

He folded the paper and put it in his bag. Pippa went up to him, shook his hand and kissed him goodbye.

"That's it then," the old publisher said, looking around, as if he were afraid of having forgotten something. "I'd better go. Trnf."

"Won't you miss publishing, Charles?" Pippa asked from the door.

"To tell you the truth," Randall replied after a pause, stopping midway up the stairs, "I've had enough of it. And I don't think I belong in it any more." He gave a tentative smile. "Have you ever heard of a chap called Arthur Rimbaud? It's time for me to go and see the world."

15

The International Book Awards – or Quillies as they are commonly called by people in the book industry – are regarded as the publishing world's equivalent of the Oscars or the Baftas. The ceremony is a very grand affair attended by more than a thousand publishers, booksellers and authors, and accompanied by a celebrity chef's dinner costing each guest a little less than an arm and a leg. To celebrate the thirtieth year of the Awards, the organizers had once again chosen the Grosvenor House Hotel in Park Lane. The room was full to the brim, and the host – a minor celebrity himself – had started his spiel, desperately trying to be funny.

Although the Awards are seen as a frivolous self-celebratory event by most people inside and outside the publishing world, they succeed in bringing together a large cross-section of the book-trade "family" – and this year was no exception. Sitting side by side with some of the most established authors and influential people in the publishing industry were all the cogs and wheels of the book-supply chain, as well as the usual breed of Young Turks, chancers and brown-nosers.

James Payne-Turner, in his new capacity as Assistant Director of Corporate Responsibility for the Triton Publishing Group, could be spotted at one of the front tables. During the past twelve months, the young executive had let his hair grow a few inches, regaining his former Kurt Cobain looks, and had managed to keep his riverside flat and even buy a small sailing boat.

Towards the back of the room, at a composite table of printers, packagers, typographers and self-published authors, sat Nick and Holly Tinsley. At the end of her maternity leave, Holly had decided to leave Tetragon Press and join Nick's consultancy agency, adding her editorial and PR skills to his financial and managerial savvy. In recent weeks, they had secured a lucrative contract for the restructuring of an academic publisher. Nick had heard through the grapevine that Goosen's paper-manufacturing empire was on the brink of collapse, and that an imminent takeover was the most logical conclusion. According to some unconfirmed rumours, the reason behind this sudden downfall was not so much the global credit crisis, but a DTI investigation into some of the group's activities in Ethiopian territory. Samson was reportedly on the run, and had been last sighted at a disco in Guadalajara. Nick was glad he had managed to "jump" off the sinking ship before it was too late.

At the front, near the podium, stood the giant table of the Croesus Publishing Group, one of the main sponsors of the Awards. Geoff Dyson had somehow contrived to have Tetragon short-listed for the Small Imprint of the Year category, although 2008 had hardly been the most remarkable year in the illustrious history of the press. The acquisition process had been far from smooth, with a storm of bad publicity following the switch of editorial focus from literary fiction to crime, humour and self-help. There had also been an unpleasant, if short-lived dispute with a self-styled agent who demanded the acceptance of – or compensation for – a book contract signed with the previous managing director. A couple of letters from the head office's legal department had brought the matter to a swift close. As Geoff Dyson himself said later in the evening, when he stepped up to the podium to collect the award, "It's been a rollercoaster-ride year for Tetragon Press, but the important thing is that the bottom line now looks extremely good. In a very short period – thanks to defining books such as *The Twenty-First Century Guide to Filth* and *Make Tomorrow Happen Today!* – the company has become one of the most profitable imprints of the group. That's a real mark of success."

To the left of the podium was another massive round table, lined with expensive bottles of wine and champagne. Towering above all the other heads and shouting louder than anybody else in the room, including the host, Vanitas's publishing director William Gascoigne-Pees seemed the king of the place. His spirits were riding very high, and he thought himself in a very strong position for a few podium walks with the Douglas sisters, who had been short-listed for four major gongs, including the Book of the Year and the Author of the Year Awards. *I Want to Be Lily Allen* had been a runaway success from the day of its first publication, shooting straight to the top of the Bestsellers' charts both in UK and in America, and remaining there for many weeks in a row. An early review had called the book "a double bogey of a novel", and some critics had pointed out amazing textual similarities between the sisters' story and a number of other published works, suggesting the possibility of plagiarism – but any voices of dissent had been silenced by the time the book had sold its first two hundred thousand copies. Translated into forty-seven languages, the book had now sold over eight hundred thousand copies in the UK alone, and there was every chance that it would hit the one-million-copy mark before the end of the year. Thanks to appearances on various daytime shows and reality-TV programmes, the authors had become household names. A film adaptation of the novel, directed by Richard Curtis and starring Renée Zellweger and Kathy Burke, was in production, and a series of highly remunerative merchandising, music and spin-off deals had transformed the two ex coffee-shop owners into multi-millionaire stars.

Helen and Sarah were sitting left and right of Gascoigne-Pees. If Helen had been taking to her sudden rise to fame in a quiet, modest way, the opposite could be said of her sister. Sarah had thrown herself into her new life of late-night parties, champagne and excess with all the enthusiasm of a neophyte. One gossip magazine had published a picture of her snorting a line of cocaine, and another had snapped her exiting a stretch limousine without any knickers on. Although they maintained a united front for promotional and publicity reasons, the behind-the-scenes reality corresponded more closely to the storyline of their novel, with each sister secretly wishing for the disappearance of the other so that she could take centre stage and enjoy success undisturbed. Midway through the dinner, Sarah had already downed one and a half bottles of red wine, and Helen prayed to God they wouldn't get any awards, shuddering at the thought that her sister might make a spectacle of herself on live TV.

Charles Randall, the most unlikely of guests, was also present at the ceremony. It was his first appearance at the Quillies, and rather than enjoying the evening, he sat in morose silence and drank far too much wine for Pat's and

Pippa's liking. To help with the publicity of the MacKenna book – which had been one of the great success stories of 2008, with more than a hundred and twenty thousand copies sold in hardback alone – Pippa had employed the services of a PR company that was also involved in the organization of the International Book Awards. They had suggested putting forward Randall for the Lifetime Achievement Award, *The Great and the Damned* for Book of the Year, and Vivus Press for Newcomer of the Year. To their own surprise, the three entries had all made the shortlist. In the weeks leading up to the event, Pippa had asked Charles to prepare a short speech in case he won. He had taken the task so seriously that he had spent two weeks in creative confinement. He said that he wanted to say something he would be remembered for.

When everyone was roundly drunk, the awards started to be dished out. Juliet Fenton of Dada Books scooped a deserved third Quillie in four years when she received the Outstanding Achievement Award for her Dadablog; Princes Street Press won the Small Publisher of the Year Award, and an apparently inebriated Barry Newman went up to the podium to refuse the honour, saying that his company's turnover was well above that of a small publisher, and threatening to sack the person or people, in his organization, who had submitted Princes Street in this category; the Personality of the Year Award was predictably awarded to Tony Ritchie of Perdita Books, described by one of the judges as "an excellent man with a very honourable and successful track record as a publisher".

More awards followed in quick succession, building up to the most coveted prizes. What with the wine, the strong lights and the noise, Charles had sunk into a sort of open-eyed reverie. He imagined what it would be like if, say, Dante or Milton were sitting there next to him, in the middle of this pitiful masquerade representing the highest echelons of today's book world. What would they think? Would they laugh? Would they cry? Would even they have enough power in their language, in their style, to describe the absurdity and vacuity of the scene?

Just as he was lost in these thoughts, a high-pitched clamour around him made him come back to the present, and he was gently helped towards the podium by Pippa. Only when he was in front of the microphone and the host congratulated him on the result, did he realize that Vivus had just been given the Newcomer of the Year Award.

"Would you like to say a word?" the host asked, adding in an aside: "Make it brief, please... we are running behind schedule."

Randall's hand fumbled around in his pocket for his notes. The other winners had jumped onto the podium, cracked a ten-second joke, collected the award and returned briskly to their tables among the applause. Ponderously he smoothed out three large sheets of paper.

"Ladies and Gentlemen," he began in a hoarse, shaky voice.

To hell with it. These people had *not* been listening to him for thirty years: they might as well open their ears now, for once.

"Ladies and Gentlemen... The last time I received a prize, it was in Stockholm, almost twenty-five years ago, so I suppose I should be grateful for the honour that is being conferred on me tonight by the powers that be in today's publishing world."

There was some booing, wolf-whistling and clapping of hands from the back tables.

"Oh – my – God," thought Pippa.

"What is a publisher? Is it a profession, a trade, a vocation or an occupation for gentlemen? Well, certainly not the latter any more. In 1978 I considered myself to be entering a profession. It is no longer that, ladies and gentlemen. It is now a much debased branch of globalized corporate business – with a few honourable exceptions. I have always admired those who see publishing as a way to support a political, humanitarian or cultural cause, to make the world more civilized, to advance education and further progress in literature, philosophy, science and the arts – subjects much neglected by our rulers today – and for thirty years I have tried to fight that part of our human nature that links us to the animal world. Trnf."

The host, smiling to the public, appeared to whisper something in Charles's ear.

"I am talking of course about the innate tribalism that lies behind all the stupid wars we engage in, the greed that poisons us, the massacres and the holocausts, the ethnic cleansings and the pacifications – an instinct that we find in every animal species... that makes us dislike, hate or feel different from and superior to others of our own species because of nationality, culture, race, colour, religion, language or some other difference."

A stray giggle resounded through the room.

"In different ways I have tried to internationalize culture and help people understand each other. I have tried to resist fashions and the dictatorship of mobocracy, and I have only published what I really believed in... often in an uncommercial way... books that could inspire the individual to think beyond the limits set by convention or society. Obviously I have failed, ladies and gentlemen, because the world has not become a better place to live in."

"Shut up!" shouted a girl from a distant table.

"Instead of striving for the best, we are told we must not be elitist. The arts, which are the driving force of all progress in human history and evolution, are considered to be too difficult for the young, so we no longer teach them seriously. No one talks of literature any more. Reading, which is an active occupation that engages thought and intellectual curiosity, has been replaced by passive screen-watching, while information is increasingly fragmented, commercialized and distorted – and is rendered meaningless by a lack of context and critical understanding."

A couple of black-attired individuals stationed to the left of the podium were gesturing frantically to get Charles's attention, one of them using a pair of imaginary scissors to make cutting motions in the air, the other simulating first a hanging and then a decapitation with his left hand.

"Ladies and gentlemen, you have given me not only a worthless honour, but also, perhaps for the last time in my life—"

"Get *off*!"

"...last time in my life, an opportunity to make my ideas, views and feelings public to the world. In my last thirty years, I've had experience as an editor, as a writer and a publisher. I would be very happy if some of the books I have written, edited or published will still be read in thirty years' time... preferably on paper. Thank you."

As he left the podium, there was some sparse cheering, more like a cry of relief, but no real applause. The host

– widening his eyes, grimacing and raising his eyebrows comically – hastened to introduce the next award, and the evening continued to its ineluctable end, marked by the Douglas sisters' double-whammy: Author of the Year and Book of the Year.

Randall followed the rest of the proceedings in sulky silence. A handful of people – some of them completely drunk – came to congratulate him and to shake his hands. Pippa and Pat told him that it had been a very fine and moving speech. But he knew he hadn't got through to anyone.

Soon the evening of glamour and glitter was over, and everything was forgotten. In the following days a London paper described Charles's ceremony outburst en passant as a grotesque incident, and in the *Bookpage* International Book Awards special feature there was not a single mention of his speech or even of his award, as if the jury had retrospectively decided to scrap it. To compensate for that, a short but positive review of his book of poetry appeared in the Times Literary Supplement – completely unexpected, and not by one of his friends. As he read it, his eyes filled with tears, and later that evening Pat listened, with a polite smile on her face, to his passionate declamations on the breezy terrace of her flat.

"He's such a good man," Pat was thinking, with half-closed eyes. "An incorrigible idealist. Not the greatest poet… but a very good man. If he asks me to marry him, I may even say yes."

* * *

Only a few miles from Twickenham, in the densely populated concrete island of Roehampton, surrounded by three of the largest parks in the Greater London area, there is a facility for the treatment of complex mental health problems, an unprepossessing red-brick structure of modern build which the locals refer to as the "loony bin". On the first floor, towards the back of the building, there is a small bright room with white walls, mauve curtains, pine furniture and a bed with a cream duvet cover. This is where Jim is gradually regaining his equilibrium, after some of the most trying months of his life.

The loss of his publishing contract with Tetragon had not only put a dampener on his intellectual aspirations, but had generated the undesired effect of making him bankrupt. His advance cheque had been returned unpaid and, as a consequence, Tom's cheque had also bounced. Jim had expected the Irishman to come barging through the front door of his mother's house any minute to make him pay his debt to the last penny, on pain of licking the asphalt from the house to the station. But for some reason Tom didn't show up – which was almost as bad, if not worse. Jim hadn't felt comfortable going out any more, fearing a sudden assault. His paranoia mounted to the point that he was afraid to walk downstairs, and one day Uncle George – having not seen him for close to forty-eight hours – had entered his room and found him hiding under his own bed, wrapped up in his bed sheets.

The situation at home had deteriorated further, with a mother who cried from morning to night in the throes of her own clinical depression, and an unforgiving uncle who wouldn't stop poking fun at him in an awkward attempt to shake him up a bit. The news from the outside world of Helen and Sarah's stellar success had finished him off. Jim had cracked up, and Uncle George had found his nephew supine on the floor with eyes wide open, a yellow rivulet dribbling from his mouth and a half-empty bottle of Fairy "Lemon Twister" in his right hand.

His admission to the Roehampton hospital had offered him a sanctuary against the pressures and preoccupations of the world, where he could cultivate his interests in peace and lead a life of almost monastic simplicity. He received regular visits, especially during the weekend, from his mum and uncle, who brought him home-made cakes and CDs from the library.

Helen was also a sporadic visitor at the clinic. She had made an arrangement with the hospital's management and, feeling partly responsible for what had happened to Jim, paid for his fees. That afternoon she was there to see Jim after an absence of more than two months, having just returned from a book tour in Europe and America. She was accompanied by her two bodyguards, as her agent wouldn't let her visit her former friend on her own. She gave a gentle knock on his door, and a muffled voice invited her to come in.

"Hi Jim, it's me," she said softly as she stepped inside the room.

"Helen... how nice to see you," he said with a weak voice.

In two months, Jim had undergone the most dramatic transformation. His hair, which had been thinning anyway, was now completely gone. His face was blanched and stony, and his already thin body seemed to have shrunk even more since the last time she had seen him. Tears welled up in Helen's eyes as she gave him a hug and sat down in front of him.

"So how are you?" she asked, without looking at him.

"Oh I'm good, I'm good, yeah."

"You seem to have lost a bit of weight."

"Well, I don't eat that much... I'm on a strict diet here..."

"I brought you a book," she said with a feeble smile, handing him a small packet.

His skeletal hands unwrapped the present bit by bit, until the front cover was revealed.

"*Treasure Island,*" he said pensively.

"I thought you might like a lighter read from time to time..."

Last time she had visited him, she had noticed some of the volumes lying around in the room, such as *Ulysses*, *The Man without Qualities*, *In Search of Lost Time*, *Nausea*, *Journey to the End of the Night* and tome after tome of philosophy, from Nietzsche to Schopenhauer, from Hegel to Heidegger. These were hardly the books that one would recommend to someone recovering from a mental breakdown. Luckily they seemed to have disappeared.

"I don't think I've read it," Jim said at last. "Thank you."

There was a long pause.

"So... when do you think they are going to discharge you?" Helen finally asked.

"Oh, I dunno... But I'm in no hurry. I'm fine here, I'm fine. They're taking care of me. I've got my own room, no distractions... I've got my mental space here... I can think, read, write..."

"They let you write?" Helen exclaimed in surprise.

"Only longhand, unfortunately... but that's OK – I find it relaxing... I've also started to make drawings."

He pointed at some sheets on his desk.

"And what are you writing?"

"Well, for a start, I'm helping my uncle with this novel he

wrote many years ago… and you know what? It's not bad. It's not bad at all… We may even be able to find a publisher once we've finished going through it. Then I have a number of projects on the go… I've started a technological thriller set in the Middle East… very topical… terrorists, mujahidin… and I've also got a long work in progress… a sort of spiritual history of mankind… a posthumous book, I think… and then I'm keeping a diary, which I suppose could also be published one day… not that I'm that desperate to see my stuff in print any more…"

"How's your mum?" Helen asked, trying to change subject. "Is she recovering?"

"She's all right, yeah. She manages on her own now… which is good, because that means my uncle can go back to Bristol soon… How're things with you?"

"I'm getting married next month," she said, immediately regretting the disclosure. "To a Swedish artist. He does abstract paintings. Very beautiful. The paintings, I mean. We met at a party a few months ago. We'll be moving out of London… possibly even out of the UK…"

There was another long, awkward silence, which Jim was the first to break.

"Do you think you could do me a favour, Helen?"

"Sure."

"Do you think you could sign this for me?"

Helen went purple when she saw him take out a copy of *I Want to Be Lily Allen* from a drawer.

"Well, Jim, I…" she tried weakly.

"It's all right Helen, it's all right. Here please, on the title page. If you could inscribe it for me… that would be great… Thanks."

As Helen racked her brains trying to come up with something anodyne enough or intelligent enough, Jim continued:

"I've read it, you know... not just once... five or six times... it's actually... good... it's very good... it's superb... my hat off to you and Sarah... you've done a wonderful job... you've pulled it off magnificently... a natural writer... you deserve every inch of your success... well done."

"I'm sorry... I..." Helen said, thinking that this was definitely the last time she would come to see him.

"It's fine, Helen... it's absolutely fine. I have no regrets. You had an opportunity, and you took it. It's fine. It's life. As I say, well done and good luck to you."

Helen gave him back the inscribed copy of *I Want to Be Lily Allen*. She had only managed a lame "To Jim, with all my warmest wishes".

"That's great. Thank you," he said, putting the book back in the drawer, then he added, after a short pause: "So, what is your next project, if I may ask?"

"To be honest, I haven't even started thinking about it, because we're still busy promoting our first book... My sister says she wants to write a kind of memoir, an autobiography... so I may have to do my own book next year... a novel, perhaps."

"If you need any help..." Jim said with a smile. "Only joking..."

Helen rose to leave.

"Before you go, Helen, can I ask you another favour?" Jim said.

This time, the girl didn't rush to answer "Sure", but stared at him uneasily. Jim was not put off by her silence.

"I was wondering… if it's not too much hassle for you… do you think you could have a quick look at the first few chapters of my latest novel?… I'd like to have an impartial opinion… And if you think it's any good, maybe you could recommend it to someone you know… one of your contacts…"

Helen thought it through, with a sad smile on her face.

"I don't think I've got time, Jim. I don't think that's a good idea. Sorry," she said, shaking her head.

"No? I thought so. Don't worry, Helen, don't worry. It's cool. It's still too raw to be submitted anyway. Maybe you can have a look at it once it's finished, uh?"

"I'm afraid I've got to go now. I have an appointment in central London in half an hour."

"Have you? OK. Thanks for coming to see me. I appreciate it."

Helen embraced his almost insubstantial shape, gave him a quick kiss on his hollow cheeks and slipped out of the room without looking back.

When he was alone, Jim took Helen's book from the drawer, had another long look at the inscription and then put it away again with a sickly smile. Then he opened another drawer and took out a large manuscript, each page crammed with tiny handwriting, with many words and entire paragraphs crossed out, and yellow Post-it notes sticking out at the margins. He read a few bits in silence and chuckled. "This is good," he said to himself. "This is really good." Then, with a sweeping gesture, he moved the manuscript to one side, unpacked a brand new ream of A4 paper and placed it on the desk. He picked up a biro from the top drawer and started writing on the top sheet of the ream slowly, with a careful hand: "CHAPTER ONE". He raised his head and looked out of the window at the bright April sky with a dreamy expression on his face.

"One day..." he mumbled out loud through gritted teeth, "one day..."

Acknowledgements

My thanks go to the many people who read and commented on the early drafts of this novel. In particular, I would like to thank Mike Stocks for his astute criticism and his sagacious observations. William Chamberlain, Christian Müller and Alex Middleton have offered invaluable advice that has helped make this book much better than it originally was. A special thank you goes to Tim Bates, who has read this book through many drafts and has given me constant encouragement to see this project through during some of the busiest years of my life.

ALESSANDRO GALLENZI IS THE FOUNDER OF HESPERUS Press, Alma Books and Oneworld Classics, and the successor of John Calder at the helm of Calder Publications. As well as being a literary publisher with ten years of experience, he is a prize-winning translator, a poet, a playwright and a novelist. His collection of poetry, *Modern Bestiary – Ars Poetastrica*, was published in 2005 to critical acclaim. He lives in Richmond with his wife and two children.

www.almabooks.com